# Ghosts of the Empire

## Parisian Ghosts

**Janna Ruth**

PARISIAN GHOSTS 8

# GHOSTS OF THE EMPIRE

## JANNA RUTH

# Grab your free copy

**When an undead movie star asks you for a small favour, you know you're gonna be in deep trouble.**

Seeing ghosts is just something I've learnt to live with. They're everywhere I go, especially since I chose to study history at the Sorbonne, one of the oldest universities in the world. While on a class trip to the Pantheon, where France's great men—and women!—reside, I get introduced to the fabulous Josephine Baker! One of her war medals has gone missing, and she wants me to find its whereabouts.

Who could say no to a flapper girl turned movie star turned war hero? Little do I know agreeing to do so will send me on a wild-goose chase across the country with a ghostly pet cheetah, hidden walkways, and a murder attempt.

.

**Follow Alix on her first big ghost adventure two years prior to the events of Parisian Ghosts.**

.

Sign up to my Story Seeker mailing list at <u>www.janna-ruth.com/</u> <u>newsletter</u> and grab the prequel for free

# A Note on Sensitive Topics

Dear Reader,

This is a book about ghosts, so naturally death plays a rather large part in it. If you don't like spoilers and are cool with everything, skip this note and start the book. If you want to be prepared, read on. I'm writing this because reading should be fun, not a nasty surprise.

*Ghosts of the Empire* is the penultimate book of the *Parisian Ghosts* series and things are heating up. That also means a lot of dark secrets are coming out. With resurrections going rampant, there's plenty of dark magic, using bones and blood in copious amounts.

An old fiend will return and bring back horrible visions of characters' individual deaths by drowning, car accident, and electrocution.

A battle will be fought with salt violence, shredding a ghost's identity, head bashing, and sword slashing. None of it's too graphic, though your imagination may run wild.

One character will reveal a tragic backstory of child abuse in moderate detail, including a near-death experience, a failing justice system, and the mention of suicide. The character still reacts to the trauma they experienced, though no physical child abuse will happen on page.

When we start, we're still dealing with the loss of Olivier, and the grief and guilt associated for Gaby and Alix.

Lastly, the language can get a bit rough when tempers rise.

Happy to tag along? Then join Alix on this new ghostly adventure as she faces the Chevalier and Napoleon and all the fresh horrors they bring.

Love, Janna

# Chapter 1

"I still can't believe he's gone."

Birds sing outside my window, their song ringing out over the constant buzz of motorists on nearby streets. Sunlight filters through the gaps in the closed curtains, desperate to creep in and fill the room with warmth. It seems wrong the world outside should be so gloriously summery when it's so dark and cold inside us.

Gaby cuddles deeper into my armpit, cradling a sleeping Malou in her hands. She's barely left the room since her brother met a sudden and violent death of his own making.

I still shudder thinking about it. The desperation in his voice, the terror in his eyes, knowing he was about to suffer the same fate as the king he'd so recklessly bonded himself to. I'd hoped to save him, that if we could've just calmed Olivier down, he'd recover and survive the abrupt separation. But his heart was under too much strain, and he passed in the hospital where it all started for him.

My first ghost whisperer mentee was a complete and utter failure, and I can't help think I'm the one to blame. If only I'd dedicated more time to the living Olivier, instead of solely focusing on his whisper ghost. Then again, it was the whisper ghost who let himself be tempted by the Chevalier's fancy promises, not knowing it'd spell the end for him.

As my mind scratches at the Chevalier's name, I feel a wave of anger surging through my body. He promised to meet me halfway, to be more ethical about his choices—heck, he even promised to stall resurrections altogether unless he could figure out how to do them safely. And then he turned around, cut off Ollie, and tied Olivier's life to King Louis XVI so they'd perish or live together. What kind of improvement is that supposed to be?

Gaby sniffles and I put an arm around her, pressing her closer to me, while I whisper sweet comfort into her hair. Nothing will take this pain away. Her brother is gone, and while his ghost is still out there, he's left a world in which they both can be.

The doorbell rings and I sigh. Sébastien and Dix are at work and will be for the better part of the day. Their days have been even more packed since the Chevalier stole the royal bones before coming for freaking Napoleon. I can't imagine how mad the new headquarters must be as GoPol fumbles to get the situation under control.

"You stay here," I tell Gaby, before extracting myself from the bed. My bones ache from lying for so long and I feel a little guilty at much I relish this chance to stretch.

The doorbell rings again and I speed up the process, stepping into the hallway. Just then, Gaspar walks through the closed door. Our gazes meet and he winces. "It's Séb's boss, the Bézier guy."

I sigh. My track record with GoPol agents, or in this case Interpol agents, isn't great. This isn't the first time Thomas Bézier has sprung an unwanted visit on me, either. I'd like to think he's here for Sébastien but that's highly unlikely, given that the GoPol offices should've been his first stop if he was looking for my boyfriend.

"I'll inform Séb," Gaspar says, vanishing through the door as I let the Interpol agent up.

Maybe I should've pretended to be out, but in my experience, that'll just prolong the inevitable. Still, I can't help but hug myself as I hear his heavy steps on the staircase. Soon his close-cropped curls come into sight. He looks up and gives me the faintest smile.

"Bonjour, Mademoiselle Dubois."

"Bonjour."

He reaches the top, his judgemental gaze taking in the creased clothes I threw on sometime in the morning before climbing back into bed with Gaby. "I hope I haven't rung you out of bed," he says with a frown. Apparently, it's unacceptable to still be in bed after noon.

"What brings you here?" I ask, not exactly welcoming.

"I was hoping we could talk. Things have been crazy over at GoPol so I couldn't follow up with you until now, but I believe a chat is in order." His tone makes it clear he's not to be refused.

While I'd love nothing more than to shut the door into his face, I push it open instead. "Would you like a coffee?" Because I definitely can't do this without caffeine in my veins.

"I'd love one."

He follows me into the living room. I offer him a seat at the dining table while I go put on some coffee. As I watch him glancing around through the small window connecting the kitchen and living room, I'm kind of glad Sébastien has such a spartan, impersonal style. The apartment has changed a little since I moved in—most of the stuff lying around is mine—but we haven't really had time to redecorate yet. If Bézier's looking for photo clues or guilty pleasure hints, he'll come up short.

The smell of coffee fills the kitchen and it's time for me to face the music. I set a cup in front of him and hug my own as I take a seat. "How can I be of help?"

"Jumping straight in, huh? I appreciate it."

I just want to be done with it.

Bézier takes out a sleek little notebook. "Why don't we start with what truly happened at Versailles?"

"Didn't Séb tell you?"

"I'd like to hear it from you. As I understand it, you're always at the heart of every ghost hubbub, and his account is limited due to his unfortunate fall."

A cold shower still washes over me whenever I think of the moment Sébastien was dragged through a window and fell three stories deep onto the gravel ground. He was lucky he got away with a broken arm and cracked ribs, because for a moment, I'd thought I'd lost him.

"May I ask what the purpose of this is? Am I in trouble or something?" It would be so like GoPol to blame it all on me.

"I guess that depends on what you tell me." Bézier's eyes soften. "But right now I'm just trying to understand the situation a little better. You were working with King Louis for the event?"

This is where we're start off? "No! I'd never even talked to Louis beforehand. The exhibition was about the royal women, not the men."

"I see. But he's Marie Antoinette's husband, isn't he? So, I'd assume she'd bring him to a big event like this."

"She's the one who killed him." And I had to watch as the queens doled out their punishment after Louis' betrayal.

Bézier's eyes widen. "Tell me more."

But before I can launch into my reluctant tale, the door to the living room slams open, and Gaby storms in, still in her pyjamas. "It wasn't Alix's fault!"

"Gaby—"

"My idiot brother is to blame for the mess at Versailles. *He* was the one who went to the Chevalier, who gambled his ghost and his life away, and who did something so horrendously stupid as to bond with Louis XVI! I mean of all the kings—him?"

Bézier turns to her with interest. "Gabrielle Lemel, right?"

"Gaby, it's okay. I've got this."

But Gaby isn't ready to let this go. "You lot always love to point the finger at Alix and blame her for everything that's wrong in the world, when she's just a woman trying to help the ghosts only she can see."

"I'm pretty sure GoPol—"

"GoPol doesn't do shit for ghosts. All they care about is using them for their spy work or ruining every independent whisperer's life."

My back goes rigid at her bluntness. "Gaby, please."

"No, Alix! I'm sick of you catching stray bullets from every side. No one cares for the ghosts like you. You're the only one they can turn to with their problems and issues, and you deserve a bloody medal for it, not to be cornered in your own home."

"So, you'd say she'd put ghosts' needs in front of the needs of the living?" Bézier asks, his voice giving me chills.

"A hundred per cent!" Gaby says with unbridled passion.

I wince, too late to stop her. As much as I appreciate her defence, I'm not sure it's helping.

Bézier turns to me. "So, which side are you on, Mademoiselle Dubois? Ours? Or the ghosts'?"

My eyes bulge at his conclusion. "I wasn't aware there were sides."

His eyebrows crawl up. "Really? The GoPol headquarters are attacked by a ghost after another manages to build an invisible machine that can warp reality? The whole building was levelled—sinkhole, my ass. And then mere weeks later, ghosts come back to life, trying to subjugate the living and take their bloody revenge for something that happened over two hundred years ago."

"One ghost."

"You think it's going to stop at one ghost when the bones of Napoleon are missing from his grave, the great emperor of France, conqueror of Europe? You think he and every other ghost saw King Louis' failure and decided it wasn't worth it?"

So far, that seems to be exactly what Napoleon is doing. At least, I haven't heard rumours of a revived emperor yet. Louis was brought back within hours of his bones being stolen, but Napoleon's vanished as thoroughly as his bones.

"And what about your friends at the Panthéon? Don't they want to come back and regal us with their superiority? Wouldn't you help them? You know, if they're asking nicely?"

I'm too stunned by his accusations to react properly.

Gaby has no such inhibitions. "That's not what Alix does. Yes, of course, she helps ghosts, but not blindly and not every request.

We're talking about proper care for their resting places or that one time we drove to the Dordogne to find Josephine Baker's stolen war medals. The curator hadn't even noticed they'd been replaced by fakes and would've done nothing. That's why we need people like Alix, who keep an open mind and listen."

*Too much information,* I think. She's giving Bézier way too much detail.

"Or that one time she risked her life in the catacombs to retrieve a ghost's dead body to uncover a crime that would've been lost to the darkness, the ghost forever suffering from the injustice."

I'm almost grateful she's leaving out the fact the ghost tricked me with this request, letting me believe I was only going after some sentimental bauble, not her whole-ass body after she'd been murdered.

"Gaby, would you like some coffee?" I ask in a terse voice, all but dragging her with me before she can run her mouth some more.

Clattering the dishes extra loudly, I hiss, "What are you doing?"

"I told you—I'm tired of you and everybody else blaming you for everything that goes wrong in the ghost world when you're just trying to help."

I can't help but notice how different her reaction is from my sister's Hélène. When I was indirectly involved with her fiancé's death, she blamed me for dragging him into my world—ignoring the fact he'd wanted to join that world for longer than any of us even knew him. Meanwhile, Gaby, who has every reason to be mad at me for failing her brother as he navigated his new existence as a whisperer, won't let me go anywhere near the guilt calling out to me.

"And I'm grateful for it, but you're painting me as a ghosts-first radical."

"A ghosts advocate," Gaby corrects, adamantly. "You want ghosts to be acknowledged, valued, and respected. We both know you wouldn't stand for anything harmful."

"We do, but *he* doesn't." I pour her a cup of coffee, though my fingers are shaking. It's happening all over again. Just like Charles Roubert, Bézier's going to hold me responsible for every ghost activity and roadblock in GoPol's way. "Just... tone it down a little. He doesn't need to know how far I'm willing to go to help ghosts."

If you looked too closely at all the times I've helped ghosts, you'd find a multitude of transgressions and rule breaking I was willing to commit in order to help, starting from sneaking into my workplace outside opening hours, to full on grave-digging to return missing bones and the likes. Never mind all my excursions into the off-limits part of the catacombs.

I think the rules don't really apply when you consider my special ability and unique nature of the requests—I've always broken them for good reason—but let's be honest here, that wouldn't hold up in court.

Gaby crosses her arms, looking at me coolly. "You deserve better, Alix, and it's high time these law enforcers accepted that."

I sigh. Looks like there's no reasoning with Gaby today. She's lost her brother and now she's willing to burn down the world; anything to ease the pain and make his death a little less meaningless. "Let's get this over with."

We return to the living room, where Bézier's writing into his notebook. He looks up, acknowledging the alibi cup, and asks, "Ready to continue?"

"What do you want?" I ask, still sore from my talk with Gaby.

"What do you know about Napoleon?"

"Nothing." Okay, that's far from the truth. "I mean, I'm a history student, so, obviously I know a lot *about* him, but I've never met his ghost, if that's what you mean."

Bézier raises his eyebrow. "Such a famous person? I would've assumed you'd be all over him."

"Why? The Napoleonic Wars aren't a special interest of mine and I doubt we have much in common. He's not exactly known for being a big feminist who's keen to pour his heart out to a woman."

"Did he approach you about the resurrections?"

"She just said no," Gaby barks. "Stop pinning this on her. Alix isn't planning on taking over the world. She's helped Émile Zola and Paul Cézanne to reconcile after a hundred years of strife, allowing their relationship to blossom, and she's helped Abelard and Héloïse have a child after eight hundred years of yearning, which GoPol promptly tore for them, mindlessly destroying one of the greatest love stories in history. She's not trying to cause trouble but ease suffering. Heck, the girl would jigsaw puzzle the skeletons in the catacombs if you'd let her."

"I won't," I say quickly, throwing a firm glance at Gaby. "But if you wanted to neutralise some ghosts and alleviate suffering, you could start there. It's really horrible how they're being held in this world despite having already forgotten who they were—if you could see them, with their multiple limbs or headless bodies. It'd be much kinder to burn the bones and let them rest."

Now Gaby's passion has gotten to me, too. The ghosts of the catacombs are still heavy on my mind ever since I came face to face with their plight. I still haven't figured out how to help them, but maybe this could be it. I just need to take a page out of the GoPol book and paint them as the threat Bézier so clearly craves.

But Bézier shakes his head. "We're getting off-track here. I'm not worried about headless ghosts in the catacombs, but boneless ghosts in the hands of the Chevalier. What's your relationship with the Chevalier d'Os? Or Romain Coullier?"

I'm saved from answering by the sound of the keys in the door. Before it even opens, Dix barges into the living room, quickly followed by Gaspar, both looking ready to throw down and seemingly perplexed to find us all having a nice cup of coffee.

Not too soon after, Sébastien arrives, still sporting a cast. "What's the meaning of this?"

Bézier empties his cup, then levels a stare at me. "Did you send your whisper ghost to call him?"

"Petite Alix is a toddler." Unlike the GoPol agents, I can rely on more than one ghost.

There's a weird energy in the room as Sébastien waits for his answer and Bézier stews in annoyance at having his interrogation disrupted. The whole situation isn't helped by Gaspar and Dix flanking me, as if there was anything they could do if this turned violent.

Gaby feels it, too, despite being as blind to the ghosts as Bézier. "I'm going to need more coffee."

Bézier closes his little notebook and slips it into the pocket of his dress shirt. "There was no need to rush home from work, Roubert. Mademoiselle Dubois and I were just having a chat."

"Don't you think she's faced enough abuse from the police already?" Someone's not taking prisoners today.

Unfazed, Bézier stands. "I'm just doing my job. And if it turns out that Mademoiselle Dubois is at the core of all this recent ghost activity, we need to keep an eye on her. Clearly, *your* judgement is clouded in this case. Her intense focus on the needs of ghosts is worrying, especially as we're still trying to understand how powerful this secret society of ghosts truly is."

"You know there's this thing against ignorance," I say. "It's called learning."

Bézier snorts softly. "But are you the right person to teach us or are you just pushing your ghost agenda?"

"What ghost agenda?" Dix asks. "Doesn't he realise there's literally millions of ghosts in this city with very different ideas on how to spend their afterlife?"

"No," I say to Dix, disregarding Bézier's sensibilities about only hearing half the conversation. If he wants to keep an eye on me, he'd better get used to it. "Instead of accepting the fact ghosts are real people who just happen to be dead already, they're being treated as a homogeneous entity, and as a threat. It's typical for humans. Instead of trying to understand each other, we destroy each other."

Dix rolls his eyes. "And here I thought we were finally moving forward."

"We are," Sébastien says, his voice still like steel. "Moving forward, that is," he says for Bézier's benefit. "Any potential threat will be investigated, but the goal isn't to neutralise all ghost activity, but to benefit from each other. Wouldn't you agree, Thomas?"

Bézier's looking from Sébastien to me and into the general direction in which Dix waits. "And if Mademoiselle Alix turns out to be a threat?"

What have I ever done to GoPol? "To answer your earlier question: I detest what the Chevalier is doing with these resurrections. We are not the same."

"Far from it," Sébastien agrees.

"He's in it for power, maybe revenge. I'm here for the ghosts."

# CHAPTER 2

Bézier's surprise interrogation and something the Chevalier said earlier this year has gotten me thinking. Right now, ghost mania is still in full swing. It doesn't completely overwhelm the news cycle anymore, but people still crave new information. GoPol's clearly trying to paint the ghosts as a threat, something that needs to be controlled and held at bay. If I let them, nothing much will change.

It's time to give Voltaire what he wants.

Before my next ghost tour, I take the stairs up to Monsieur Passard's office. and knock on the door. He looks up from his desk and takes off his glasses. "Alix, how may I help you? Or is it the ghosts who have a request?"

I can't help but smile. He's gotten on board admirably fast, and it just warms my heart to have someone who can't even see ghosts appreciate them. "I was thinking."

"Uh-uh."

"The ghosts tours have been going so well I had an idea for our social media account." He looks interested, so I feel emboldened. "What if I were to introduce our inhabitants. Have little interviews, regular Q&As, or even present some of their work?"

I see the wheels turning in Monsieur Passard's mind. "That sounds like a lot of work."

"My sister Odile is a bit of a social media expert. She runs two very successful accounts and would be delighted to help."

"Unpaid?"

"Maybe we could budget a little bit for her?" I don't want Odile to put all this work in without getting something out of it, especially when I haven't even asked her yet.

He's pulling up something on his screen and studies it for a minute. I wait patiently while he crunches the numbers. "Costs have gone up with the additional load on the conservator, but the tours are doing very well—we're still booked for weeks. I'd assume interest would increase with the added social media. Too bad you're still studying."

"I've got summer break coming up. That's two months, almost three, where I could do more shifts." That reminds me I need to study for my exams.

"You want to work full-time over summer?" Monsieur Passard asks.

My heart skips a beat. "Are you offering me a full-time position?"

He grins. "Right now, you're my top employee, Alix; I don't need a degree from you. Any chance I can convince you to make this a permanent position?"

My head's swimming, and I really have to fight off the grin this time. I've just been offered a well-paid, permanent, full-time position in my favourite workplace—to work with ghosts! But if I've learnt anything these last few months, it's how quickly things can change. The interest in ghosts could wane. Other ghost whisperers could go public and create competition. I might have other opportunities, or not, if I don't have a full degree. The situation is far too new to risk my career on it.

"Let's do the summer first. Maybe we can work something out with the Sorbonne after that."

"Sounds good. Well, I'll make a draft for what your summer position could look like. I reckon you'll want *some* time off to actually enjoy summer..."

"Yes, please." Now he's said it, I wonder if Sébastien, Gaspar, and I could go away. Somewhere warm and sunny—and full of ghosts.

Monsieur Passard nods with a twinkle in his eyes. He knows there are limits to how much I can do. Even if I detest them at the moment. "And yes, to the social media content. I'll add you to the moderator list and loop in our social media manager. Let's trial this for a few weeks before we fully commit. If the engagement numbers go up, I might have a summer job for your sister, as well."

The grin is back—not that it ever truly left. "You'd better brace yourself. Odi has a lot of ideas."

"Seems to run in your family."

As soon as the ghost tour and all the guests have left, I tell my ghosts about my new master plan.

"Finally!" Voltaire exclaims, throwing his hands up and pacing. "I thought it was never going to happen."

"Does that mean I get to share my thoughts and ideas with the living once more?" Jean-Jacques Rousseau asks, a painful note of hope in his voice.

Voltaire returns immediately. "Oh, please, no. The last thing the world needs are more of your idiotic ideas."

"*My* ideas are idiotic? You're the one behind the times—still harping on about enlightenment when the whole world shines bright."

"You call this generation enlightened? These people who forget their own history and still struggle with the same concepts as they did when we were alive? Who value financial success, comfort, and vanity above science and fact?"

I roll my eyes and move to the writers' crypt where I can't hear the two of them fighting. There, I find Petite Alix on Alexandre Dumas' knees, listening to what sounds like a story about hedgehog musketeers—the Malou crossover we've all needed. She immediately stretches out her arms to have a cuddle with me, and I indulge her. Though I've lived most of my ghost whispering life without her, I can't imagine ever doing so again. We'd been separated long enough she feels less like a part of me and more like a baby sister.

"Did you bring Malou?" she asks.

"No, she's off fighting Milady d'Escargot, isn't she?"

Alexandre Dumas smiles. "Indeed. Do you think she'll win this time?"

Petite Alix immediately returns to his knees, eyes shining. "Malou will get that evil snail this time!"

I turn to Victor with a smile, thinking if Bézier could only see this, he wouldn't be so scared of ghosts. But there might be a good reason for his fear, and while I don't plan on joining the GoPol efforts anytime soon, I should cover all my bases. "Can we talk about Napoleon?"

Victor sighs. "What's there to talk about? He's a short, little man with a god complex."

"Yeah, maybe that's exactly what we should talk about, considering he might be coming back to life soon." I'm still amazed he hasn't already. "What do you think he'll do?"

Never one to miss trash-talking another ghost, Voltaire appears at my side. "Same as always. Try to take over the world."

"Same as always? You mean when he was alive?"

Voltaire shakes his head. "He spends his eternity cooking up harebrained schemes, each more moronic than the one before. If Napoleon doesn't plan on taking over the world once every decade, it wouldn't be the afterlife."

Surprised, I gape at him. "This is a regular thing?"

"Told you he's got a god complex," Victor says, not sounding particularly worried. "It's only grown worse since they buried him in that fancy, giant tomb of his."

"So, who stops him? How has nothing happened before?" I can't believe everyone's so nonchalant about it.

Voltaire snorts. "Mostly, the lack of an army."

"That fancy, giant tomb isn't just for decoration either," Victor points out. "It was meant to keep him inside, severely restricting his ghost's movements."

"Well, he's no longer inside."

Voltaire waves me off. "It's only superstition. Napoleon's no more powerful than any other long-lasting ghost. Without an army, he's just a little man dreaming of bigger things."

"So, you're not worried what he might do if he came to life?"

"Is his army alive, too?" Voltaire asks.

I shrug. "Maybe not the whole army, but I doubt the Chevalier will stop with one last resurrection."

"Now that's a man who worries me," Victor says. "He's ambitious and smart. A dangerous combination."

"He's about to have a strategic mastermind at his side." Say what you will about Napoleon, the guy knew how to win wars.

"On paper, yes," Victor concedes, "but what the Chevalier happens to forget is we ghosts are more than just our accomplishments. We're still human, prone to mistakes." It's rare for him to show some real humility. "This alliance might not be as fruitful as the Chevalier hopes it'll be. I can't imagine Napoleon working for him—or even listening to anything he's got to say. Like I said, we're talking about a man with a god complex; *two* men with god complexes."

I can see how that might be a recipe for disaster. It's hard to imagine Napoleon submitting to the Chevalier or listening to reason, but it's far from impossible. If someone knows how to rise through the ranks, it's our former emperor. He didn't come from nothing, but his origins are comparably humble and would've been unthinkable before the revolution blew the field wide open.

"The problem is we have no idea what the Chevalier is planning. Or Napoleon, for that matter." I look over my shoulder, looking for one of the Napoleonic generals buried in the Panthéon. They're all keeping to themselves these days. "We need information."

"I'm telling you: it's just one of his usual schemes." Voltaire waves his hand in an affected manner. "They gather steam fast then fizzle out for lack of support. He can't recreate the magic. It's not his time."

"What if it's his time now?"

I don't want to sound paranoid but there's definitely something going on. Louis XVI and Olivier may have been a test run, born out of opportunity, but the theft of Napoleon's bones was long planned, and considering how Marie Antoinette simply demanded her bones back, the fact Napoleon hasn't means he's in on this plan. I bet that snivelling Mathieu, the Chevalier's right-hand man, has been courting him while I was busy in St Denis.

Victor puts a hand on my shoulder, looking deep into my eyes. "Don't worry, Alix. We've had almost two hundred years of his antics. It'll be the same as every other time. The world isn't in danger."

Only it is. "What about Nostradamus' prophecy?" I was told I'd bring chaos and destruction to France. Will that be by courtesy of Napoleon?

"That prophecy is nothing but superstition—" Victor starts.

"Something Napoleon might believe" Voltaire adds.

"But even if it *were* true," Victor stresses for my benefit, "the prophecy mentioned you'd do that, not him. So, unless you're planning on teaming up with Napoleon and conquering the world for yourself, I don't see it happening."

Neither teaming up with Napoleon nor conquering the world are on my bucket list, so I probably should stop worrying. If only someone would tell my brain to shut up and stop overthinking.

"Listen," a new voice adds to the chorus—Jean Moulin, "if it makes you feel better, I could look into the matter, gather information, find out his plans."

I let out a sigh of relief. "That would make me feel a lot better." Nothing like having France's best spy on the case.

He salutes me. "Consider it done."

"Alright. Time for me to head home."

I give Victor a hug and then an even longer one to Petite Alix, promising to tell Malou to stop by once she's back from her adventures in 17th century France. Pack-down goes fairly fast, since most of it was already done before I ran my tour, and soon I'm out on the stairs, breathing in the warm night air.

I'm about to unlock my bike when a shadow peels away from the fence and steps into the light. "I thought you'd never come out."

Freezing, I stare at the woman in front of me, recognising her by her ginger curls. "Madame Humbert."

She's a journalist, who snuck into one of my early tours to get the inside scoop on ghost mechanics. The Panthéon ghosts had to remove her to stop her from hounding me, but she turned up in Versailles at the night of the royal ball.

"Bonsoir, Mademoiselle Dubois. I was wondering if you had some time for me."

I continue unlocking my bike as if she doesn't faze me at all. For all I know, she's just a stubborn journalist. I know the type; I grew up with one. "Not really. I'm on my way home."

"How about tomorrow? We could meet at a café."

I sigh. "For what?"

She smiles, slightly irritated. "For an exclusive interview about ghosts and ghost whisperers."

"I don't do interviews." I yank my bike from the fence, not that it needed so much force, only to find my path blocked. "What are you doing?"

"I don't care what the others say: you're the real deal, the best source there is for the truth about ghosts. And I intend to be the one to uncover it."

"My father has all the rights in that regard."

Félice Humbert winces. "I'm, of course, familiar with your father, Mademoiselle Dubois. Great journalist. That exposé? Groundbreaking. But he's your father first and a journalist second. His takes are biased. It shows in that exposé, which so deftly buried your actual role in ghost matters. I understand you value your privacy, but I think this could benefit us both."

"I don't think so." To mark my words, I push the bike around her, swinging one leg over the seat.

"I know you're in a relationship with a ghost."

My movements come to a sudden stop. What did she just say? "That's ridiculous."

"Is it?" she asks, sounding slightly amused. "For you, they're just like every other person, aren't they? It makes sense your dating pool would be twice as large. I don't see a problem with it."

She hesitates slightly before plunging the dagger in. "But others might."

Slowly, I turn around. "And I assume you've got irrefutable proof?"

She taps her phone and shows me a video. Sure enough, it's me at Versailles, lying in Gaspar's arms, seeking comfort after dealing with Olivier, before sending him to take care of Sébastien instead. And while only a ghost whisperer can see Gaspar, my movements and words give his presence away—or make me look like a crazy woman.

"Since you value your privacy so much—"

I won't even let her finish. "Tomorrow morning, 8am, *Chambelland*. You've got half an hour before I have to go to class."

Her face breaks into a wide grin. "I'll be there eight sharp."

# CHAPTER 3

I'm still pissed about the whole thing when I roll into *Chambelland* the next morning. Félice is already there, occupying a table at the window. She's positively beaming and waves as if we're just two friends catching up. I give her the slightest smile of recognition, then turn away to order at the counter, not that I have to spell it out. Marie knows exactly what I'm getting.

"Have here or take away?" is the only question she needs.

With an eye-roll in Félice's general direction, I say, "Have here. But I might need you to rescue me if this interview goes terribly wrong."

Marie grins. "I've got you."

I take my order and sit opposite Félice. Last night, I called my father to ask his advice, and he gave me a quick refresher of how to make a journalist happy while not telling them anything I wouldn't want printed in the newspapers. He wasn't too pleased with how Félice approached me, going as far as calling her unethical, but agreed the best way to deal with her would be to get it over and done with.

"Thank you for meeting me, Mademoiselle Dubois." She's all smiles this morning, looking positively excited. "Do you mind if I record our session? Just tell me if anything is off the record, but you probably know your way around interviews."

"This is my first," I remind her, "but yes, I do know the rules of recording." The question is, does she? Ethically, she's not allowed to use anything I've explicitly said was off the record, but the best way to avoid any surprises is to not say anything at all.

Félice grins. "Wonderful. Then let's get started." She puts a small recording device on the table and takes a sip from her coffee. "I'm so excited to speak to a real ghost whisperer. So, let me ask this first: when did you first realise you were able to see ghosts?"

I'm not going to go into my family history, so all I say is, "I could practically see them all my life. When I was younger, everyone assumed they were standard imaginary friends, so I guess I was about seven or eight when I realised mine weren't like anybody else's."

"Did you always feel different because of it? I can imagine it's quite a burden to see a whole host of people no one else can and—I don't know. How did people react?"

Question two and we're already fishing for deep-seated trauma. How do I answer this question without using my "no comment" card? "Well, I guess, I definitely didn't have your usual childhood. While others went to the playground, I went to the cemetery."

"You sought ghosts out?"

"They were more interesting."

Félice laughs. "I bet. No, seriously. If I could see ghosts, I'd spend all my time with them, too. Was that how it was for you? Did you feel more comfortable around ghosts than the living?"

The answer is a big fat "Yes!" but I'm not sure I want that in the paper. "I guess the ghosts didn't judge, because they knew they were ghosts and they could see the living, whereas for the living, I was basically talking to myself."

The laughter fades away and I see concern enter her eyes. "I can only imagine how hard that must've been." Damn, she's good at this, using empathy to break down my walls. "Has that changed for you since the World Fair apparitions? I mean, I was on one of your ghost tours and you were so confident and comfortable."

"Sure. It's still early days, but I'm hopeful about where we're headed. Being able to share my ghosts with the world has been a relief, but also a great joy. I think they still have so much to offer this world."

Papa mentioned the best way to deal with an interview would be to direct it to the topics you *want* to talk about. It can be a tug-of-war if the interviewer and interviewee want different things, or it can be a respectful open conversation that brings things to light naturally.

Félice leans forward, intrigued. "What would a world full of ghosts look like? What can we expect? What do you hope for?"

Hook, line, and sinker. "Oh, ghosts carry all kinds of potential. The important thing people need to realise is when we talk about ghosts, we aren't referring to paranormal phenomena. These aren't fragments of a life, evil poltergeists, or vengeful spirits: they're human. In fact, they're just like us. They've just already died. So, once you wrap your head around that, there's a ton of possibilities. Just going by the ghosts who reside in the Panthéon, we've got Marie Curie, who's been continuing her research, currently specialising in spectral radiometry, or Paul Langevin, who's still obsessed with magnetism."

So obsessed, he rarely leaves his crypt.

"I know Victor Hugo, Alexandre Dumas, and Émile Zola have a ton of books still waiting to be written. Hidden masterpieces, perhaps. And people like Jean-Jacques Rousseau are extremely interested in the meaning of the afterlife, and would love to share their ideas with living philosophers. If we can find a way to connect more humans with ghosts, we can advance science into the stratosphere. Just imagine, thousands of researchers, who can work around the clock, no longer require payment, and continue contributing."

"Wouldn't that put our living researchers out of their jobs? I mean, you're making a valid point about ghosts being the better alternative."

I'm speechless for a moment. That's absolutely not the point I was making. "I'm talking about collaborations, not replacements. Science, like all fields, needs new voices and eyes as much as it needs experience and expertise."

"But let's be honest. If you were able to 'employ'"—she uses her fingers for air quotes—"ghosts, saving you tons of money, why would you bother with the living equivalent?"

I'm completely baffled by the argument, and yet, there's some truth to it. Idiotic humans that we are, we'd absolutely do such a thing. "Sounds to me like capitalism is the problem, not ghosts."

"So, your dreamworld would be a socialist one then, where everyone just contributes to society from the goodness of their heart?"

That'd be exactly what the ghosts would do. I fail to see how that's a bad thing. But I can already see the headline: *Ghost whisperer's delusional socialist dreams.*

"Maybe it'll be something new. We've never lived in a society where everyone was aware of ghosts. Sure, we can always assume the worst, but if I've learnt anything from history, it's how adaptable humans are. This discovery falls in the same veins as the Industrial Revolution and other shifts in society. Things change—hopefully for the better—and we'll develop new standards, new codes, a new way of living."

"Such as..."

"One that's connected to the past, showing ghosts respect and dignity, while using this concentrated boost in knowledge and thinkers to forge a path into the future. It's hard to tell what the world is going to look like at this point."

Félice nods understandingly, but there's a little crease on her forehead. "But you're certain the world will change?"

"How could it not?" With ghosts proven to stick around, I can't see a future that continues to ignore their existence.

"It's a bit scary, isn't it?"

"Change often is." I hope if she puts that in her article it comes across as a message of hope, not an inevitable fact everyone freaks out about. Like death itself.

Félice laughs nervously. "Well, you've certainly embraced the change with your ghost tours and that exciting ghost exhibition at Versailles... Speaking of Versailles, can you tell me what happened there? I know the official version is you hired an actor to impersonate Louis XVI, but that doesn't seem in line with your usual work."

"What do you mean?" I sip my coffee, which has already gone cold, watching her anxiously. Versailles was a giant mess, a sore topic with repercussions far beyond anything I could've imagined.

She leans back, oozing confidence. "Well, you put on this magnificent exhibition about the royal women, and I remember you telling us at one of your tours that the royals were being led by a Triad of Queens,"—curse my stupid mouth—"so, it doesn't really make a lot of sense for you to hire a male actor to impersonate a king, and not just any king, but Louis XVI, who we got... well, rid of."

So close. She's too close to the truth. There's no way I can tell her more than that. For one, because it's so incredibly haunting, and second, because I signed a contract with the government not to pass on any detail of ongoing investigations or paint ghosts as something to be afraid of. Something I didn't think I'd be in danger off until the three queens ruling St Denis proved me wrong.

It's time for my get-out-of-jail-free card. "I'm not at liberty to say."

Intrigued, she leans forward again. "Is that because a ghost asked you for privacy in the matter, or—"

"I signed an NDA," I say, intending to stop her in her tracks.

"For whom?"

Raising an eyebrow, I don't even deign her with an answer.

"Sorry." Félice laughs. "You can't fault a journalist for asking." She checks her watch. "Not much time left, I'm afraid. So, let me ask one more thing: what's going on with Napoleon?"

A chill creeps into my bones. Wouldn't we all like to know? "You mean the disappearance of his bones?"

"Exactly."

"I don't know any more than you. Apparently, a group of people broke into Les Invalides the night of the ball and stole them."

Félice is practically hanging off my lips, but she won't learn much more than that. "For what purpose?"

I shrug. "Beats me."

"You don't know?" When I shake my head, she crosses her arms. "What does his ghost say? Is he worried?"

"I haven't talked to his ghost. We're not familiar."

Now, she's outright pouting. "Is that so?"

"I'm telling the truth. I'm not acquainted with Napoleon."

"And the ghosts? I mean, you're practically surrounded by his generals. Haven't they said anything? Do ghosts gossip?"

"Oh, yes, very much so. But no, all I've heard from the ghosts is I shouldn't worry about it." I hope Bézier's happy with this answer as I'm doing my very best to minimise the danger.

Félice is still pouting. "And you believe that?"

"I trust my ghosts, yes." Quickly, I empty my cup and grab my untouched pain au chocolat. "But I'm afraid I have to run now. I expect you'll send me the article for approval?" She should.

With a forced smile, she nods. "Of course. Thank you for your time, Mademoiselle Dubois. I wish I could pick your brain for longer. Maybe some other time? We could talk more about your personal relationships with ghosts."

Forming a thin line with my mouth, I nod sharply. "Maybe." I can't believe she's going to keep holding my relationship with Gaspar over me. "But I've got exams coming up and a demanding job going through lots of changes. It might be a while."

"I understand." The smile is almost genuine.

Relief washes over me as soon as I turn my back on her. It wasn't as bad as I'd thought it might be, and hopefully she'll portray me truthfully rather than build a narrative of anti-capitalistic, job-stealing ghosts. But after experiencing how GoPol twists my every word and I'm almost exclusively met with fear and suspicion, I don't really have high hopes. And it annoys me that someone else gets to tell my story, painting it with their own biased brush. Never mind the ghosts' stories.

"You got through that one well," Marie says as she packs the pastry into a bag and pours another coffee to-go.

"I'm glad it's over."

"I bet." Marie's smile wavers, and suddenly, her eyes water.

Alarmed, I jump to the nearest conclusion. "Did something happen to Gaby?

"Oh, no." She quickly shakes her head. "All considered, she's doing amazing. I'm glad she's got you. I mean, sure, I wish she'd lean a little more on me, but we've only been together for a half a year, and I didn't even really know Olivier."

"Neither did I," I say softly. At least not before his near-fatal accident.

She sighs. "I just wish there was something I could do for her, something to make it all better."

I reach over the counter and rub her arm. "Gaby's going to come back from this. She's strong, resilient. She just needs a little time away from the world."

Marie smiles, but it's the same sad smile she had after Gaspar's death, when I thought she was the saddest barista I'd ever met. "I know. And she knows I'm here for her, right?"

"Absolutely." And in case she forgot, I plan on telling Gaby that Marie asked about her.

The smile grows a little in strength. "Thank you." She takes a deep breath. "We'll all get through this."

At least until the Chevalier unleashes Napoleon.

# Chapter 4

After classes, I visit my parents, or rather Odile, who I find occupying the dining table with her head over flash cards, folders, and her laptop. I've been so busy with everything else, I'd completely forgotten she's in crunch time for her bac. She must be halfway through her written exams with only the specialised subjects and her grand oral ahead of her.

"Is this a bad time?" I ask, holding up a bag of crisps. "I brought sustenance."

Odile snatches the bag from my hands and breaks into it. "Save me."

"From what?" I ask, laughing.

"I can't do any more exams. I'm pretty sure, I failed French and Economics and—"

I put my hands on her shoulders and search her gaze. "Odi, I'm sure you aced those. That's just normal bac madness." I should know. I was a bundle of nerves throughout my last month of school. "Two more weeks and you're done."

"If I pass."

"You're going to pass."

Odile might not be the most academically inclined person, but she's never truly struggled in school, and I know she's passionate about her specialisations. The grand oral, which nearly made me puke back then, will be a total breeze for her.

I sit at her table, quickly overlooking the various subjects. "Do you want me to help you study?"

Crumbs fly from Odile's mouth when she speaks. "Nah, I've already got Hélène on my case." There's a key in the door. "Speak of the devil."

"I'm back!" my older sister calls. She no longer lives here and returned to her old apartment with a friend, but apparently, still visits frequently. "I got you some boba and some *healthy* food for your brain." She stops cold when she walks into the room and finds Odile with her hand in the crisps. "You need proper sustenance." There's a shy smile for me. "Hello, Alix. Are you here to help Odi? History was last week, wasn't it?"

"Yep, that's done. I think I did pretty well," Odile says, proudly. "Why *are* you here?"

It's still a bit awkward between Hélène and me. While I've forgiven her—and she's forgiven me, though I never did anything wrong—she's still put me through so much hurt. Most of it was well-meaning, but I wish she'd spent less time worrying about me and more time listening. Specifically, when it comes to ghosts, which makes the following a lot harder than it should be.

"Look, you need to concentrate on your exams, but once you're done, I might have an exciting project for you."

Odile's eyes light up. "Tell me!"

I share another glance with Hélène, which annoys me, because I don't need her permission. "Well, I've decided to start a social media channel."

Nothing could've prepared me for Odile's squeal and euphoric embrace. "Finally! Give me your phone. Which platform are you thinking? Content? Ghosts, of course."

"Slow down, please!" I say, laughing, her enthusiasm quickly blowing all my doubts away. "So, two things: first off, my boss gave me access to the Panthéon's social media. I want to do a series on our ghostly inhabitants. And he said there might be a summer project in it for you."

"For me?" Odile's grin grows even wider. "I'm in."

"You don't even know the details," Hélène says, always the voice of reason.

I try to practise some restraint for both their benefit. "We'll have a meeting with our social media manager and get you in for an interview: *after* you're finished with exams."

Odile pouts. "I don't need to learn anymore. I already know everything."

That's an impressive turn from the wild panic only a few minutes ago. "Yeah, I still think it'll be better afterwards." Which is exactly when my finals are—add it to my growing list. "The second thing is I want to have my own channel. Educational, but more about ghosts in general, my experience and relationships, not all the famous people I know." I'm thinking of tea with my grandmother and Beatrice, rainy Chopin concerts in Père Lachaise, or the ghosts of the catacombs.

"Alix," Hélène says, her distinctive brand of worry thickening her voice. "Do you really want to put yourself out there like that?"

"Well, it looks like I don't really have a choice." Bézier was right about one thing. "Whether I want this or not, I'm at the heart of the ghost movement. I can't escape it, and frankly, I don't want to. But if my story has to be told, I'd rather it be in my own words." I don't want the Félice Humberts of this world to paint my picture, nor the Thomas Béziers to muzzle me.

Odile has tears in her eyes. She makes excited little mini claps and hugs me again. "I knew you'd come around. I'm so proud of you."

Hélène uses Odile's show of affection to secretly wipe a tear from her cheek. "I just hate the fact I can't protect you."

"From what?" It's not like Hélène has ever truly done so.

"The world, I guess." She shrugs. "To me, you're still the little girl who fell in the river and nearly died. Only now you've got crazy people coming after you with guns, ghosts trying to blow you up, and..." Another tear rolls down her cheek. "It's all going to be worth it, right?"

I'd be lying if I said I wasn't scared. This whole thing, this rapid change I see in the world around me, and my growing list of people I'd rather only see on the other side of the Seine, scares the shit out of me. But I truly believe we can build something great if only we learn to embrace rather than fight it.

"It will be. Eventually."

"Okay." Odile claps her hands, then pulls up a paper. "Let's draw up a plan for your channel and brainstorm your first few videos. Malou will share you, of course."

"What about your exams?" Hélène complains, ever the voice of reason.

Glad that's not my role. "It'll be good for her. Take her mind off it for a bit. Breaks are important."

"What she said," Odile says, and we both burst out laughing.

Hélène looks a bit affronted at first, but then she smiles, too. "Alright. Let's do this."

Later that night, I show off my first video to Sébastien and Gaspar. Wedged in between the two, we're snuggling on the couch, two wine glasses on the table. As so often, Dix is in my room, getting his daily dose of double hedgehog fun, and keeping far away from what he calls the "gross throuple stuff".

Life has been good lately. Sure, there are worrisome things underfoot, but when I see how far the three of us have come, and how much respect we have for each other, I couldn't be happier. Somehow, this throuple thing is working. It's not just two guys who are in love with me and tolerate the other to make me happy, they actually carry a lot of love for each other. And while they haven't been physical with each other, as far as I know, I've definitely seen some glances in that direction.

My video's a fun little intro, poking fun at how seeing ghosts used to be frowned upon and is the hottest shit right now.

"What do you think?" I ask. I had way too much fun with my sisters. The video might not be groundbreaking, but we needed it.

"Very cool!" Gaspar says. "But next time, I'm in charge of the music."

"Since when do you listen to on-trend music?"

He pulls the most adorable face, and I nuzzle my nose against his, then kiss him softly.

On my other side, Sébastien's started reading the comments. There aren't many yet since this is literally my first public post. "Are you sure you want to do this?"

I put my arm around him and tousle his blond hair. "Don't worry, I can handle the scrutiny. But yes, I'd rather tell my own story than have it told by the newspapers or people like your boss."

He winces. "Sorry about that." He apologises at least once a day for it.

"We knew that was coming. GoPol—or Interpol—can't wrap their heads around the fact anyone outside of the organisation could have a valid point."

"I can." He leans his head on my arm, turning his face to me. "In my opinion, your points are the most valid, and I wish we had more of that in GoPol."

I tousle his hair some more, gazing into his blue eyes, just as Gaspar presses his lips on my neck. A gasp escapes my mouth, and I lurch forward, leaning more into Sébastien. He captures my mouth with his lips, and for a moment, I forget all about GoPol. But I'm still buzzing too much from my new ideas, and manage to extract myself from their double-pronged approach.

"How are things at GoPol?"

"Seriously?" Gaspar complains.

Sébastien, however, sighs. "Not so great. The talks have stalled, and I've got a ton to do investigating the stolen bones."

"You're not back in the field, are you?" It's only been a few weeks since I watched him fall out of a window. He's still wearing a cast, for that matter.

He shakes his head. "No, but I'm coordinating the efforts. I've sent half of our Parisian force and their whisper ghosts into the catacombs to try and find the Chevalier."

"Find him? Is he not at the Crossroad or in his lab?"

I haven't been back in the catacombs after my last altercation with the Chevalier. I thought we were building something good, but he only used me to lure powerful ghosts towards his scheme, then had the audacity to berate me about loyalty, only to stab me in the back by bringing back Louis XVI and sacrificing Olivier.

Worry flashes in Sébastien's eyes, but it's gone so quick, I wonder how serious this truly is. What's he keeping from me? "He's gone. We checked all the known places, even crawled back into Ossa Arida, but there's no trace of the Chevalier. Dix picked up enough ghost rumours to know he's *somewhere* in the catacombs, but the ghosts are pretty tight-lipped, unfortunately. They're hiding him."

"Do you want me to ask?"

"No!" His outrage is joined by Gaspar, who shakes his head. Sébastien's eyes are wide, as if I've just offered to become the next experiment in the Chevalier's hands.

I sink into the couch, taken aback by their violent reactions. "Jeez, it was only an idea." After all, my relationships with ghosts are arguably the best of the three of us—yes, even counting Gaspar's inherent ghostliness.

Sébastien shifts to bring his knee up next to me, then puts his healthy hand on my cheek, a warm smile on his lips. "And I appreciate it, but this is literally a standard GoPol mission. I've got the manpower, everyone's doing their job, and no ghosts are getting harmed. We all know the Chevalier has taken a special interest in you, which is why I want you as far away from him as possible. I can't think of a reason good enough to expose you to this danger again." He leans in to kiss the corner of my mouth. "Please."

I can't quite resist the kiss, cherishing the rare moments when Sébastien takes charge. But there's something more powerful inside me, yearning to get out: my guilt.

"I should've done more to earn his trust. Then I might've known about his plans surrounding Napoleon. I could've stopped him."

A low growl builds in Sébastien's throat. "Don't you dare take the blame for this. Once again, that's a GoPol job. You're not an agent."

"But maybe I should've been. You wanted me to work for you and—"

"Not like that!" His eyes are blazing. "Alix, the man's dangerous. He's playing fast and loose with people's lives, and he's obsessed with you. I don't care what intel you might be able to get for us, I'm not going to risk you, agent or not."

A hand lands on my thigh, slowly stroking up, just as Gaspar resumes kissing my neck again. His whispers are almost hot in my ear. "Leave the spy work to Séb and Dix. You're needed here."

"I've got it under control," Sébastien says in a slow seductive tone, then cocks his head to kiss the other side of my neck. "Don't worry about it."

Grasping a coherent thought is becoming increasingly hard, especially when Gaspar's hand strokes more up than down. And somehow Sébastien's hand is under my shirt.

"Um... okay. I mean... okay." Yeah, my brain has definitely left the building. A stray thought floats up. "Family dinner."

"What?" Sébastien lifts his head, his hot breath blazing across my lips.

"Um, family dinner. My mother wants us all to come to dinner on Saturday. Getting the whole family together."

"You mean she wants *you* to come?"

I shake my head. While Sébastien has stopped for the moment, Gaspar is not letting me off the hook that easily, continuing his foray into my nether regions. "I... Oh! Um, no, she... she wants you to come, too. You live with me, so you're part of the family. I mean we are—ah... together."

Sébastien winces. Coming from a two-person family where he's only ever experienced abuse, the whole family business is still foreign to him. He probably doesn't believe he's really wanted. For that reason alone—and the fact Gaspar is about to rob me of all my brain capacity—I grab Sébastien's face with both hands. "You're coming."

Then I pull his lips onto mine and drown out any further doubt with my tongue.

# Chapter 5

After Gaby spent last night in her flat with Marie, she feels ready to face classes again. According to her, she can't afford to miss any more, especially not with exams creeping up on us. To brace ourselves, we meet up at *Chambelland* for an early morning coffee.

"Saw the video," Gaby greets me from behind the counter. Apparently, she's been helping Marie opening the store. "Loved it. Odi's signature?"

"Of course."

Overnight, my video's gathered some surprising steam. I blame the trending sound and current interest in ghosts, but I've already got a bunch of questions I can reply to without even having to touch the other content we've planned.

Some of the comments are a bit nasty, but after everything I've been through with GoPol and the Chevalier, they don't cut nearly as deep as I'd thought they would. Who cares about some internet trolls and self-proclaimed gatekeepers? I'm just going to ignore the negative nancies and focus on the things that bring me joy.

"I knew it! You need to tell me what you've got planned before class. If you want, I can help you moderate. You've got so much else to do and I'd love to be part of this."

A bit overwhelmed, I glance at Marie. It's as if overnight Gaby has completely wiped off her grief and been reborn a new woman. The wary look in Marie's eyes tells me I'm right, so I treat the offer with caution. "Sure, let's see if we can work something out." One thing's for sure: I trust Gaby a lot more than the likes of Félice Humbert.

"Alright, I'll take a quick trip to the loo and then we can go."

As soon as she's gone, I ask Marie, "Is everything okay?"

"She's really determined to go back to class and leave it all behind her. I'm worried it's still too early. I mean, they buried him only last week." Marie hugs herself.

"I know." As a friend of the family, and Gaby in particular, I was there. Olivier's ghost, meanwhile, has kept his distance. I haven't quite figured out where he's off to, and to be fair, part of me doesn't care. While I could've probably done more to help him, he acted like a real ass, even before he fell for the Chevalier's promises. He's probably somewhere drowning in shame and guilt, which he totally should. Bonding with Louis XVI against all reason was exceptionally stupid.

It makes me wonder who the unlucky guy the Chevalier plans to bond Napoleon with is. But then I already have an inkling who it might be. After all, he's already chomping at the bit.

"I wonder what Mathieu's whisper ghost is like," I think out loud.

"Who?" Marie stares at me in confusion.

I wave her off. "Sorry, just thinking about the next step in the Chevalier's plan."

Marie hugs herself. "He's going to bring Napoleon back, isn't he? I talked to my uncle about it and, apparently, the sarcophagus Napoleon was buried in was designed by the Knights Hospitallers. It was supposed to seal his power."

Voltaire said something similar. "But now that seal's broken."

"What's broken?" Gaby returns.

Marie and I share a quick glance and non-verbally decide not to worry Gaby right now. "The coffee seal. Whole load is ruined. Are you ready to go?"

Gaby gives us a megawatt smile, as if we're off to Disneyland rather than a fairly boring method lecture. "As ready as I'll ever be."

I guess there's no sense in stopping her. There's only so long you can lie in bed and wallow. "Alright. Let's go, then."

The lecture goes surprisingly well. If anything, Gaby is incredibly focused and eager. I've never seen her take so many notes or keep her eyes fixed on the board. The problem is I can't quite tell whether that's because she wants to forget about Olivier or because she desperately needs to catch up.

"That was a good one," she declares at the end, still jotting down notes. "I feel like I've got a much better grasp on restoration than before. It's interesting, too, isn't it? The care that goes into conserving historical buildings and sculptures."

"Sure." It's not exactly a topic I'm passionate about, though the Panthéon's conservator would probably beg to differ. "I'd rather do it than write about it, though."

Her eyes light up for some reason. "Oh, I wonder if we'll be doing anything at the lab later today. Damn, I've missed so much."

"Only a few weeks." Just then, my phone pings, and I get it out of my bag. "Oh, she must be kidding me."

"Who?"

"Félice Humbert." I show Gaby a message containing a link to an article—a *published* article. "She was supposed to send me this for review."

Gaby clicks on the link and gives the article a quick read before handing the phone back. "Yeah, no, that's live."

I sink back against the chair and dive into the portrait of me as some expert medium, "the one ghosts trust", as the article calls me. It's a mess. My quotes are ripped from context, and more importantly, they're sensationalised, as if there's a ghost revolution underfoot, and I'm in charge, or if I'm the only one who knows about it—the article isn't very decisive. The good news is the article doesn't make ghosts look particularly dangerous. Just me—a dangerous lunatic, that is.

The things I've said about potential outcomes of a pro-ghost society are presented as fact, and every nuance is missing—some of it's just plain wrong. And of course, she went with the socialist angle. Tomorrow, people will cry about ghosts stealing their jobs—if they believe anything written here.

Théo approaches our row while I'm still engrossed in this horrible sham of an article. He smiles at both of us before levelling his gaze at Gaby. "Hey, Gaby. Good to see you back."

"I'm glad to *be* back," she declares proudly, packing her stuff. "Come on, Alix. Just delete it."

"I'm so sorry for what happened to your brother. I can't imagine losing mine, so if you need anything..." He looks up, frowning. "You okay?"

Gaby has frozen, all the fake excitement and enthusiasm draining out of her, like soft ice cream melting in the sun. "You... I'm sorry. I think I'm getting a headache."

I quickly put my phone away. "Gaby..."

But it's too late. She grabs her bag and high-tails it out of the lecture hall. My heart breaks for her anew. This'll take a lot longer than she's ready for.

"Did I say something wrong?" Théo asks.

With a sigh, I shake my head. "Not necessarily. It's just too soon."

His face falls. "If there's anything I can do..."

"She just needs time. And stellar notes to study for the exams—*if* she's going to sit them."

I grab my bag and join Théo on the way out, trying to forget all about the article. We talk a little about the method lecture and which classes we have next, deciding on a study date in the library later, when a door opens behind me and Madame Canet sticks her head out. "Alix?"

Whirling around, I flash her a quick smile. "Yes?" I don't have any classes with her this semester, but I really enjoyed her History of Paris module last term.

"Do you have time for a quick chat?"

Surprised, I nod. Seems like everyone wants to talk to me these days.

"Go ahead," Théo says. "I'll text you where we're going for lunch."

I let him go and follow Madame Canet to her office, curious what this might be about. Since she's not teaching me, it can't be about the exams. There are currently no TA positions available, but maybe it's about my master's thesis next year? Whatever it is, colour me intrigued.

She closes the door and offers me a seat in front of her desk. "Would you like some grapes? They're delicious."

There's a bowl of fruit, glistening with redness. Sure enough, they're chock-full of flavour. "Thank you."

"Now, Alix." She flashes me a quick smile as she settles behind her desk. "Things are a bit wild at the moment, aren't they?"

I'm starting to get a hunch where this chat is truly headed. "Do you mean... the ghosts?"

For all my publicity lately, it still feels strange to say it out loud. Maybe because all this time, I'd kept my two worlds separate. University is the path of reason, the feasible long-term career, serious, in a way. The ghosts were my indulgence, my fanciful passion no one really knew about. And while I've already started to meld the two on the outside with my tours and exhibitions, it's different within these ancient halls.

Madame Canet sighs. "Yes, that. I know it's a hot topic at the moment, a trend, especially with young folks, such as you."

"A trend?"

"I understand our museums are in crisis and often hop on these trends to entice people to come and visit. Normally, I'm all for it—go creative marketing—but I feel like people are taking it a little too far this time. I mean, telling ghost stories is one thing, but claiming to speak for the deceased? Putting on *exhibitions,* presenting made-up material, talking to the press..."

Of course, she's seen the article. My face quickly turns bright red.

"I have to say, Alix, you were the last person I thought would do such a thing. I thought you had more respect for our discipline. The way you wrote and spoke last year gave a different impression than what I'm seeing now."

My eyes probably can't get any bigger. I don't even care about the rebuke, it's the sheer disassociation. "Madame Canet, firstly, please ignore that article. My words were taken wildly out of context, and I didn't get final approval, otherwise it would've never seen the light of day." I take a deep breath to fight the embarrassment. "I can assure you, I deeply respect our department, history itself, and especially those that came before us..." Softly, I add, "The ghosts. It might be a trend for everybody else, but I've been seeing ghosts since I was a young girl. No one else could see them, so I kept quiet about it, but they're the reason I wanted to become a historian."

It's not every day someone tells you they can talk to ghosts, and Madame Canet clearly doesn't believe ghosts are real, which makes me sound like a lunatic.

"Alix..." she says slowly, considering her words. "I think you're a bright, young woman, but I'm worried this will ruin your chances at being taken seriously. It might be lucrative now, and I certainly see the appeal, but you need to think long-term, and the historic society is notoriously stuffy about these things. I don't want you to throw your career away for a temporary fad."

I'm equal parts charmed and offended. I didn't know she was so invested in my future, yet she's clearly in the wrong. Will I have to do another ghostly hide-and-seek game to prove myself? Or can I convince her otherwise.

"Look, I know it sounds wild—believe me, no one knows more than me. Every time I mentioned it, people turned up their noses. My own sister—and mother—were begging me to see a therapist because they believed I'd made it all up, but I hadn't. Ghosts are real. They're tied to this world by memory alone. Once those fade, they move on, but for ghosts, like the people we study here, that doesn't happen. So, they tend to stick around for much longer." I see I'm losing her, but how to make her understand? It's too bad I don't have a ghost handy.

"I could tell you what happened in May. When everyone saw ghosts for a hot minute. Actually, do you have access to the footage?"

Madame Canet looks doubtful. Without letting me out of her eye, she opens her laptop and pulls up a quick search. "What exactly am I looking for?"

It's a moment I'd rather forget but it might come in handy now. "May I?"

Wordlessly, she turns the laptop around. It doesn't take long to find one of the shaky videos under the Eiffel Tower. I place the laptop back in front of her and press play. The audio is horrible. There are too many people and too many questions, but suddenly, the crowd parts and Sébastien appears, dragging me behind him. Madame Canet gasps when she recognises me.

We hurry towards Eiffel's resonator, and for a few minutes we're seen struggling with turning the thing off. And then half the people in the video vanish and the World Fair settles down—at least for Madame Canet. The video follows me and Sébastien a little longer, but we quickly disappear in the direction of the elevators.

"What am I seeing here?" she asks breathlessly.

"Well, for one, you can see Gustave Eiffel." I rewind the video a little to point him out. Her eyes widen when she recognises him. "At the time of this video, he was putting on this masterpiece, recreating the 1889 World Fair for the ghosts. I got to visit it, and it was magnificent, a mix of historical memories and ghost innovation. It was made possible by a new invention called the Spectral Resonator. That's the machine you saw here." Again, I point at the video. "I'm probably making a mess of the explanation, but it uses collective ghost memory to recreate the past. Unfortunately, someone sabotaged it, and it overreacted, superimposing the past on the present. That's why everyone saw glimpses of the Ghost World Fair suddenly, and why Sébastien and I rushed over to turn it off. Which we succeeded in."

It's a lot. I've practically gone from claiming I can see ghosts to telling a fantastic story about ghostly events, invisible saboteurs, and imaginary adventure. It might be time to summon a ghost for some good old-fashioned proof.

Madame Canet rewatches the video once, twice, then one last time. Her face tells a whole story of doubt and disbelief, through undeniability, and at last, acceptance. She looks out of breath when she finally closes the laptop. "This is real?"

I nod.

"You can see ghosts? Talk to them?"

I nod again.

"At the Versailles exhibition, you actually got those answers from the dead queens?"

"If they're in the right mood, I mean, yes. If they're in a heads-off mood, I simply come back another day. I'm not making anything up."

She swallows heavily. "And at the Panthéon…?"

"Absolute dream job. I still can't believe I get to work with the likes of Victor Hugo, Voltaire, or Jean Moulin. And they're so keen to have their words transcribed once more. My boss has actually agreed to do a little video series on it."

It's a little too much too fast. Madame Canet massages her temples, considering everything again. "But you could say anything. Without another resonator, no one could prove your claims. We wouldn't know if those were really Voltaire's words."

"Yes, which is why I've never used anything I couldn't also prove through other means in my work at school."

There's a flash of relief, as if I've just proven myself worthy of our esteemed discipline. "Still... Wait, at the ball, that wasn't the *real* Louis XVI, was it?"

I think reincarnations are a step too far. I've already been far more open with her than I was with Félice Humbert. "Unfortunately, that's classified information I can't share."

"Classified? The government knows about this?"

"Naturally." I bite my lip. It's not like I can tell her all about GoPol.

She stares me down, but unlike Félice, she accepts it. "And you're involved with them?" When I neither nod nor shake my head, she massages her temples again. "So, all this time, they've been hiding ghosts from us? All this information?"

"I know!" I say, a little too passionately. "They don't think of the ghosts at all. To them they're just tools, but we're talking real people. Just because they're dead doesn't mean they've stopped being real."

"The dignity of the dead," she whispers, looking at me with big eyes.

"Yes!" I feel like I've finally got her on board. "Listen, when I went to the catacombs, it was awful. Normally, when ghosts are remembered, they look and behave like normal people, but the people in the catacombs aren't truly remembered—their real identities have been long lost, but since the catacombs see such a heavy load of tourists, their collective memory has survived, and it's had horrifying effects on them. They don't even remember what proper human beings look like because their bones are all jumbled up—I'm talking headless ghosts and ghosts with three legs. They're all looking for the rest of their bodies, but to match them up would be insanity. It would involve extensive DNA testing and manpower, and... It would really just be easier to burn them all and let them rest instead of this travesty."

Madame Canet rubs her face, still processing the barrage of information I've spilt over her head. "I... I think I understand your perspective a lot better now," she says in a feeble voice. She's so pale I fear she's about to pass out. "Not that you didn't make a convincing case without mentioning ghosts, but this changes... everything."

My enthusiasm ebbs away and I nod meekly. "They're suffering terribly."

"I-I'm sorry to hear that."

"Is there any way we can convince the city to shut the catacombs down?"

Her eyes bulge. "Shut them down? Uh... Sorry." Trying to clear the cobwebs, she shakes her head. "I'm afraid not... at the moment. It's all a bit too new, you see. I mean, you've made some great arguments, but... there's no way to prove you're right."

"And you won't just take my word for it," I surmise, trying my hardest not to let the disappointment get to me.

"I want to, Alix. I really do. But this is a lot, and I don't have the power to do such a thing, nor do I know where I'd even start." She watches me with a mixture of befuddlement and exhaustion. This has really pulled a number on her. "I'm afraid I still need a moment to wrap my head around all of this. If it's true... the catacombs, speaking sources..." Huffing, she shakes her head. "This could change everything."

I give her gentle smile. "Yeah."

"Well, then. Thanks for clarifying this for me. I'm really sorry I doubted you." Slowly, she returns my smile. "Sounds like we're going to hear a lot from you in the future."

The future. I know Madame Canet is only one person, but her words warm my heart and fill me with hope. Maybe I can change the world for the better: one person at a time.

# Chapter 6

It's Saturday afternoon and time is fleeting. Between my new social media account, the Panthéon account, and exam prep, there's not enough hours in the day—especially not today when we're expected at my parents' in an hour or so. I still need to get ready. Guess, it's break time.

I stretch my neck, put the flashcards away, and turn my chair around, only to get a big fright, because Dix's in my room, watching the hedgehogs. "You scared me."

There's the sheepish smile I love so much. "Ghost perks."

Snorting, I get up and tousle his hair, knowing how much he hates it. "Are you coming?"

"Coming where?" he asks, desperately trying to straighten out his hair again.

"To my parents'."

His shoulders tighten. He's watching the hedgehogs a little too intently. "What good would that do?"

I get the hedgehog bag and carefully lift Malou out of her cage. This is a family dinner after all. "You're also invited."

"Really? By whom?"

Technically, there's no such invitation—I don't think my mum is even aware of Dix's existence. "By me."

He snorts and gets out Squishy, hugging him jealously to his chest. "Ghosts don't do family meetings."

"Um, yeah, they do. They do it all the time." For some ghosts, it's all they do. Take Gaspar's family crypt, for example.

His shoulders fall and he whispers so low I almost don't catch it, "Whisper ghosts don't. We were never part of the family, so we don't get to hang out with them when they die, either. I mean, once the whisperer dies, we're gone, anyway."

I hug him before he can say even more awful things. "Dix..."

My throat tightens, thinking of the inevitable. Although Sébastien has preserved the piece of bone that could provide Dix with a full ghost future, that avenue has been shut down by the Chevalier—none of us trust him enough for something so delicate. Dix deserves his dream to be realised, not to end up on the cutting floor after another failed experiment.

Unfortunately, that means everything will stay the same. Dix will exist until Sébastien's death, upon which he'll simply cease to be; like dying. I should just accept it as the normal way of things, but it seems so unfair. He never did anything wrong before he was ripped away from Sébastien, and now he doesn't even get the full afterlife experience. I want him and Séb to hang out as ghosts in the far, far future, not be separated completely.

He puts a hand on my arm, squeezing it slightly. "It's okay, Alix. That's just the way things are."

"Well, the way things are sucks." Why is this the one thing we can't change?

A grin splits his face. "Majorly, yes!"

"You should still come." Before he can protest, I tousle his hair once more. "You're family, Dix. *My* family—along with Séb, and Gaspar, and Malou and Squishy. We might not look like a picture-book family, but that doesn't make it any less real. If anything, it makes us more real, because we chose to be together, and I'll choose you every day."

He swallows, then makes a retching sound. "Fine, if it makes you happy, I'll keep the hedgehogs company."

I squeeze him once more, grinning. "Good boy."

Then I finally let go and get ready. Gaspar had much of the same reservations about the dinner, but I told him I wouldn't lie to my parents and sisters about him and Sébastien. Just because we look like a normal straight couple on paper, doesn't mean we are. While I don't want to go public with my ghost relationships, my loved ones need to know. I've already told my grandmother and she's over the moon, congratulating me on bagging two such devoted men. If my dead grandma can get on board with polyamory, the rest of them will have to deal with it, too.

Gaspar and Dix are ready to go when I'm dressed, but the one who actually needs to put his clothes on is still in the living room pouring over the map of the catacombs we've put together from various sources. I see scribbles all over it, denoting the places GoPol has looked at, I assume.

"Still can't find the Chevalier?"

There's a quiet harrumph, which I assume means "no".

"Can you at least find a shirt?" I tease.

Sébastien must've been in the middle of getting ready before the siren call of work pulled him back in. I don't mind his abs on full display, but it might not work so well for a first impression.

The comment gets him out of his stupor. He snorts, then grabs the dress-shirt hanging over a chair nearby. "Better?"

"If you'd put on some shoes so we can go, it'd be perfect."

He throws me a long glance. "I need to figure out where to send people. Some of these places exist according to the map, but we haven't been able to find a way in. This is really important, so maybe I should stay and—"

Do they all have the jitters? "You know, if it's so important, why don't you send me? I bet the Chevalier *wants* me to find him. He always does. We could get to the bottom of this in no time."

"No," Sébastien says, softly but determined. "Good try, though."

"Better than your try of getting out of this?"

I'm not mad he won't send me into the field. While I want to help and resolve the whole situation, I don't relish the thought of meeting the Chevalier again. Unless it's necessary, I won't even *think* of setting a foot in the catacombs.

Sébastien throws me such a puppy look, as if it's *his* father we're meeting for dinner. "Do I have to?"

"Of course not, but I promise it'll be fun. Hélène will probably say something stupid, and then Odi and I'll have a fight, and you'll look like the only sane person at the table." I sincerely hope this isn't how tonight's going to go, but if it does, it'd be on brand for the Dubois sisters. I reach out my hand. "Come on. I *want* you there."

That seems to make all the difference. Sébastien smiles and rolls up his map. Time to go meet the parents.

My parents know Sébastien. They met him at Hélène's engagement party, when he picked me up for the opera, and at the wedding, of course. My father even knows him quite well after working with him on the exposé that brought down GoPol, and so does Odile, who's constantly popping into our flat as if she lives here. I really don't know what he's so nervous about. Maybe because this is the first time he's not just meeting them as a friend—or fake boyfriend—but my *actual* boyfriend.

Now that I think about it, I'm getting a little nervous, too. Hélène and Maman had such a hard time with the whole ghost thing. To make matters worse, Hélène has never been a big fan of Sébastien. Granted, she always viewed him through Cédric's lens, but I can't tell how much his death has changed that.

With my heart in my throat, I press the doorbell, only to remember I still have a key. What am I even doing here?

The door's half-opened by me and half by my mother, who laughs at us when she sees us standing in the hallway. "Did you have to announce yourself before you opened the door?"

"Something like that," I mumble, then kiss her cheeks before letting her loose on Sébastien.

He awkwardly hands her the bunch of flowers he insisted on getting and is pulled into a joyous greeting. "It's so exciting to have you at dinner tonight. Alix has never brought a guy home." She leans into me. "By the way, Gaby's here, too. I thought it only right to invite her after what happened."

Gaby's an honorary Dubois daughter and I'm more than fine with it. I give Maman a hug. "Thank you." It's nice to see her taking her honorary mother role just as seriously.

She smiles warmly at me, and we move into the living room, where we make the rounds to greet everyone. Before we settle around the dining table, I make sure to alert them to the two invisible guests. "Just so you know, Gaspar and Dix are here as well."

Sure enough, Maman frowns. "The guy you brought to the wedding? Wait a minute. Wasn't he alive? Why—"

Papa puts a hand on hers. "It's complicated, Marguerite. Gaspar has practically always been a ghost. I don't claim to know what happened at the wedding, but he's been Alix's steady companion for a while."

"Actually, he's my boyfriend," I say softly.

Gaby sits up straight, as if on high alert. Knowing she's got my back makes waiting for my family's reaction a little less daunting.

"I thought Sébastien was your boyfriend," Hélène says, cautious to keep the typical judgemental note out of her voice.

"And he is. They both are." That was a lot easier than I thought it'd be. I realise I don't really care if they judge me. Obviously, it would suck if they did, but I'm secure in this odd relationship I've formed and don't need their approval.

Maman's eyes widen. "Both of them?"

Odile rolls her eyes. "Seriously. That's so old news. They've been living together for weeks!"

"Well, maybe to you it is," Hélène snipes back at her, "but the rest of us learn things a little later these days."

"You're just not observant enough," Odile says with her nose turned up.

And there it is, the first Dubois sister fight of the night. I can't help but giggle, which naturally draws Hélène's ire. "What's so funny?"

"Nothing," I say, trying to control my giddiness. "It's just I already knew you'd react like this."

"Well, how am I supposed to react? You've barely walked in the door before telling us you're officially in a threesome with a ghost." She pauses for a quick moment, glancing at Sébastien. "And you're okay with it?"

It warms my heart to find him smiling. "I quite like the guy myself."

Gaspar wriggles his eyebrows, matching the smile with a wide grin, then slips an arm around my waist and kisses my cheek. "The fun thing about a ghost boyfriend is I get to do all these things to you while everyone's watching."

His suggestion takes my breath away, leaving me mortified and aroused all the same. "Don't you dare!"

"Yeah, not cool, bro," Dix complains. "You're not invisible to everyone."

"Right, have to think of the children," Gaspar says with a deadpan expression.

I laugh at Dix's outraged face, while Sébastien massages the bridge of his nose. "It's going to be a long night."

It's only then I notice my family still staring. As if I caught my maman doing something bad, she clears her throat and puts on a big smile. "Well, I'd better get two more chairs then." And just like that, my relationship has been accepted.

Odile jumps forward and takes my bag from me. "While you do all the talky bits, I'm going to grab these little hedgehogs—and *Gaspar*—for some photo shoots. You still love helping out, don't you?"

"Always," Gaspar says.

"I want to do hedgehog photos, too!" Dix cries.

When I tell Odile, she grins. "Awesome. I can assign one ghost to each hedgehog then."

"Don't take too long," Maman calls after her. "Dinner will be ready soon."

Now that the normal craziness has taken hold, I sit next to Gaby and hold her hand. "How's your day been?"

"Not too bad. I had a long chat with our master's rep at uni today, and we discussed how we're going to handle exams. Apparently, most of our lecturers are happy for me to submit alternative assessments at the end of July, so I can take some more time off."

"Oh, that's good to hear. I'm proud of you for asking."

"Well, that one day showed me I'm not ready yet. But I will be. And between yours and Théo's notes, I don't even need the textbook."

"Half of it is wrong anyway," I joke.

It's so beautiful to hear Gaby laugh. She might not be ready yet, but she will be eventually. Her gaze turns a little more introspective as she takes a deep breath. "Once I'm ready, I'd like you to help me find Ollie. I want to talk to him. Not now, but in a while."

I squeeze her hand. "Absolutely. Whenever you're ready."

I notice Hélène watching me and hope she's not thinking of setting up a meeting between her and Cédric, because that guy is dead to me—literally and figuratively. When she notices me, she clears her throat and strikes up conversation about work with Maman, while Papa and Sébastien discuss the developments at GoPol. I catch them mentioning my name and scoot over.

"Don't worry," Sébastien says, "GoPol killed the article and there's an alert on her. No more will go out without pre-approval."

My father nods. "I'm glad to hear that." As am I. "If needed, we can publish a counter article. But we should definitely consider taking formal action."

"Oh, she's done for." Sébastien notices me and slips an arm around my hip. "You let me know if we need to put out a restraining order."

Though I appreciate the effort, it all sounds a little extreme. "Don't worry, she won't be getting any more material. Not directly from me." Unless, she starts watching my new channel, but then again, the videos will be widely accessible, so everyone can see what a hack she is. "I prefer fighting this my way—with information rather than suppression." But it's nice to know she can't actually publish lies anymore.

"That's my girl," Papa says, and toasts me.

Later, when we're all around the table—including Dix and Gaspar—and eating some delicious pork tenderloin with potato gratin and a summer salad, everyone seems to be at ease with the two ghosts at the table. My father's even having a three-way conversation with Dix and Sébastien about some show they all watched ten years ago when Sébastien and Dix were still one. The older only remembers bits and pieces, but Dix is outright obsessed with it.

On the other side, my mother's enlisted my help to talk to Gaspar. "I'm just curious," she starts, "what do you do as a ghost all day?"

Gaspar shoots me a cheeky look. "Are we giving her the full version or the abridged one?" One stern look from me has him laughing. "Sorry, I'll try to keep it PG."

"I just won't translate anything I don't want them to know."

He clicks his tongue. "Censorship! Wait until I tell Émile and Victor."

"What *do* you do all day, Gaspar?" I ask pointedly. As much as he likes to joke about it, he doesn't hang around me at all times, much less doing naughty things.

The smile fades a little and he starts taking the question more seriously. "I've been exploring a lot. You know how you said I needed to go out more, meet some ghosts. Well, that's what I've been doing. Sometimes, Dix tags along, but most of the time, I go alone, try to immerse myself in ghost society and figure out how it all comes together."

I'm so fascinated I completely forget to pass on what he says until my mother clears her throat.

"Oh," she says, once I fill her in. "Colour me intrigued. What's ghost society like?"

"Much more complex than I'd originally thought. In a way, it reminds me of the Italian republics during the Renaissance. You know, Florence, Venice, Milano... Just on a much smaller but denser scale. Every necropolis has their own little rules and laws, but they all kind of agreed to them. That's where it gets truly fascinating, because none have a ruling body. They're more communes where everyone's free to be themselves, while still fostering a community spirit. In the vaguest sense, the Panthéon is the highest instance, but that's based purely on respect. People listen when Victor Hugo speaks. Or Voltaire." He's really getting into it, making it hard for me to repeat and process at the same time.

"My theory is once you take away food, shelter, and most importantly money, there's not much left to fight about. Ghosts don't have the same needs as the living. You can't get rich as a ghost, you know? And you can't kill each other either. So, all those imaginary lines that separate the living—that puts one group in charge of the other or forces people to go against their moral instincts to survive—are blurred once you're dead. It's kind of wonderful when you think about it."

"Fascinating." Maman's not just saying it. Her eyes glisten and she keeps nodding away. She still mostly looks at me rather than the empty chair to my side, but she's into this. "You know, I work in urban planning, so I've often wondered how we can strengthen our communities. Obviously, we can't take food, money, and shelter away, but it's nice to hear people get along a little better in the afterlife."

Gaspar nudges my side. "You never told me your mother was a sociologist."

"She's not. I mean, she studied something completely different."

Even though she didn't hear Gaspar's comment, she answers mine. "Oh, yes. I started studying politics, but that wasn't for me, and so I got a job in admin. Honestly, it's been a long road, but I think I've finally found my niche."

"I feel like I'm getting close to mine, too," Gaspar says with a wistful smile.

A fuzzy warmth builds in my chest as I look across the table. Gaspar finding his way in the ghost world and finding common interests with my mother, my father geeking out with Sébastien and Dix, putting the light back into Sébastien's eyes I see way too rarely, Hélène having a quiet, surprisingly emphatic conversation with Gaby, and Odile stuffing her face, while she briefs the hedgehogs on her grand oral topic, as if they're judging her… I can't believe how lucky I am I'm surrounded by such a loving, supportive family—and for Gaspar, Sébastien, and Dix to experience all that, too.

# Chapter 7

Since Odile is still busy with exam prep, Gaspar helps me create the first Panthéon videos. Not that he can physically make or edit the video or would appear any more visible, but he's happy to coach the ghosts on social media, doing a fantastic job deterring Rousseau from demanding a half-hour long speech transcription. They all huff at the notion of keeping it short and juicy but nod understandingly when Gaspar mentions our short attention span.

Personally, I find it hilarious. The ghosts here owe their prolonged existence to an exceptionally large attention span, but they're always eager to pass judgement.

We try to sit down with everyone to discuss potential videos, then shoot the first of many. Monsieur Passard has provided me with a list of what he thinks is the most interesting order, but I'm happy to adapt that list to my ghosts' needs. The first round will be an introduction to as many ghosts as possible, giving them a unique ghostly spin to garner interest, such as the increasingly unhinged list of titles for Victor's unwritten novels.

Some of the ghosts have brilliant ideas themselves—"Tales from an Undercover Résistante" by Josephine Baker for example—others need to be cautiously nudged towards an engaging format.

"I think the two of you should team up for a weekly debate," I tell Rousseau and Voltaire, who both regard me with scepticism. "We'll cover a few contentious topics at first but will go with requests once engagement is up."

"Contentious, such as the freedom of speech?" Voltaire asks, raising an eyebrow. "Which should not be contentious at all," he adds sharply, in Rousseau's direction. "It needs to be unlimited, no argument."

Rousseau, ever one to rise to the occasion, shoots back, "It can't be completely unlimited when we enter a social contract. For a community to exist in peace, limits are a necessity."

Knowing how vicious these two can get once they've started, I quickly redirect them, "Yeah, let's keep it a bit lighter than that. I was thinking more day-to-day truths—like are you an early morning riser or a late-night owl?"

They both look at me with the contempt I deserve. "Fine. Big societal commentary on hot topics it is, then." Let the shit storms drive up engagement.

I notice not all ghosts are eager to join in the fun. Once again, the Napoleonic generals keep themselves separate from the rest of the group. "Is everything okay with the generals?" I ask Voltaire.

He snorts. "They're embarrassed. The abduction of Napoleon's bones has once again raised doubt about the legitimacy of their inclusion in these sacred halls. I mean what have they really done apart from loyally follow a madman's grand vision? They're not here on merit but on favouritism."

I nearly roll my eyes at him. There's always been a separation between those who were interred here based on martial merit and everyone else. Very few visitors care for them—they're here to see humanity's scions. The famous minds who brought us the modern age, then built on it with innovation, creativity, and vision. Defiance in light of an oppressive regime has always been a favourite, too, hence all the deserved hero worship for our resistance fighters. In comparison, military officers who were "lucky" they died while their lord was still in power seem to add little to the prestige. People hardly recognise their names, much less remember their deeds. They know the one who gave the orders, not the followers who made sure those orders were completed to perfection.

Still, they are occupants of the Panthéon, and after two hundred years, you'd think the ghosts would've stopped caring. They've always been happy to have the generals as the executive arm of the Panthéon's will, whether that was to bring order to the throng of favour-seeking ghosts or help make the Panthéon a safe space for me and Petite Alix. In my opinion, they're more now than they might've been in life, and I intend to treat them that way.

I excuse myself from the philosophers, leaving them to Gaspar, and approach Jean Lannes' vault. While many crypts look the same with their vaulted ceilings and cream-coloured sarcophagi, boasting very little decoration, the marshal's crypt is different. First off, he's the only occupant with no space or plans to include anyone else; second, his resting place is heavily decorated. An array of French flags sticks out of the wall above the coffin, creating a tri-coloured curtain. The coffin itself looks fancier, with almost a golden sheen on top of black marble. And then there are two red pillows with filigree sculptures of branches: one laurel, the other olive. Only Voltaire and Rousseau have bigger and fancier displays. Jean was Napoleon's favourite, after all.

"Is this a bad time?"

Lannes raises his head, giving me a tortured look. "I don't think it'd be a good idea for me to join your new venture."

I wish there was a door I could close to give ourselves some privacy. "It's not about that."

While I definitely want to include him—and others—in the introductory series, I don't really know what he could offer for long-term content. People these days aren't necessarily looking for "Strategies on the Battlefield from Someone Who Died from a Shot to the Knee". Actually, phrased like that, it might draw some interest, but I don't want to diminish Lannes' military successes with the way he died.

He leans against the wall, looking tired. "What is it, then?"

"Your old buddy went missing." Now I think of it, Lannes might be able to help with Sébastien's dilemma. "Or I guess, his bones did." I don't really know whether his ghost has also vanished.

"And now you're asking what I know about that? Whether I was privy to the plan and could've warned you?"

The hairs on the back of my neck rise. "Were you?" How close is he truly to the former emperor?

"I was not. Privy to it, that is. If Napoleon had a hand in this, he did not confide in me."

I can't quite tell whether he's hurt by or proud of it. Cocking my head, I ask, "Are you saying he might not have been a willing participant?"

The Chevalier has a knack for the occult. Marie Antoinette summoned her bones back, but what if he'd taken more precaution with Napoleon's bones, effectively trapping the emperor?

"That I don't know." Lannes' face becomes painfully tense. "I don't know anything. Not his mind, not his plans, nothing of note."

"Are you okay?" I can't help myself. He sounds devastated.

"You'd think if he had such important plans he'd share them with his trusted marshal, don't you? But I died prematurely, so maybe he'd replaced me by the time he passed in St. Helen's. It's not like he shared everything with me."

Definitely hurt. "Has he shared anything with others?" A shake of the head. "And prior? I've heard... rumours that Napoleon's made..." I have to be really careful here how I phrase things. "...big plans before. Were you privy to those? Did he include you?"

There's that flash of pain again. "He failed last time because I leaked his plans."

"Right."

Lannes is quick to defend himself. "It was ridiculous. He wanted to start a ghost revolution to storm St Denis and bring the ire of the Triad over all of us."

Yeah, that would've been ridiculous. Constance doesn't play when it comes to skirmishes.

"We don't need a war," he says, a little more calmly. "Heck, we didn't need half the ones he started then." He shakes his head and sighs. "That makes me a terrible marshal, doesn't it? Detesting war?"

"Maybe. But it makes you a wonderful human being in my eyes."

A soft smile plays on his lips. "I just saw too many die," he explains. "So many soldiers, friends, comrades. He used to say it'd all be worth it, but when you look at it now... was it?" As if I have the answer to that. "The empire didn't even last another decade before it all came crumbling down."

True. The 19th century brought many changes. Especially for France. "Do the others feel the same?"

"It's difficult, Mademoiselle Dubois. We're all here, while Napoleon is... *was* buried at Les Invalides. He's still our commander. You know how it is; those things never really change. Our loyalty *is* to the Panthéon—even if we're not appreciated." So, he's well aware of Voltaire's opinion. "It's a strange situation. Something's afoot, but none of us have had word. If Napoleon's planning something... I guess, we're all waiting for orders or something. Instead, silence." Lannes frowns. "Maybe you're right. Maybe he *isn't* a willing part of this scheme. In that case, we'll have to rescue him."

I'm not sure I like where this is going. On the one hand, I don't want to judge Napoleon too quickly. He might be the victim here, but that doesn't really fit his brand.

"If that were the case, would you do me the favour?"

I suck air in sharply. If Napoleon's been captured by the Chevalier, rescuing him should become our top priority. There's no telling the atrocities the Chevalier would do in the name of science. And there's no good reason for him to steal the bones. At least none I can think of. But taking on this favour means more than just finding out where the Chevalier is hiding—it means facing him, potentially even fighting him. And I don't think that's something I want to do.

Refusing a favour is always hard—I get a lot of impractical ones or outright impossible ones that make it a bit easier. But ones I can genuinely help with? Not quite so easy. "Sébastien... I mean, GoPol are looking for the bones," I say in what I hope is a fair compromise, "If they find anything regarding Napoleon's whereabouts, I'll let you know."

Lannes straightens, standing to attention. With a sharp nod, he salutes me. "Thank you. It means a lot."

"One way or the other, we'll get to the bottom of this."

Gaspar and I are buzzing on the way home. My head is exploding with ideas of possible content for both my private and professional channels. There's so much the ghosts have to offer despite most of them having died before the internet was even a pipe dream, much less social media. I'm starting to get why Odile is so into it; the possibilities are endless.

We have to stop chatting about ghosts when we arrive at the apartment. There's a neighbour in the courtyard when I lock up my bike, and I politely greet her while Gaspar hops off the carrier. He weighs practically nothing when he's not touching me, so it's easy to travel this way—plus no one complains about me talking to myself while I ride.

"There was a woman looking for you earlier," my neighbour says.

"Oh, what did she want?" Not Félice again. She's been hounding me daily with messages. As if I'd want to talk to her after that sham of an article.

Gaspar stands behind me and runs his hands down my arms, making my hairs stand to attention. "Let's go upstairs," he whispers, his breath hitting my ear just right.

What the hell does he think he's doing?

"She didn't say," my neighbour says in a cheerful way that tells me she's enjoying the chance to chat with me. "I told her you were still at work."

"Thanks." I huff because Gaspar has just wrapped his arms around me and kissed the nape of my neck. "Um, I guess, she'll be back some other time." I'm sure there's a mystery here, but I can hardly remember what we're talking about.

The neighbour follows me as I turn towards the stairwell. "Maybe you know her. She was about this height, coiffed brown hair, very elegant." She sounds impressed. "Definitely a designer bag." Not Félice then.

"Are you sure she was looking for me?"

I don't know such fancy people. The stairwell is tightly wound, allowing Gaspar to keep at least one hand on me at all times. It's currently sitting on my thigh just above the knee, but it's slowly riding up my skirt as I desperately try to keep a steady pace. Why did it have to be the neighbour opposite?

"Oh, yes, she knew your name and described you very well. I thought she was a relative. Maybe a rich aunt?"

I press my legs together, trapping Gaspar's hand before it can visibly lift my skirt. "An aunt?" Why do I need an aunt? Oh, right, the mystery visitor. "I don't have an aunt." Actually, I do, but those details are terribly hard to hold onto when your ghost boyfriend is being naughty in public.

"If you ask me, she was looking a bit... shall I say gaunt? Probably just a rich person diet or so. It wasn't doing her any favours." My neighbour is so blissfully unaware, it's almost painful.

I manage to slap Gaspar's hand away as we take the final set of stairs. When I catch his grin, I almost wish I hadn't. That boy is going to be the death of me.

"Maybe she's sick."

To be honest, I've already forgotten who we're talking about.

"Maybe." We finally reach our respective apartments, but my neighbour pauses at her door, not even reaching for her key yet. "I finally made it to that Versailles exhibition Sébastien told me about. The one you put on?"

"Right!" Now we're static, Gaspar has resumed kissing my exposed skin, only he's no longer interested in my neck.

"It was so good! I really enjoyed all the displays. And to think this has all been done with the help of real ghosts. How do you even get into that?"

Getting into that is sort of the phrase of the hour with Gaspar kneeling in front of me and following the trail of his hand with his tongue. But we were talking about my exhibition. And ghosts, I think. Just not this ghost in particular.

"Um, long story." And one I absolutely do not have the necessary eloquence for right now. "Maybe we can sit down sometime... other." I fumble for my keys, promptly dropping them at my feet. "Sorry, I really need to"—*get inside right now*—"pee." Okay, slightly embarrassing, but not nearly as embarrassing as it would be if my panties were next to drop.

"Oh, sorry. I didn't mean to keep you. You should totally come over sometime. Have some wine."

While she launches into her long-winded goodbye, I bent down to pick up my keys, noticing Gaspar has moved his knee over them. He looks up at me coyly and grins.

"But I'll leave you to it, now. We'll chat later."

Her keys jangle in the door, while I mouth at Gaspar, "Seriously?"

I force his knee aside to grab the key, hoping my neighbour doesn't notice the weird movement.

She's already halfway into her apartment and waves at me as I straighten again. I swallow hard when Gaspar presses his body against my back while I try to open my door. A very dangerous part of me wants to give in and let him pleasure me in this semi-public space, but a fragment of reason has managed to survive, and I push the door open, practically falling inside.

"You can't do tha—"

Gaspar captures my mouth with his merely a split-second after the door's fallen shut. I drop the keys again, vaguely aiming at the cupboard in the hallway, and throw my arms around him. Together, we crash into the wall behind me.

"Admit it. You thought it was hot."

My brain's practically fried at this point, so I just nod and search for the handle of my door instead. We stumble into my room, ignoring the hedgehogs, nearly falling over our feet. Gaspar grabs my ass and lifts me onto my desk, swiping a pile of flashcards off the table.

"That skirt's been calling to me all afternoon," Gaspar confesses between kisses, his hands now firmly under the guilty garment.

"Has it?"

Just then the doorbell rings. Is it my neighbour again? Surely, she can't expect me to be done so quickly?

"Just ignore it."

I try to, but less than a minute later, it rings again. "She probably forgot something."

"Alix," he calls in a siren voice, his fingers getting dangerously close to their target.

"Please," I whisper, not quite sure what exactly I'm begging for. "I'll just deal with it quickly."

He pulls back with a groan, and I hop off the table, frantically straightening my skirt.

"You stay here!" I don't think I'll last long if he continues.

Eager to get it done with, I rush to the door and nearly rip it off its hinges. "Did you forget—Oh, sorry."

The woman in front of my door is *not* my neighbour, but she fits the description from earlier: a tall, thin woman with a perfectly curled bob of brown hair. Everything about her screams money—the polite smile, the business attire, the tasteful jewellery, the Chanel bag. But she looks tired, her make-up barely hiding the shadows under her eyes.

"Mademoiselle Dubois?"

"Yes?" Despite my neighbour's description, I have no idea who she is.

Her polite smile makes place for one of relief. "I'm so glad I found you. When I got here, I only saw 'Roubert' on the sign outside. But you're associated, right?"

"Can I help you?"

"I sure hope so," she says, a hidden strength in her voice. This woman knows how to get what she wants. "You talk to ghosts, right? Well, I'd like to hire your services."

What in the seven hells? "My services?"

"Yes, I'd like you to find a ghost for me."

Behind me, Gaspar steps into the corridor, having grown impatient in my room. "Maman?"

# Chapter 8

"Would you like some coffee?" My voice is a little shaky, while my brain is still trying to switch from sexy times with my ghost boyfriend to unexpectedly meeting said-boyfriend's grieving mother.

She's standing in the living room, taking in the furniture, silently passing judgement. I'm keenly aware of the empty wine glasses on the coffee table and mess of lecture notes covering the dining table. It doesn't help that Gaspar's standing near the windows, arms crossed, glowering at the woman who gave birth to him.

It's hard to see their resemblance. Not because he hasn't inherited her features—they've got the same shade of brown and curl in the hair, the same kind of nose and chin—but because their styles are so wildly different. Gaspar's mother is all poised elegance, oozing style and manners—and money. Meanwhile, Gaspar's hunched over in his band hoodie, hair a little messy, and black-painted nails.

"Yes, please," she says with a practised smile.

"Please, take a seat." I offer her the armchair opposite the couch, then pick up the wine glasses, and make my way into the kitchen.

Gaspar follows me, barely waiting for me to leave the room, before he asks, "Why would you let her in?"

Is he for real? How could I not? But then I remember all he's ever told me about his parents, and my heart goes out to him. Still... "She's here for you," I whisper softly, praying the coffee machine covers every word. What other ghosts would she be looking for?

"Oh, please. She's here for herself. Probably heard about the ghosts and now wants to take advantage of having one in her family. I'd be a curiosity for her Friday Book and Wine Club. Or maybe she wants to make you her new project."

I hate the sound of that. "I take it you don't want me to let her know about you then?"

"Do you want to tell her what you were doing with her son before she knocked?"

My face flushes so heavily my cheeks burn. No. No, I definitely do *not* want to tell this posh woman I'm sleeping with her dead son.

Pouring the coffee, I glare at Gaspar for being the unhelpful cause of this situation. "No toying."

He looks as if I've just suggested throwing Malou out the window. "Wouldn't think of it!"

I slap on my tour guide smile and carry the coffee into the living room. "Sorry that took a moment."

While I was busy in the kitchen, she's been sitting prim and proper in the armchair, neither leaning back nor resting her arms, but constantly hovering on the edge as if I previously spilt coffee over it. "Not at all. I was admiring all these accomplishments." Sébastien's certificates and successes still adorn the wall. "He's quite the catch, isn't he?"

Gaspar rolls his eyes heavily, and dramatically falls on the couch making retching motions. "The only thing that matters," he complains.

I try to keep a straight face and place the coffee down before taking a seat on the couch, subconsciously mimicking her posture to avoid sitting on Gaspar's legs. "Well, yes, I guess."

"Not that you're far behind," she says with a practised smile. "Twenty-three, about to get your degree in history, and already the mastermind behind that wonderful exhibition at Versailles and ghost tours at the Panthéon. I sadly couldn't make the royal ball, but I've only heard good things."

If she'd seen me at the end of the ball, her attitude towards me would've been a lot different. "I'm sorry, this might be terribly rude, but do I know you?"

"Be ruder!" Gaspar says, assuming a sitting position next to me. "Make her leave."

"Oh, no, that's my fault. I was so nervous about coming here I forgot to introduce myself." Nothing in her voice indicates even the slightest bit of nerves. She extends a hand. "Sophie du Charbonneau. I'm an art curator, and we haven't met yet, don't worry. I simply did my research."

"Oh, she knows everything about you," Gaspar whispers in my ear. "Probably hired a private investigator to uncover every speck of dirt you could possibly have."

As it turns out, I'm practically steeped in dirt. After all, I was arrested, witnessed a gruesome murder, and was essentially the ghost police's prime suspect for the better part of the year. Hopefully, she *didn't* hire someone, or I might be in more trouble than I thought.

"And why's that?" I wish my voice was as secure as hers.

Madame du Charbonneau—there's no way I'll ever think of her as Sophie—folds her hands in her lap. "Well, in a sea of impostors and nutcases, you seem to be the only reliable source when it comes to ghosts. Your interactions with them are genuine, and your claims make sense, as outrageous as they seem."

"Can't make a case without passing judgement," Gaspar says snidely.

I wish he'd stop. This is hard enough without his angry commentary in my ear. "Are you planning on involving ghosts in an art exhibition or—"

"Oh, god, no. This is all way too new to risk my reputation on something like that. Those museums might be able to get away with it, but I'm a serious curator. If I started talking about ghosts, I'd lose the trust of all my clients."

I'm starting to get why Gaspar is so hostile towards his mother. She really puts down everything in her reach. Now prestigious museums aren't serious enough. "How else might I be of help then?" The displeasure I feel makes my voice stronger.

She has to take a little breath, her eyelids fluttering. "My research showed me you're familiar with a large variety of ghosts, not just historical figures, but... I guess you could call them 'normal ghosts'."

I really want to know where all this research's coming from.

"Nearly a year ago, I lost someone very dear to my heart."

Gaspar snorts.

"My son."

"Don't believe her," Gaspar claims loudly. "I was only dear to her when I showed up as arm candy for her vernissages, and even then, only as long as I dressed *properly.*"

My heart's growing heavy. There's so much resentment in him. He truly believes his parents didn't care for him, and yet his mother's sitting right here, going to great lengths to connect with her only child. I've seen this before, seen the dead parents regretting what they failed to value in life. It's not until it's all stripped away we recognise what really mattered.

"I'm sorry to hear that." While he's alive and well to me, she was bereft of his wonderful presence.

Madame du Charbonneau nods with a wan smile. "He was involved in a car accident last October. He was on a bicycle. I knew this was going to happen, but he refused the car we bought him for his eighteenth."

As if cars have less chances of accidents, especially those given to spoiled rich kids on the cusp of adulthood. The Gaspar she's talking about is entirely unfamiliar to me. We might as well know two different people, which makes it a bit easier to disassociate her story from the ghost sitting next to me.

"He was so young. Just turned twenty-two. And deep in his rebellious phase."

"And here we go," Gaspar drawls. "May I present my mother, keeper of all my flaws."

But Madame du Charbonneau doesn't rattle off a list. Instead, she swallows, her eyes becoming a bit glassy. "I guess you could say we were estranged. It's a weird thing, an accident like that. You think you have all the time in the world to make things right, that he'll come to his senses sooner or later, and then... gone. One morning, and all that potential, all that promise, is wiped from the earth. Or so I thought," she adds quickly, as if indulging in her sadness is a capital sin.

Not meeting my eyes, she opens her bag and pulls out a folder. "I've prepared a little something for you. This includes pictures of him, where we buried him, and places he liked to frequent, as far as we knew. Also, friends, fellow students, and everyone I could find to make this easier for you."

"Easier for me?" I stare at the folder, curiosity blooming in my heart. I know so little about the guy Gaspar was before his death; so much of his afterlife was spent dealing with my drama. "What exactly do you want me to do?"

"Find him, of course." Nervous laughter escapes her lips, causing her to tense immediately. "Sorry, I should've been more straightforward," she says with a business-like attitude. The grieving mother has to take a backseat in this transaction. "I'd like you to use your unique gift to locate my son and facilitate a meeting with him. There are things I'd like to tell him, and maybe... ask how he is." The mother slips back in at the end.

"Oh, so now she wants to talk?" Gaspar snorts.

The temptation to simply tell her he's right here is growing, but then I'd have to explain the nature of our relationship, and I'm not sure I'm ready for that kind of conversation; I can hardly handle this one.

I grab my cup of coffee, nearly brushing the folder off the table, and take a sip to buy myself some time.

"Of course, I'm happy to reimburse you for your efforts. I understand it'll take time, and you're a very busy young woman with lots of other responsibilities and interests. And, of course, there's the uniqueness of your gift. What do you think about 20,000 euros, half of that upfront, to cover your expenses?"

I nearly spit out my coffee. As it is, I swallow too much of it and start coughing. I quickly put the cup down and hide my embarrassing lack of composure behind my hand.

Madame du Charbonneau has the grace not to comment or react on it. Judging by how quickly she puts others down—more than the money—shows how desperate she is.

This might be the easiest money I've ever made. Heck, this is *more* money than I've ever made. 20,000 euros are like a jackpot for a student. And yet, I feel strangely uncomfortable taking any money from her, simply for reuniting her with her son. Especially when said son is sitting right there, rolling his eyes. The only effort I'd have to expend is getting him to agree to this meeting.

"I can't take your money."

"Yes, you can," Gaspar says coldly, once more glowering at his mother. "Ask for double."

I will certainly *not* do that.

Madame du Charbonneau gifts me a rare true smile. "That honours you, Mademoiselle Dubois, but you need to know your value. You have a skill no one else possesses." Not quite true, though I doubt GoPol wants to branch out to missing person cases. "Though your profession is yet to be recognised, you're definitely an expert. And you will incur expenses. Take the money. You deserve it."

"I've never done anything like this." And to be honest, I don't relish the idea of working in this particular field, incredibly high fees or not.

"He does exist, though, doesn't he? My Gaspar, I mean?" It's the first time doubt has crept into her voice. "You said in that article—"

"Oh, please, not that article. That journalist twisted everything I said."

Madame du Charbonneau raises an eyebrow. "I figured as much. But I'm talking about the big exposé. Your father's work. You claimed everyone becomes a ghost, at least until they're forgotten. But he wouldn't be forgotten yet. I still remember him."

I just can't take this anymore. Madame du Charbonneau's tugging on my heartstrings, despite what Gaspar's said. I so desperately want to tell her the truth, but she probably wouldn't believe me if I claimed to have found him already. And Gaspar clearly doesn't want to be found.

But I can give her some comfort. "He wouldn't be forgotten yet. As long as ghosts have living relatives, they're safe, and even afterwards, it takes time. I mean, he has a grave and everything, right?"

She nods eagerly. "Yes, and I'm planning to create a music fund in his name, and looking into other options to make sure he'll never be forgotten."

That's actually surprisingly sweet. Gaspar's life was cut too short to leave much of an impression on his own, but those measures *would* help prolong his afterlife.

Not that he's appreciative. "I don't want to be remembered as a prick who's only got his name on a number of buildings to keep a meaningless memory alive."

I sigh heavily, unable to block him out completely. "As I said, I've never done anything like this and I'm not sure it's something I want to do."

"You need some time to think about it," she says understandingly. "That's fair. I've practically jumped this on you. Well, here's my number and my e-mail." She hands me her card and picks up the untouched folder, stowing it in her bag again. "Have a think and call me once you've made a decision. I'm also happy to negotiate if you think it'd take too much of an emotional toll."

Regardless of the Gaspar situation, that's exactly why I don't want to take on cases like this. I'm not a psychologist, much less a grief specialist, I'm a historian who enjoys getting to know ghosts. Even with the favours I do, I've stayed away from contacting living relatives as much as possible. There have been exceptions, but generally it's too much to deal with. But what amount of money would make it worth entrenching myself in other people's grief?

The more I think about it, the less I want to go down this road. "I'll be in touch, and if... if I should come across your Gaspar... I'll let you know."

"Thank you! I appreciate it a lot." She drinks her coffee and stands. "I won't impose on you much longer. You've probably had a long day. I can't imagine how exciting all this must be for someone already familiar with this world."

"It changes every day," I say politely as I lead her to the door.

"I bet. Hey, and maybe in a few years, when everything's found its rightful place, I *will* hire you to help with an exhibition. I know some great artists you could involve."

That sounds a lot more exciting than connecting dead and living family members. "We'll see."

The door falls shut, and I hear the click-clack of her heels on the stairs as she leaves. Exhausted, I turn, finding myself face-to-face with Gaspar. "Well, that was awkward."

"Sorry. I should've checked the door before you opened it, so you could've pretended to not be home."

I roll my eyes. "She would've just come back another time." Madame du Charbonneau proved she was nothing if not persistent.

"Yeah, probably, but we would've been a bit more prepared. Unfortunately, she always does this—just makes a decision and expects everyone to follow along, as if people don't have their own time constraints or desires. One time, she entered me into a prestigious piano competition, which I only found out when a teacher turned up at the door to go through the selection of pieces my mother had put together."

That *does* make it sound like she curates lives as carefully as she curates art.

"My mother's the worst. She's nothing like yours, open-minded, welcoming, always eager to bring her family together."

"I don't think she's the worst," I say, returning to the living room.

"Yeah, okay, Sébastien has me beat there," Gaspar admits, "but you've seen her: waltzes into a stranger's home unannounced, throws a huge amount of money at you, and expects you to drop everything else to cater to her whims."

"I don't think it was a whim," I say cautiously. "She really wants to reconnect with you. She misses you."

He crosses his arms and snorts. "No way. She just wants to relieve herself from whatever residue of guilt she's feeling. There's probably some novelty factor, the fact she *could* talk to me—look what a good mother she is, reaching out to her son beyond the grave. Can't you see how much she cares? It'll make for a wonderful story for Sunday brunch. Plus, it'll make her the envy of all the ladies, the only one who connected with a ghost. Don't expect her to pass your details on, no, she'll jealously guard them until she sees fit to present you as her new little pet."

I didn't get those vibes from her at all, but he obviously knows his mother better. "What about you? Don't you want the chance to talk to her... your parents? Maybe tell them all this." Whatever this ball of resentment, anger, and hurt is.

"And risk them turning on you for telling the truth?" His eyes widen. "Alix, they'd sue you if you told them what I truly think of them. My mother doesn't want to be confronted with her failings, she wants the tearful reunion, the assurance of how much I love her, and how sorry I am for not living up to all my wonderful *potential*." He spits the word out as if it's poison.

I hate to see Gaspar this upset. All the vitriol can't hide the fact how much the visit has rattled him. When he died, he shed his old life like a snake—he's never been interested in revisiting old friends, his parents, or all those spots in that folder Madame du Charbonneau took away with her. I always felt it was a bit unhealthy to detach so completely from the life he had, but for him, it was the escape he'd been looking for. An absolute and finite escape from his parents—until they become ghosts themselves.

I step towards him and thread my hands around his middle, pulling him close. "They're your family."

Gaspar looks into my eyes, a gentle smile on his lips. "No, they're not. You're my family: you, Séb, and Dix. And the hedgehogs, of course. My hedgehog family."

My heart melts for my hedgehog boy. "Gaspar."

He kisses my forehead then pulls away again. "I know it sounds outrageous, but dying and meeting you was the best thing to ever happen to me. I don't think I truly lived until the day I met you."

# CHAPTER 9

Gaspar remains adamant he doesn't want to meet his parents, so I shelve the unorthodox favour until he's had time to mull it over. In the meantime, Odile excels at her grand oral, while my exams are approaching quickly. I'm fairly relaxed this time around. Most of the exams don't count for more than fifty per cent, the rest of the grade already determined by cooler tasks such as the World Fair presentation Gaby, Théo, and I aced, or the fake research proposal we had to write for another course. Half the exams we *do* have are open-book, meaning we can take our notes and even textbooks in. Of course, that means they're more about understanding the material and demonstrating good reasoning, but that's something I'm fairly confident with.

For the rest, I study with Gaby, who's been feeling better by the day and is thinking of sitting normal exams rather than her special arrangements. Or rather, we *were* planning on studying.

Instead, we're sitting on the little balcony looking out on the street, hunched over my phone to read the comments on my latest videos.

"Oh, that's a good question!" Gaby points at my introductory video of Pierre and Marie Curie.

It's from a user called *SpectralFlo* and starts with: "low-key jelly you get to hang with THE Marie Curie. This might be too geeky, but how does radioactivity affect ghosts? And if it does, which kind do they most react to?"

"Marie would love to answer that," Gaby says.

"Well, I hope *SpectralFlo* will understand her answer, because I can transcribe for the ghosts, but I can't translate them."

Gaby giggles. "That'll only add to your authenticity."

I'm making a note to reply to *SpectralFlo,* when I hear the door open. Sébastien's home and it's still light outside. Today must be my lucky day. He doesn't come straight to the living room, but I hear him moving through the apartment.

Gaby puts her head on my shoulder and scrolls through other comments. "Ugh, that one needs to be blocked." It's a comment about how I'm going to hell for talking to ghosts.

"Yeah, for sure."

A sudden smacking sound has me sitting up straight. "What was that?"

The sound is repeated in quick succession, then silence. I'm just about to relax again when I hear a grunt, followed by another smack.

This time, I get up to investigate. "I'll be back in a minute." The smacks continue. "Séb?"

I run into Dix in the corridor. He's outside Sébastien's door, arms crossed, managing to look both tense and bored at the same time. "I wouldn't go in there if I were you. He's in a particularly crabby mood."

I start to realise what the noise means. When I moved into Sébastien's apartment, he gave up his fitness room for me. Some of the equipment moved to GoPol, one machine is sitting in the living room, and the rest were moved into his bedroom, including the sandbag. Only trouble is, Sébastien still has a broken arm.

Worried, I knock on the door, then open it cautiously. Sure enough, Sébastien's back is turned to me as he attacks the sandbag with his good arm, his dress shirt sort of hanging halfway over his shoulder, as if he couldn't be bothered to drag it over his cast before he went at his training equipment.

I close the door behind me, shutting Dix out, and climb onto Sébastien's bed, where I'm safe from his swinging.

The creak of the springs betrays me, and he pauses, breathing hard for several seconds before he faces me. "What are you doing?"

"Waiting for you to finish and tell me what's wrong."

Instead of answering, Sébastien hits the sack again. Judging by his face, he's not happy about the blow he landed. "I'm annoyed I still have this stupid arm."

"Did you want them to amputate it?"

My silly answer stops him cold, and I see some of the tension ease out of his shoulders. "No, of course not. But it's taking so long to heal. Even when it finally comes off, I'm facing weeks of physical therapy, maybe even months. And it'll probably always stay weak."

"You're going to be fine. Lots of people break their arm and recover full function. Just give it time."

"I don't have time."

I stare at him, confused. "Why not?"

He looks at me warily, and I see the temptation to lie in his eyes. Now I'm on edge. Clearly, it's something that has to do with me, but I'm not supposed to know. "Séb, what's going on at GoPol?"

"Nothing." He looks so tired. Then he throws his good arm in the air. "I'm just a colossal failure who's going to ruin the whole agency."

"Did someone say that to you?" That someone will have to answer to me. Sébastien's doing a damn good job of dragging the ghost police out of the mud Charles and his predecessors deliberately stuck it in. "I swear. If—"

He gives me a tortured smile. "No one has to say it. It's obvious. I'm not only failing at bringing the actual change we need to the agency, I'm also losing agents."

"Are people quitting?"

I can think of two types of GoPol officers to jump ship: those who hate the change Sébastien is trying to evoke and are loyal to Charles or something, and those who've realised how terribly wrong they were and can't live with themselves.

Sébastien plucks his shirt from his injured arm. "I don't know."

"What do you mean you don't know?"

He drops his shirt and sighs. "Maybe they quit, like you said, or maybe they're dead or worse."

My worry only grows. "Séb, what's going on? Talk to me."

Another tortured grimace. If he thinks I'll let him off the hook now, he's sorely mistaken. I reach out with my hands until he gives in and lets me pull him onto the bed. Kneeling, I massage his shoulders. "I promise I won't tell anyone. Not even Gaby." Which is ironic considering she's only a room away.

"You know I'm looking for the Chevalier, right?" He sighs again. "Or rather, I'm sending agents into the catacombs to look for the Chevalier, because there's no way I can crawl into them like this."

"It's not long to go now." If everything goes well, the cast will be off in two weeks.

"I know, but it's not nearly soon enough." He leans into me and closes his eyes for a moment, allowing my fingers to do their magic. "They're getting lost down there," he admits softly. "We've lost touch with almost every GoPol agent I sent into the catacombs to search for the Chevalier's whereabouts or information about Napoleon's bones."

"What?" I pause massaging.

Sébastien nods, another grimace distorting his face. "Sandrine's the latest. She begged me to send her in, then, three days later, no contact. Neither her nor her whisper ghost are anywhere to be found or summoned. And I don't know if she simply jumped ship or got herself killed. Weeks of searching and I still don't know anything. Eight agents are currently missing in action. Surely, that's a GoPol record."

I throw my arms around him and hug him tight. "It's not your fault."

"Yes. Yes, it is, Alix. I'm the acting commander. They followed my orders. They're my responsibility. And I failed them. I can't even go look for them them myself." He throws his head back, resting it on my shoulder. "Man, I hate this cast."

I kiss his jaw, trying to comfort him. "I'm sorry. But you can't blame yourself for everything. That's usually my thing."

A smile makes his lips twitch. "True."

Chuckling, I continue, "What I'm saying is we both know these aren't normal times. The world is changing and something sinister's afoot. If anything, it means your agents are getting close to the Chevalier, and most importantly, he doesn't want to be found."

He turns his face to me and gives me a sweet little kiss. "You're right. The Chevalier's definitely still hiding in the catacombs. I just don't know how to find him without sending another agent to their doom."

"You've got to let me help."

Am I afraid of the Chevalier? Absolutely. Do I feel equipped to handle his particular brand of obsession? Absolutely not. But afraid or not, I know I can help, that I'm more likely to get to the heart of this than another ill-equipped GoPol agent.

Sébastien snorts. "You think I'm going to let you explore the catacombs after what happened to my agents?"

I refrain from pointing out I can do whatever I want. I know he didn't mean it that way, just being his usual protective self. "There are other ways, you know."

He pulls back his head. "Like what?"

I wriggle my eyebrows to indicate I'm talking about myself. "You could hire a ghost consultant."

# CHAPTER 10

We reconvene the next day at GoPol headquarters. The new premises are still partially under construction to cater to all the special needs at the agency and has yet to develop its previously warm atmosphere. People need more time to settle and adjust to the new leadership and direction. I wonder if this building also comes with a quick access to the catacombs, and if so, whether the entrance is better guarded this time around.

Sébastien's office is on the top floor, but it's missing the grandeur of Charles' old stomping ground—there's no bar, no pool table, or any fancy amenities. Practicality is Sébastien's middle name, and so his office is furnished around his work with computers, file cabinets, and a huge table to spread maps and plans on. I'd bet my whisper ghost half the rescued archives have moved in here.

The map table is fancy—it's practically a huge tablet that pulls up documents and lets you zoom in and out. With a special pen, Sébastien can scribble directly on the screen and have his handwriting transformed into text. Right now, it's showing the catacombs map in three-layers: a transparent street layout of upper-world Paris, the widely explored first level, and the deeper, broken, and more mysterious second level. The second level isn't as well documented because unlike the first, it's not a continuous web underneath Paris, instead, it's made up of patches and small parts, which are connected to the upper level by collapsed walls, wells, and secret staircases.

"You think he's hiding in one of those?" I ask, noticing the multitude of question marks.

Sébastien leans over the map, drawing his pen across the surface. "I'm all but certain of it. My agents were able to cover his usual spots with ease—they're all empty, not a trace remaining. They've been able to safely go there and leave again. It's when I sent them to check the lower access points, chances of return diminished drastically."

I blow out my cheeks, staring at the patchy lower level. For all we know, we've only mapped twenty per cent of it. It could be connected, and most importantly, there could be entire rooms hidden where nothing but emptiness is displayed on the map.

"Just send me already," Dix complains from the sidelines. Turns out I'm not the only one who's been benched.

Sébastien throws him an annoyed glance, as if they've been over this before time and time again. "The Chevalier knows you."

"He's never *seen* me."

"But his whisperers and ghosts have." Sébastien shakes his head, straightening in the process. "I'm not going to risk losing you."

Dix rolls his eyes. In true teenage fashion, he thinks the risks don't apply to him, and he knows better. But we almost lost him once, and it's already bad enough his existence is tied to Sébastien's survival. For that reason alone, I'm glad Dix's been benched as well.

"What if we pretend we're looking for the separation Old Chev promised?" Dix tries once more. "We talked about it before, and we've got the bone splinter now, so it's only natural we'd search for him."

"He's not stupid," Gaspar says. Since we're all at GoPol today, he's decided to tag along. "The Chevalier knows where your loyalties lie. He'd know it was a trap."

"Never mind that he could trap *us*," Sébastien adds sternly. "As Gaspar said, he's clever. If he can snatch up all my agents, he can build a trap for us."

Yeah, that's not happening on my watch. The last thing I want is for the Chevalier to get his grabby hands on the bond that connects Dix and Sébastien. Dix might want to be free in the long term, but the Chevalier's experiment is not the solution; it's the end.

"We're going with Alix's plan," Sébastien says in a firm voice that allows no discussion.

"What's that?"

We all whirl around. Thomas Bézier looks as if he was about to walk by but spotted me instead. "Mademoiselle Dubois. May I inquire what you're doing up here?"

"She's a consultant," Sébastien says. "I've hired her."

He insisted on doing it all professionally and officially, even making me sign a contract so I could be reimbursed for what I'd just give him for free.

"On a GoPol mission?" Bézier enters the room and nods towards the map. "Is that appropriate?"

"I consult on ghosts," I say stiffly. Bézier might not be a paranoid maniac like Charles, but his reaction to my presence is becoming dangerously similar. "Like Napoleon. I think it's really important we talk to his ghost. As far as we know, he hasn't been resurrected yet. We could still convince him to step away." If he's free to do so.

Bézier regards me with a frown. "I don't care about Napoleon—he's just another ghost who doesn't know when to rest. Should he *be* resurrected, he'll pose no more danger than any other random lunatic."

Gaspar moves behind me to rub my upper arms. "Just ignore him," he whispers. "He doesn't know anything about ghosts."

And most importantly, he doesn't care.

"I want to know what the Chevalier's doing and what he's planning. He needs to be brought in. Whether that's by force or deal I don't care. However,"—Bézier stabs the map with his finger—"no more agents or whisper ghosts are to be sent into the catacombs until we have more information.”

“And that information’s just going to drop from the sky?” Dix asks sarcastically.

He’s got a point. Or he would’ve, if Sébastien and I weren’t already a step ahead of Bézier. “That’s where I come in.”

“You want to go into the catacombs?” Bézier asks doubtfully.

“No,” Sébastien, Dix, and Gaspar say as one, as if the mere mention will kill me.

“Relax guys, we’ve already talked about this.” I hold Bézier’s gaze. “GoPol’s whisper agents and ghosts are too obvious. They don’t fit in. The same isn’t true for other ghosts. There are millions in the catacombs—they’re bound to know something. Don’t worry, I *won’t* go in there myself, but we’ve built this whole ghost network with Jean Moulin at the helm. He’s a spy. He knows how to approach this.”

Bézier holds up a hand, frowning heavily. “Wait, what’s this about a spy network?”

I bite my lip. “It’s not really a spy network, just a network of ghosts, picking up gossip and filtering it through Jean Moulin in case... well, in case something happens in the ghost world.”

“Let me get this right, Mademoiselle Dubois: there’s a network of ghosts collecting information on the living and dead alike, under the oversight of Jean Moulin, who’s a ghost himself, with no further regulating body or anyone to report to but you?”

"They were invaluable in collecting evidence on my father," Sébastien chimes in. "I've worked with them before."

"So, they were spying on GoPol?" Bézier takes a step back and runs his hands across his head before massaging his temples with his palms. "This is such a massive security leak, I can't even wrap my head around it." He points at Sébastien. "GoPol assured us the only ghostly surveillance threat came from foreign whisperers and their ghosts. You said normal ghosts wouldn't be interested in us—they'd be too flaky, too wrapped up in their own little worlds to care what we do."

"What're you gonna do?" Dix asks, though Bézier doesn't hear him. "Eliminate all of us?"

A chill travels down my spine. I know for a fact he'd consider it if he had the ability. Better to destroy a ghost than try to establish a positive relationship with them. There's still so much work to do.

"Most ghosts *are* too flaky," Sébastien assures. "They aren't interested in us. And they've always refused to work with us, which is why we've come to rely on our whisper ghosts and former police officers."

"But they won't refuse to work for Mademoiselle Dubois," Bézier concludes.

I almost grunt in frustration. The reason the ghosts won't is because I've spent years building a reputation and, in many cases, individual relationships. "I'm not some ghost puppet master who's ordering them around and has them dancing around my fingers; I'm part of their community. You need to let go of this idea all ghosts are against you and working to bring down the living. They're normal people who lead normal afterlives, and who take care of each other."

"Yet, they've founded a spy network."

"To protect me. I doubt it's permanent. Look, I'm not helping the ghosts take over the world,"—prophecies be damned—"I'm helping them fix their graves, right old wrongs, or find forgiveness. Please don't make an enemy of me." I can't do this all over again.

Bézier's eyes darken. "Is that a threat?"

Gaspar's fingers tighten painfully around my shoulders, but I shake my head. "Not a threat. Just a plea." I don't know what to do if GoPol goes after me again.

Surprisingly, Bézier's face softens. There's a human in him, after all. "I'm sorry. This is all terribly new to me, and dealing with something I can't see, hear, or sense in any kind of way requires a lot of trust. I *want* to believe you, and maybe it's not fair for me to focus on the ghost threats I *do* know about. I guess the grand majority is exactly as you say: harmless." He sighs and rubs the root of his nose as he thinks through the new information. "To be honest, the idea of sending normal ghosts in there isn't a bad one. It'd keep our agents safe and pose little risk to us. Can we trust these ghosts?"

Sébastien meets his gaze. "Can we trust our agents?"

I nearly gasp. We both know Samira wasn't an isolated case—in fact, she was loyal to GoPol until Charles decided to eliminate her. But there *are* ex-GoPol officers in the Chevalier's ranks. Heck, the Chevalier himself is ex-GoPol. And yet the idea of all the missing agents defecting under Sébastien's nose is a scary one.

Bézier raises an eyebrow and nods at me. "Obviously not."

Sébastien snorts, a small smile playing around his lips. "Rest assured everything I do is for the good of this country. It just happens to include more than those who are alive."

I want to run over and kiss him. It's the first time he's completely bridged the divide, acknowledging the dead as part of our country's fabric, instead of an invisible threat lying in wait.

Bézier breathes in sharply, then nods. "I see where the definition might become a bit blurry. Very well, if the ghosts are going to be a part of our society, it's high time I learn more about them." He turns to me. "Since you're the expert, please tell me all about existing ghost structures and their allegiances. I want to know what we're dealing with. Oh, and I guess, if you think it's worth it, please *do* work your magic on Napoleon."

# Chapter 11

Before I deal with Napoleon, I pay a visit to Père Lachaise, where most of my non-Panthéon ghost friends reside. I've already informed Jean Moulin about the new deal I struck with GoPol, and we're striding through the cemetery together. Now the warm weather has arrived, the rows aren't just full of ghosts, but tourists as well. I'm lucky my grandmother's grave is in a spot without many big names around, though the ghosts of said-names flock to me as I make my way there.

"Any news on Napoleon?" I'm asked by Chopin.

I shake my head. "You know as much as I do."

"That man can't be allowed to return," Héloïse exclaims. "We might as well hand the necropolis over to the GoPol agents."

Yeah, there's a reason I'm doing this without Sébastien. I'm afraid he's still very much persona non grata here, especially now he's the official face of GoPol—imminent changes or not.

"We won't do that," I promise. To cover my chats with thin air, I've got my earbuds in, pretending to be on a call. "That's why we're here: to form an emergency response, right?"

Jean Moulin nods. "Exactly. It's better to be prepared than find yourself overrun by the enemy."

Unlike the Panthéon and GoPol, the ghosts here seem to take the threat of Napoleon more seriously. I suppose the general ghost population suffered under Napoleon's many previous attempts at world dominion, while my privileged friends at the Panthéon barely caught a whiff. As for Jean Moulin—he's always at war.

We reach the secluded area where my grandmother and Beatrice are, and find them sitting with a bunch of other older ladies and my grandmother's beau, Alexandre de Beauharnais, who just so happens to be a contemporary of Napoleon. They both served in the revolution, after all.

Seizing the opportunity, as no tourists or visitors are currently coming down this path, I weave between the tombstones and give my grandmother and Beatrice a quick kiss on the cheeks before waving at the other old biddies. "Salut."

"Salut, ma chérie," my grandmother says. "You're a busy young lady. Living people, right?"

There's a cackle around the graves and I can't help but snort. "Wouldn't you know it?"

"We're not busy. We're just sitting here, chatting, and passing judgement. Like, did you see those Americans? Or rather *hear* them? So loud!"

If people could hear ghosts, they'd probably complain about the ruckus, especially the one coming from this corner. I love that for them. Sadly, I'm not here to gossip today.

"Alexandre, do *you* have any information on Napoleon?"

The revolutionary general looks up, shielding his face against the sun. "I never met the man, but you know who did." There's a layer of pain in his voice.

And then I remember—of course! What's a good Napoleon story without the love of his life, Joséphine? Who just so happens to have been Alexandre's wife first.

"She's buried in Malmaison, right?"

After their divorce, Joséphine retreated to a big mansion called Malmaison, now part of one of Paris' most affluent suburbs. There, she grew roses, her namesake flowers—she went by Rose before Napoleon fell for her and insisted on calling her Joséphine.

"I believe so."

"You don't talk?" I ask curiously. Usually, the mutual memories draw ghosts together.

Another flash of pain. "I wasn't exactly what you'd call a good husband."

My grandmother pats his arm. "That was many, many years ago. Unlike other men, you've evolved." She throws a pointed glance at Héloïse.

"It's not my fault the man devolved." Héloïse shrugs. "Throw a bunch of salt at your man and he'll turn into an ass again, too."

It still hurts me to know one of the greatest love stories of all time which lasted a thousand years was destroyed in one fateful night, all because, once again, the potential of a threat was enough for GoPol to act.

I put talking to Joséphine on my list of options if Napoleon proves uncooperative. Unlike Alexandre, I bet he's over in Malmaison as often as he can be. The guy might've been a genius strategist in battle, but when it came to love, he was a smitten schoolboy at best. Joséphine might well be the ace we need in this latest of his conquests.

Beatrice pats the tombstone next to her, but there's a family of four walking by who'd probably take offence to me casually sitting on the graves. I wait until they're out of earshot before saying, "We need to reactivate the whisper network." Unlike what Bézier likes to think, the ghosts have little interest in long-term employment. The network exists when it's needed or not at all.

Héloïse tenses. "Are the ghost police after you again?"

"No. The ghost police are making a lot of promising changes. They're more inclined to work with ghosts rather than use and discard them at will these days."

Beatrice snorts. "I'll believe it when I see it—the whole bunch, not just your agent lover."

"My agent... You know about Sébastien?" I mean, of course they know about him since I told them about my relationship, but I kept his GoPol affiliation a secret.

"Please. What good is a spy network if you can't use it to spy on your favourite granddaughter's boyfriends?" my grandmother says. So much for the network lying dormant. "We had to make sure they were good boys, didn't we? And yes, we had a talk about your Sébastien, and all agreed the evidence is in favour of him being one of the good ones." She smiles at Alexandre. "After all, we do believe people can change; whether they're dead or alive."

I let out a sigh of relief. It never sat quite right with me to keep Sébastien's job from them, it felt like a shameful secret, but my grandmother is right. He *has* changed, and now GoPol's changing with him.

"Now we've cleared that up, you *need* to bring him along and properly introduce him. We only know his naughty side, the little whisper teen."

While there's undoubtedly something cheeky about Dix, they have *not* seen Sébastien's naughty side, the one he's only just discovering himself.

"Look at her blush," my grandmother whispers, loud enough for everyone to hear. "She's finally having some fun."

If I wasn't blushing before, I definitely am now. "Grandma!"

A bunch of tourists look my way, startled. I grimace and take extra care to look like I'm on the phone. "You can't say things like that."

"I'll say whatever I want to say. If you can't speak your mind in death, what's it even for?"

I know better than to argue. The tourists have gone past and no one else seems to be heading this way, so I'd better get to the point. "Alright. Things are underfoot in Paris—literally underfoot. The Chevalier's stolen Napoleon's bones and we know he's into resurrections, but he hasn't resurrected him yet, which worries me more than it comforts me. Something's happening, and we need to find out what."

"GoPol's useless." Jean picks up my thread, allowing me to remain quiet when a new group of visitors walks past. "They're not equipped for a ghost-human coalition of evil."

You'd think a bunch of ghost whisperers would be, but they've always ignored the ghost community and kept to their own for standard-issue intelligence work. It's coming back to bite them now, though, as they stick out like sore thumbs in the catacombs.

"We need men—and women—on the ground in the catacombs to find out what the Chevalier or Napoleon are planning. What's the end goal? Where are their outposts? Who's with them? I want to know everything."

Jean's commanding voice makes even my back straighten. He sure knows how to run an operation. Or maybe not, because the ghosts are all looking baffled, throwing unsure glances at each other.

Only Alexandre stands to attention. "Yes, Sir!"

I guess grandmas, nuns, and musicians aren't quite as used to military speak.

"What's the matter?" I ask. "If you're scared, that's okay. You don't have to do anything." I won't force anyone to help me after what happened last time.

"It's not that," Héloïse says. "I'm not scared of those sad little men, but I've never been to the catacombs." They didn't even exist in her time.

"Me, neither," Chopin adds.

Beatrice winces, "Sorry, love. I mean, I guess it'd be fun to stick our noses in there, but I honestly wouldn't even know where to start."

Lots of ghosts have made the catacombs their home, most of whom were buried there, but it's not their natural habitat. I vaguely remember all the different innovations at the fair, trying to extend people's haunting space, and I realise our whisper network has hit a sizeable snag.

"Well, I do."

I turn at the vaguely familiar voice and come face to face with one of my worst nightmares: Emily Durant, the ghost who started it all.

Back in October, I took on an innocuous little favour to retrieve something dear for her. What Emily failed to mention was that that "something" was her dead body. It's the reason I'm now acquainted with the Chevalier, and how GoPol found me after years of peaceful ghost whispering. Sure, one could argue I also wouldn't have met Sébastien and Dix, but let's not give her too much credit, because Emily was bloody useless in the catacombs.

"What do you want?" I ask, guarding my face.

Jean Moulin moves ever so slightly closer, as if to assure me he's got my back.

Emily steps closer. "I want to repay the favour. You don't like me and that's fair—I was a brat and you didn't invoke much confidence. Now look at you, a bonafide cataphile yourself." She gives me a respectful nod. "I haven't forgotten you took on my favour and brought my case to the police's attention, nor that you were involved in the demise of the woman who pulled the trigger on me. Thanks for that, I guess."

To be fair, I haven't really paid Emily much mind after our ill-fated adventure in the catacombs. I was always glad she and I parted ways after that.

"Unlike these old biddies here, I'm a catacombs crawler. I know those tunnels like the back of my hands, even better than I used to when I was alive. Over the last eight months I've explored far and deep—it's even cooler if you can simply walk through stone, but don't worry, I've made an effort to look for mortal access points, too. Just in case, you know."

As much as I hate it, this sounds exactly like the kind of skill set we're looking for. And if I'd forgotten Emily, the Chevalier will have, too. Plus, the catacombs ghosts would be used to her, seeing her as one of their own.

"You're willing to help us?"

She shrugs and blows the sweep of green hair out of her face. "Why not? I owe you, and it could be cool. Find even more places." She grins at me. "Oh, you wouldn't believe the cool stuff I've come across already."

"She makes a good case," Jean mutters in my ear.

I know. This is gold. But I can't quite ignore the little voice in my head telling me not to trust her. Then again, what do I have to lose?

"Alright. You heard Jean: we need all the information about the Chevalier and Napoleon we can gather, most importantly where they're holed up and what they're planning."

"You've got it, little girl." She winks, taking some of the bite out of her disdainful remark, and sinks straight through the graves into the ground. I hope when she finds the Chevalier she makes good on her promise to look for living access.

"That's a good asset to have," Jean says appreciatively.

I sigh heavily. "Potentially. Keep a close eye on her, because last time I worked with Emily, my safety was her lowest priority."

# CHAPTER 12

After I've put my whisper network back into action, I ride my bike across town to meet Sébastien at Les Invalides. I arrive before him at the backside of the big palace at Place Vauban since it's closest to Napoleon's tomb, under the golden cupola high above the palace. Peering through the wrought-iron fence, I notice the tomb is still closed off and guarded by gendarmes. That doesn't stop tourists and school classes from walking the grounds, though.

A taxi stops near me, delivering Sébastien. While he's paying the driver, Dix joins me. "I can't wait for his cast to come off so he can get back on his bike. We're missing all the good road weather."

"There's still enough summer left for the two of you." That said, I miss Sébastien's motorbike, too.

Sébastien makes his way over and leans in to kiss me. Dix teases, "Not in public."

"Shush," Sébastien says, his lips quirking up. "How was your meeting with Moulin?"

"Very good. The network is employed, and we've even got a dead cataphile on the case." I swallow. "Emily Durant."

He raises an eyebrow. "The dead body you stumbled over in Ossa Arida." Swaying his head, he shrugs. "I guess she'd be a good ally."

"We'll see. We didn't really get along back then, but she thinks she owes me, and I'm not above taking her up on it."

"What did Thomas call it? Your magic?"

I stare at him, not amused. "Any whisperer could wield the same; they just don't want to."

Instead of being offended, Sébastien's smile widens. He slips his good arm around me and pulls me in. "But none could do it as well as you."

I graciously allow him to kiss me, ignoring Dix's gagging noises in the background.

"Alright. Let's see if Napoleon's about."

We enter the grounds courtesy of Sébastien's badge and make our way to the dome at the back of the large military museum. It's completely cordoned off from the public, which makes me sad for the museum staff who'll have to cope with the lack of visitors. I notice a boy on the lawn staring at us, but before I can get a better look, he joins one of the classes. Shrugging, I enter the dome behind Sébastien.

Our steps sound hollow on the marble floor under the vaulted roofs. Light enters through windows high above our heads, giving it a church-like glow. Carved and painted frescoes adorn the walls and the ceiling above the tomb. The tomb itself isn't visible from the entrance—it sits on a lower level, viewable from a circular hole in the centre, and accessible via a set of stairs at the back. In each of the four corners under the cupola is a separate resting space for Napoleon's brothers and comrades in arms. Their tombs aren't nearly as fancy, but they're still massive. A few ghosts watch our approach but no one bothers us.

Together, we traverse the room until we reach the giant hole in the middle. The dome sits on top of us, its ceiling painted similarly to the one in the Panthéon. It's pretty, but the real prize is below. From above, Napoleon's tomb looks exactly like the pictures, a fancy mahogany tomb with curly details. However, no picture could do its size justice—it's just so *massive*. I know he wasn't the one who put himself here, but I can't stop myself from comparing the tomb to his ego.

"They broke in from the bottom," a voice says next to me.

"Jean!"

My friend, Jean Lannes, is hanging out in Napoleon's tomb site. He gives me a tired smile and Sébastien and Dix a short nod. "Salut, Mademoiselle Dubois, Messieurs Roubert."

"I didn't know you came here often."

He raises an eyebrow. "There's a whole section dedicated to my memory over at the museum. Lately, I've been hanging out more at the Panthéon." His look turns introspective. "I wonder if that was a mistake. If I'd been here…"

I put a hand on his arm. "Don't beat yourself up. No one could've known this would happen."

"I should've known. I'm his best friend—*was*. And his brothers told me there was another ghost whisperer here."

Sébastien tenses. "Who?"

"He goes by the name of Mathieu. He never acknowledged any of them, just came for Napoleon."

The hairs on my arm stand and I bristle. "Mathieu."

"He works with the Chevalier," Sébastien explains.

"Figures." Jean sighs, a cloud of sadness still over his head. "Come on, I'll introduce you to Napoleon." He turns towards the stairs.

"So, he's here?" I ask.

After our last talk, I had small hope he'd been captured by the Chevalier, making this more a rescue mission than delicate diplomacy. There's just something chilling about the idea Napoleon might be the mastermind behind everything.

Jean nods. "We haven't had a chance to talk yet, but I've asked his brothers and he's been around."

We walk down the stairs to the round lower level. The tomb is even more impressive this close, towering above us. It has the shape of a massive chaise longue, or maybe a fancy treasure chest, in rich, polished mahogany wood. It sits in its own room on a black marble slab on a raised dais, separated from the walkway around it by a knee-high stone wall and columns. The floor displays the imperial sun around a wreath of laurels. Yellow, black, green, and the same mahogany brown dominate the centre of the room, while the walkway itself is utterly devoid of colour. It wouldn't be hard to jump the little wall and get closer, but there are security cameras all around the dome, especially down here. Still, broken crumbs of wood and marble cover the black slab, showing me where the thieves got in. The gap between it and the pedestal is big enough for a man to lie between, but I wonder how they got their equipment in there—and the bones out of it? They didn't use explosives, did they?

My stomach turns at the sight of destruction. Whether I like the man or not, to wilfully destroy a tomb that's stood the test of time for over 150 years will never sit right with me.

I don't get to mull over it for long, because Jean rounds the walkway to a bench full of fresh flowers. The dome might be closed to the public, but the staff still pay their respects. There we find Napoleon in the uniform and hat that's become synonymous with him.

People always harp on about how small Napoleon was, but he wasn't a midget. In fact, his size was pretty average for his time. Coming in at just below 5 foot 6, barely an inch shorter than me, he's not a tall man, but he's not a dwarf, either. More importantly, though, he has a presence that more than makes up for what he lacks in size. I can easily imagine how impressive he would've looked on top of a horse, charging into battle. It's the same energy he exudes now, facing me. Once a warlord, always a warlord.

"Your Majesty," Jean says, bowing sharply. "May I present to you Alix Dubois, official whisperer of the Panthéon, and Sébastien and Dix-Sept Roubert from GoPol."

Dix clears his throat. "Leaders of Go—" Napoleon's stare hits him, and the loudmouthed teen suddenly swallows. "Never mind."

"You may leave, Lannes," Napoleon dismisses, his gaze barely even touching the marshal. "I will meet with the whisperers alone."

"Very well." Jean bows once more. He flicks me an apologetic look before blinking out of existence.

I restrain myself from hugging my chest, grateful for Sébastien's confident presence. "Your majesty," I acknowledge, giving a slight curtsy. It's more than he gets from Sébastien who simply nods.

The emperor's gaze falls squarely on me. "So, we finally meet."

I feel reprimanded, as if I've already offended him by not seeking him out earlier. "So, we do," I reply, trying to replicate his tone.

There's the slightest nod of acknowledgement. "I believe we have a common friend?"

Since I doubt he means Jean Lannes or any of the other generals in the Panthéon, there's only one person he could be talking about. "The Chevalier."

"Walk with me."

Sébastien throws me a glance, and I shake my head. It doesn't seem like Napoleon's interested in talking to him—only me.

We set off around the walkway while Sébastien and Dix take the opportunity to examine the break-in. If anything happens, they're less than ten metres away, so I'm relatively safe. Still, my heart's in my throat, my pulse pounding in my ears.

"I take it you're familiar with me, then?" I ask softly, trying to make small talk with the guy who once controlled half of Europe.

"There isn't a ghost in Paris who hasn't heard of you. Yet, I'd dare say I'm not nearly as familiar with you as you are with me."

I'm not sure if he's boasting about his popularity or acknowledging my history background.

"The Chevalier has told me a great deal about you."

I try not to show how cold my blood runs at that admission.

"At first, I was doubtful. What does it matter if we have one more whisperer on our side? And a woman, no less."

There's nothing like casual misogyny to set my head straight. "But?" I ask, less than impressed.

"You've proven yourself time and time again, showing flexibility, tenacity, and most importantly conviction. It would be an honour to fight side by side with you."

We're going from misogyny to honest compliment so fast, I'm getting whiplash. "What are we fighting for?"

"A new era." He regards me sternly. "Make no mistake, Mademoiselle Dubois, when I rise, I will reward those who stood by me, but I will also punish those who tried to stop me with the utmost severity. And I *will* rise."

I practically taste the threat on my lips. "Speaking of rising, there's something you need to know about the Chevalier's process." I quickly tell him about what happened with Louis XVI—and Olivier, too.

"Are you comparing me to a weak king who couldn't even hold onto his crown while he was alive, and deservedly lost his head for it, then came back to life, only to be killed by a trio of mad women?"

I wouldn't dare call the Triad of Queens "mad women", but that might just be me. "What I'm saying is he lived less than a day."

"Are you threatening me?"

Though he doesn't raise his voice, my blood freezes in my veins. "N-no."

"Good. Because I wouldn't advise it, Mademoiselle Dubois. I don't take lightly to threats, whether from ghosts or whisperers."

"So, you're planning on going through with the resurrection?" I don't know how to convince him to stop. He sounds like he's already made up his mind.

Napoleon's face never even twitches. "My plans are of no consequence to you."

A sarcastic "Really?" slips from my mouth before I can stop myself.

Now, he's smiling, or rather smirking a little. "There's a place for you in my army when you're done catering to the living. Until then, I'm afraid you're not to be trusted. Let my marshal know once you're ready to meet with me and the Chevalier."

He marches around the next column, but when I follow him, he's gone.

My heart's still beating in my throat, fearing he'll jump out of the shadows at any moment. Napoleon and the Chevalier want me. There's going to be a fight. And he will definitely be back.

"That was short," Sébastien comments, climbing back over the fence. "Did you get him to reconsider?"

I shake my head, not quite trusting my voice.

Tension creeps into Sébastien's stance. "Did he threaten you?"

"Not like that." Technically he *did,* promising bitter retribution to his enemies. But... "He doesn't see me as an enemy—yet."

"That's good, isn't it?"

"I don't know. He seems to think I want to join him and the Chevalier."

Sébastien frowns. "Why would you do that?"

Beats me. "A place in Napoleon's army" is not exactly what I was hoping for. "There's going to be a battle," I admit, in a hushed whisper. "I'm scared."

Sébastien immediately steps forward and wraps his arms around me, holding me tight. "That's just Napoleon boasting. You've heard the other ghosts—he pulls this shit all the time."

"But this time he's got the Chevalier at his side."

"A coward who's holed up deep in the catacombs. What a fine pair they make." He strokes my hair while my heart continues to pound against his chest. "Of course they need you—you're the key to all the ghosts in this city. Without you, they're just a bunch of has-beens, dreaming of glory."

I swallow hard, trying to find comfort in Sébastien's assessment. "He said if I wanted to meet with the Chevalier, I could." Slowly, I force myself to look up at him. "He'd let me find him."

There's a flash of fear in Sébastien's eyes, but it's replaced by blue steel soon enough. "I'd rather die than let that man get his hands on you again."

I should probably fight him: this could be our opening, our only chance to find out what's really brewing in the catacombs before it's too late. But when he holds my gaze, his arms holding me even tighter, all I feel is a massive wave of relief washing over me. As long as I stay here, in Sébastien's arms, I'll be safe.

Until I no longer am.

# Chapter 13

Whatever Napoleon and the Chevalier are planning, they're not in a rush. I manage to get through my entire exam week without a ghost catastrophe. Maybe the Panthéon ghosts *were* right, and Napoleon is all talk and little action. I mean, he still hasn't even been resurrected. If I only knew what was stopping him.

I figure it can only be good for me, because all I need is time. My social media accounts are growing nicely—even Odile is impressed with how quickly they're gaining ground. That's what you get for being the on-trend topic. I still have a ways to go before I can start to plant some seeds around the benefits of closing down the catacombs or advocating for ghost rights. Right now, it's all about building awareness. And luckily, the ghosts are all on board.

As soon as I finish my last tour and meet up with Odile, there's a long line of willing participants. Victor's brought an excerpt of his newest book, Josephine tells the most amazing story about how she swindled three Nazi commanders out of their plans *and* their pocket watches, and Voltaire and Rousseau surprise me by having already gone to the effort of breaking down their latest debate to a minute—a minute, that's jam-packed with opinion and zinger lines.

"You're absolute naturals," Odile exclaims, even though she's unable to tell where each philosopher stands. You'd think it'd be pointless to take videos of ghosts, but we're using a combination of imagery, my presence, and subtitles to make the videos engaging.

We do a couple of regular videos before diving into responses, such as Marie Curie's somewhat-lengthy explanation of spectral radioactivity. Some of the comments are like *SpectralFlo's,* full of curiosity; some are weird requests we are being very selective about—the ghosts deserve their dignity after all; a few, however, range from sceptical to trolling. I want to ignore them, but Odile picks out a particularly ruthless one.

"Who wants to answer this?" she asks, then quotes, *"Antzfor-fun*—what a stupid name—thinks it's selfish for ghosts like you to stick around. Why don't you just move on and leave us alone?"

What a rude thing to say. Never mind the fact the ghosts have little choice in when they fading, it seems so petty. How do ghosts continuing to linger hurt *Antzforfun*?

Victor steps forward and I quickly tell Odile to record. This is going to be one hell of a response. He straightens his jacket and clears his throat. "Move on and bereave the world of my talent? Who's selfish now?"

Okay, humility has never been his strong suit.

Odile bends over laughing when I tell her what he said. "Oh, this is epic. Iconic really."

"I aim to please, young lady," Victor says with a benevolent smile. "In all earnestness though, when has existing ever been selfish? Or maybe it's inherently selfish?" He looks over at Rousseau and Voltaire, who immediately jump to the occasion and argue over it, whether Odile's rolling or not.

We continue with the videos until I notice Jean Lannes stalking the periphery. I know he's not interested in being part of our project, so I gather he has another reason to search for me. Perhaps news from Napoleon.

I finish recording and say my goodbyes before approaching him, leaving Odile to work on editing. "Did you want something?"

"I'm good, Mademoiselle Dubois."

"Are you?" Something's clearly bothering him, but I can't help him if he doesn't speak up.

We go upstairs, away from the hustle and bustle of the crypt. "I want to let you know we've erected a perimeter around the Panthéon," Jean says, matter-of-factly. "If there's an attack, we'll know."

"That's good," I say, acknowledging his diligence. While there's some concern about the Chevalier trying to steal more bones, I doubt he'll get into the Panthéon—the ghosts simply won't let him.

We walk a little further until it's rather obvious there's more weighing on his heart. "How are things with Napoleon?"

"We made up."

I nearly stumble over my feet. "What? What does that mean?" Has Jean switched sides?

"Terribly little, I'm afraid," he says, tension lacing his voice. "He assured me he's forgiven me and that his last venture was indeed ill-conceived, but he's a better man now with the kind of vision which will change all our afterlives."

I desperately want to know more, but I'm afraid to interrupt.

"Don't get your hopes up," Jean says, as if he's read my mind. "He didn't actually tell me what this vision entails. In fact, we both agreed on a mutual information embargo to protect each other's integrity."

"I don't understand."

He regards me with a torturous look. "It means I don't tell him anything about the Panthéon and he won't tell me anything about what's going on in the catacombs."

As much as I want—and need—a man on the inside, I see Jean's loyalty is torn. At least, this way, the Panthéon isn't compromised, but even I know it's not going to last. One day, sooner rather than later, Jean—and the other generals—will have to choose.

"He asked me to convey this to you."

You'd think it'd be impossible for a ghost to hand you an actual item, but I've long since learnt the truly powerful can. Just as I drank wine in the Boutique of Psychosis and shut off Gustav Eiffel's resonator, I can take the small piece of paper from Jean and read the single chilling line:

*If you want to see a world where ghosts can thrive, join me, Alix.*
*Yours truly, R.C.*

Romain Coullier—le Chevalier d'Os.

# Chapter 14

With no lectures or exams to distract me, I can't stop thinking about my creepy invitation. There's only so many ghost videos and tours I can do, so on my day off, I accompany Sébastien to work. He's still spending too many hours at the office, trying to figure out where his agents have vanished to, so this might be my only chance to hang out with him.

We talk through a few options, when I suddenly have an idea. "I think I've figured it out."

"You have?"

It's all falling into place. "Do you remember how the Panthéon ghosts used their power to practically seal the Panthéon off to GoPol agents and whisper ghosts? They all suddenly had something else to do."

They did the same when Félice started bothering me. She's reached out yet again, but I keep ignoring her, hoping she'll eventually take the hint and go away.

Sébastien's slowly catching on. "And you think the Chevalier could be doing something similar?"

"He's obsessed with his places of power, and we know he now has potent ghosts at his side. He might be hiding in plain sight, turning everyone looking for him away." It explains why Emily hasn't returned with anything useful yet—or she's simply abandoned the mission.

"That still doesn't explain what's happened to my agents," Sébastien says, musing over his map.

Gaspar is hanging out in a corner of the room, sitting on a file cabinet. "If they were dead, their ghosts would've returned, wouldn't they?"

"Unless the ghosts have been held back, like the whisper ghosts. They could be bound to a specific location, like what the Knights Hospitallers did with Molay. Or maybe he's destroyed them completely," Sébastien says softly.

I shudder, a chill crawling down my back. "They could've decided to switch sides." Trying to be more generous to the agents, I add, "Or gone undercover."

"Why would they do that?" Sébastien's gaze hits me, the hurt not entirely hidden. "Is it because I'm a bad leader? Have they decided to take matters into their own hands? Or would they rather join the Chevalier with his vigilante crusade than rebuild GoPol from the ground up?"

Not willing to hear more self-punishing arguments, I walk over and slip my arms around him. "This isn't on you."

"But it is, either because I sent them into an unclear, dangerous situation—"

"Which is part of their job."

"—or because I drove them to the Chevalier." Despite his words, he accepts my comfort and rests his head against my cheek. "I'm afraid I'm doing it all wrong," he whispers. "I can't get the agency changed to your standards, my agents are running away... It's all slipping through my fingers."

I hug him a little tighter, running a hand across his back. "You're too hard on yourself. The agency you've inherited was a mess."

"It's still a mess."

"Yes, but that's part of change. It takes time to sort it all out and build a strong framework. Nobody gets it right the first time. That goes for individuals as well as societies. It's why France took over a century to build a stable republic."

Sébastien snorts softly. "I'm hoping to take a little less time than that."

Chuckling, I agree, "You will." Slowly, I entangle myself from him. "In regard to the Chevalier, maybe it's time we consider using all our weapons."

"No."

I haven't even finished. "The ghosts have yet to report anything useful, and your agents are still missing."

"No."

"Jean Lannes and the other officers are in contact with Napoleon, but they've struck some weird truce-slash-information-embargo."

"The answer remains no."

The wait is killing me. I wish Napoleon would just hurry up and reveal his plan, so we could take action. Failing that... "He's invited me in."

"And you're not going."

I throw him an unimpressed stare, but before I can give him a speech about making my own decisions, Gaspar presses against my back and breathes in my ear, "I'm with Séb there. We'll tie you up, if necessary."

I nearly miss a heartbeat, suddenly keenly aware of the two bodies trapping mine. "I-I..."

Sébastien puts a finger under my chin and lifts it slightly, making me hold my breath. "You're far too valuable to risk on a reconnaissance mission. The fact he's invited you makes me even more worried. We've always known he wanted you. How long until he stops inviting nicely and takes you by force?"

His eyes blaze when he says "force", and his throat bops. His fear seeps into me. Suddenly, I have visions of the Chevalier hunting and abducting me.

Sébastien nods. "You understand. Good. That's why I'm going to teach you how to defend yourself." He steps back, leaving me strangely unbalanced. "Since my arm's still in a cast, Gaspar will be your partner."

Gaspar slings an arm around me and lifts me just enough to turn me, facing the empty space in Sébastien's office. I only now notice a thin mat's been rolled out.

"Wait, what?" Was that their plan this whole time?

"Let's take the offer to roll on the floor," Gaspar quips. "I can't promise you'll learn much fighting, though." The wink he gives me sends my pulse racing, and I glance at the door, making sure it's closed.

Sébastien clears his throat. "I'm serious, Gaspar. She needs to learn how to defend herself. We can't be with her all the time."

"Yes, sir!" Gaspar salutes, a smirk ruining the submissive gesture.

"You're almost as bad as Dix," Sébastien complains.

But for the next hour, Sébastien gets his wish, and I get my first lesson in self-defence, which leaves me sweaty and aching. It's surprisingly fun, though, especially when your opponent is a mischievous ghost who's sneaking in as many surprise kisses as possible. I know I'm supposed to defend myself against his touch, but I seem to forget that little detail the longer we're at it.

"You're supposed to fend him off, not invite him in," Sébastien says exasperated. His face is almost as red as mine, though he's not the one wrestling on the mat.

"Speak for yourself," Gaspar growls near my ear, and the most delicious chill runs down my spine.

I try to make Sébastien happy and half-heartedly place my hands on Gaspar's arms and twist. But my angle is off and all I manage is to unbalance us both. Gaspar wraps his arms tighter around me, bracing me against the fall as we tumble to the ground. I land on him, turn, and rob myself of the last bit of breath I still had by kissing him.

There's a click at the door, startling me. I push up on my arms as much as I can with Gaspar holding me, but it's only Sébastien locking his door. Guess I'm moving on to lesson two: how to "defend" myself against two attackers.

When I leave Sébastien's office—or rather the private bathroom I needed afterwards—I feel entirely too self-conscious for coherent thinking. With everyone I pass, I wonder if they know, never mind the fact no one even knocked on the door, and his office is the only one on this level. It doesn't help that Gaspar's still with me, a hand on my lower back.

A familiar laugh grabs my attention. There's another person who thankfully didn't walk in on us, and by the looks of it, he had a surprisingly similar reason. Dix's leaning against the wall in a corridor, a lazy grin on his face as he listens to an equally dead girl telling him a story with big gestures and even bigger expressions. She's got a shock-full of curly brown hair and can't be more than fifteen or sixteen, and by the looks of it, she's absolutely smitten with Dix.

"—and then he rambled on about all his past glories, as if she cared. That woman was so over him, even before they were both dead."

Dix laughs again. "True that."

It's so good to see him acting like a normal teenager, gossiping and flirting. I don't want to disturb them, but Dix notices Gaspar and me when we try to walk by.

"Alix!" he calls, and the girl spins around in response.

She's quite cute, with a smattering of freckles and a rather old-fashioned set of glasses. Her clothes look like something a young girl might've worn in the eighties. I know exactly who she is, even before Dix introduces her.

"Come and meet Lys, one of GoPol's best whisper ghosts."

Lys slaps his arm and giggles. "Don't say that. I'm just the secretary's ghost."

"Nah, don't let her fool you," Dix says with a wink. "She's a spy, alright. Tell them what you just told me."

Put on the spot, Lys is growing quite shy. I remember when Dix first told us about her—her whisperer, Louise, practically discarded her as she grew older and more mature. At fifteen, no one thought about turning Lys into a whisper agent, no one paid her much attention at all—until Dix made an effort.

"Oh, well, if you insist, Dix." Lys leans forward conspiratorially. "I saw Napoleon visit Malmaison."

"He visited Joséphine?" I ask. "Recently?"

Lys rolls her eyes. "That man's a sucker for her. Doesn't matter she never truly loved him and used him to get ahead—which honestly, more power to her." Her words quickly gain steam as she speaks. "Still, he comes back like a beaten puppy every single time, and it's always with a big gesture. One time, he made her entire garden bloom—in winter!"

That's surprisingly romantic.

"And he always promises her the world, but this time he *means* it." I catch Dix giving me a pointed look, but Lys is unstoppable now. "He told her he had a plan and he wants her by his side again, like, this time, he's gonna give fuck-all to anyone bothering him about an heir, because who needs one if you never intend to step down? So, Jojo and Poli are back on—or they would be if she had any interest in him."

"Are you friends with Joséphine?" I ask, my heart racing.

"What, me?" Lys' eyes widen. "Never! I'm not friends with anybody."

"We're friends," Dix says casually.

Lys all but melts. I'm pretty sure I hear her whisper, "You're special."

Behind her back, Gaspar gives Dix an appreciative fist bump, and I all but roll my eyes. "Well, I don't want to keep you two." I trust Dix to give me a slightly less colourful account of what he's learnt later. "It was nice meeting you, Lys."

"Same!" she says, with almost as much adoration as she has for Dix. "I can't believe I talked to *the* Alix Dubois. You're my hero."

That's a first, for sure. "Um…"

Gaspar wraps his arms around me and nuzzles his chin into the crook of my neck. "Mine, too."

"Yeah, yeah, we all love Alix," Dix says with a hefty dose of reality. "We just don't all defile offices to prove it. Seriously, I can never go in there again."

"Dix!"

My loud cry draws the attention of several GoPol employees. I throw him a dirty look—he has the audacity to grin—and quickly march off. Embarrassment makes my cheeks burn. I can't believe he knows what went on upstairs and dared throw it in my face in public. Gaspar chuckles behind me, not making it any better.

I'm about to snap at him when a young woman slips in front of me, her pale blue eyes shining with admiration. She's a little smaller than me with gorgeous ginger hair in a high ponytail, and a face filled with so many freckles I can hardly make out the pale skin beneath them. The sea of freckles extends down her neck and even her arms, which are exposed in the muscle shirt she's wearing along with her shorts. A light-weight jacket is knotted around her hips.

"You're Alix Dubois, right?" she says with a distinct British accent.

"Yes?" Unlike the two I just left behind, she's not a ghost.

"I'm Florence, but people call me Flo. You probably know me as *SpectralFlo*. I follow all your accounts. Figured you'd be GoPol, duh."

She's almost as bubbly as Lys. It takes a moment for the pieces to click into place. This is one of my online followers, the one who asked the terribly detailed question of Marie Curie—and she's affiliated with GoPol.

"I'm not GoPol, just an occasional consultant."

Flo's eyes widen even more. "That's so cool. Honestly, Paris is something else. I'm usually based in London, but with everything going on here, I had to come over. I never thought I'd meet you." She squeals. "I'm such a big fan. I've followed Malou for ages, because who wouldn't? She's the most adorable hedgehog I've ever seen. And when she started doing the ghost stunts... Such a genius idea." Her gaze lands on Gaspar. "Oh my god! You're the ghost from the videos."

Gaspar gives a mocking bow. "You're not supposed to see me."

"I know, I know, and I promise Malou's secrets are safe with me." She turns back to me. "When you started making your own channels, I immediately knew you were the real deal. There are so many hacks out there at the moment, but your material is gold. I've never really been interested in history, but it's something else when you can actually hear famous people talking. And you're familiar with Marie Curie. So jealous!"

It's rare to meet someone at GoPol who genuinely enjoys hearing about ghosts, despite it being their entire livelihood. "Are you an agent?" Did Sébastien send for reinforcements from other GoPol agencies?

Flo shakes her head. "No, my brother is, I'm just one of the engineers at the GoPol Research Centre in London. We do a lot of ghost research."

I can't help it but my opinion of her is taking a quick nosedive. If I'm wary around GoPol agents, I'm doubly so around those who research ghosts. Chalk it up to bad experiences, first with Sébastien's ruthless mother in Provence, and now with the Chevalier. Neither cared a lot about the ghosts *or* living they were willing to sacrifice for their progress.

"You experiment on ghosts?"

"Depends on what counts as a ghost experiment. I mean, technically, all we do revolves around that, but my job is a lot more theoretical. I've tried to get some of my gadgets through, but most agents sneer at them. Who needs assistive technology when you're already one of the chosen ones?"

"What's assistive technology?" Gaspar asks. Unlike me, he sounds genuinely curious.

"Oh, you know, tech that allows non-whisperers to interact with ghosts. Like me."

"You're a non-whisperer?" I would've never guessed from how she's interacting with Gaspar.

Flo nods proudly. "Yes! When my brother turned into a ghost whisperer, I became obsessed. I wanted to speak to his whisper ghost and learn about ghosts, so I figured out a way."

Though I'm still suspicious, I can't help but be impressed. If there's a way for others to see ghosts, it'd make my life a lot easier—or even more complicated. "That's cool."

Flo bends forward to whisper conspiratorially, "Honestly, I'm glad the Parisian division is working with people like you. In my opinion, GoPol could learn so much from you. As could I," she ends, with a huge grin.

My phone buzzes, giving me an opportunity to end this before my curiosity overrides my caution. "Well, it was nice to meet you, Flo, but I've got to run."

She's certainly enthusiastic, but so was Margot. And the Chevalier. Unfortunately, being a fan of my talents doesn't guarantee someone's a good person—quite the opposite, actually. As interesting as Flo seems to be, the thought of another ghost scientist taking an interest in me gives me the creeps.

Gaspar accompanies me outside, throwing a last glance at the red-headed Brit. "She seemed nice."

"They always do." I pull out my phone to read the message. "Oh, my..."

"What?" He looks over my shoulder.

"Your maman got hold of my number. She's doubling her offer."

Groaning, Gaspar pulls away. "Tell her to fuck off."

The amount of money Madame du Charbonneau is willing to throw at me is mind-boggling, but my loyalty can't be bought. If Gaspar doesn't want to meet her, there's no point in exploiting her. However... "Are you sure you don't want to talk to her? Just once?"

"There's never 'just once' with my parents. Do you think she'll be happy with one quick chat?" His mood's quickly tanking. "No! Once she's got her talons in me, she'll never let go. Same goes for you. She'll trot you out at every social event."

"You make her sound like a monster."

Gaspar opens his mouth, as if to tell me she *is* a monster, but then he shuts it again. "She's not like Séb's mother—or father," he admits, "I just don't think she's genuinely interested in meeting me. Just a version she's made up in her mind. And I'm done with that. I don't need her approval or whatever she calls love these days. It's all just show."

"I don't think so," I say softly. There's no doubt Madame du Charbonneau is very concerned with her image, but the pain in her eyes was real. She may have failed Gaspar as a mother while he was still alive, but she's regretting it now. "If you don't want me to meet her, I won't. But I'd love to see where you grew up, learn a little bit more about you..."

He grabs my hands and presses his forehead on mine, sighing deeply. "Just ask."

"It's not the same."

Another moment passes as I let him stew. As much as I'd love to explore his childhood, that isn't why I've brought it up: Gaspar needs this reconciliation just as much as his mother. He's so untethered from his old life it's affecting his afterlife. And though he's loud to proclaim otherwise, there's still so much hurt in him, hurt which will fester if left untreated. I'm happy to put myself out there, taking the brunt of any repercussions, if it helps him find a little more peace.

"It's a lot of money," he says softly.

"I don't care about that."

"You should," he insists. "You deserve it." Then he takes a deep breath, the gesture still ingrained from his living days. "Fine. I'm not saying I'm going to speak to her, but you should go. Take the money and let her show you around my room—you know to find clues or something. Just make sure you add a no-success guarantee. If she wants to lose money on a wild goose chase, that's on her."

The money doesn't entice me. Sure, 40,000 euros would be amazing to have, but I feel bad about taking it when I don't actually have to exert any effort to find the ghost in question: Gaspar is right here, in my arms. Getting him to speak to his mother, though, is a whole different wheelhouse.

# Chapter 15

Madame du Charbonneau is so excited when I get back to her, she clears her entire schedule for the next day and invites me to her home. She also wants to send me a taxi, but I assure her public transport is good enough. I have to snort, though, when I receive the address.

"Rueil-Malmaison?"

If I hadn't known Gaspar's family were rich, I definitely would now. It's one of the most affluent suburbs of Paris and home to the Chateau de Malmaison, Joséphine's resting place.

"You didn't want to mention you lived close to Joséphine all your life?" I ask Gaspar as we leave the train station behind. From the Arc de Triomphe, it's less than twenty minutes to Rueil-Malmaison.

Hands in pockets, he snorts. "First off, we weren't even concerned with her until last month, and second, it wasn't something I cared much about. Now if you ask my father…" He hesitates.

"Yes?"

Gaspar pulls a face. "Alright, heads-up: some great-grandmother of mine was Hortense de Beauharnais' lady companion."

"No way!"

Hortense is Joséphine's daughter from her first marriage to Alexandre. Oh, and she became Queen of Holland as the wife of Louis Bonaparte—yes, Napoleon married his stepdaughter off to one of his brothers—and was the mother of Napoleon III. No biggie.

"Yes!" Gaspar says enthusiastically, his sarcasm cranked up to the max. "Please don't do that in front of my parents."

I quickly school my face. "Sorry, it's just it's not every day your boyfriend tells you he's practically a descendent of Napoleon."

"That's because I'm not," Gaspar quickly clarifies. "Believe me, if the Charbonneaus were related to Napoleon, my father would never shut up about it. Our family was wealthy, noble, but they weren't the kind of makers and shakers who had their names immortalised in history books. A few were on the National Assembly, married to someone who was someone's daughter, or lost their head in the revolution, but nothing of note really—just a whole lot of pompous assery."

It's so incredibly hard to contain my inner fangirl when he talks so casually about his relatives. I've met them, and they're really not the most charming people, but still… "I know you hate your family, and that's totally valid, but from a historian's point of view, I'm so jealous! Your ancestors were part of history. Mine were just normal day-to-day people you never heard about."

But Gaspar shakes his head. "Just because you don't know them by name doesn't mean they weren't part of it. Yours probably fought for human rights and equality; mine just joined the side of shifting power that would benefit them the most."

I didn't think I could love him any more. He's absolutely right. Most of the people we learn about in history were already born into a life of notoriety—a few rose to the top from humble beginnings, but we often forget they didn't do it alone. There's always a grand mass of people who also fought in the battles, gave their lives, or carried a movement. The revolution didn't succeed because of the few whose names were immortalised with it, but the thousands of brave Parisians who joined the call.

It's easy to get carried away by names everyone recognises, but my complaint was premature. My ancestors were just as much a part of history as Napoleon himself, just as we're part of the history that's woven today.

If we weren't out on the streets, I'd run my hands through that soft brown hair and kiss Gaspar mindless. As it is, I content myself with holding his hand as we head towards the mansion-like houses that populate the area. Not many people are about but I can't help feeling watched and *judged* by the residents here.

"This is where you grew up?"

The streets are so clean, each garden meticulously manicured. Even the grass is green, despite the temperatures turning it yellow everywhere else. The houses seem to grow in size, and there's more and more space between them. For someone who's only ever lived in multi-apartment buildings with narrow winding stairs in badly lit hallways and even tinier courtyards, they all look like palaces.

Gaspar just grunts, his mood worsening with every step. I'm afraid he's going to pull back completely, but then we arrive at Maison du Charbonneau. Big chestnut trees cover the front yard, providing shade to the carefully curated flowers in the garden. While many houses in the area have opted for big stonewalls, this one has a wrought-iron fence, as if it wants to be admired.

"Is that a fountain?" Who the heck has a fountain at home?

Gaspar rolls his eyes. "Yeah, and there's a pool and a tennis court in the back."

I can't quite tell if he's joking or telling the truth, but I *can* tell how much he hates it. "Sorry," I whisper. "I'll make it quick."

His face softens and he squeezes my hand. "No, don't. Take all the time you need. I'll try not to be an ass, but I can't make any promises. There's something about this place that just gets under my skin."

I return the pressure of his fingers. "You tell me if you've had enough, and we'll leave right away."

There's a soft smile and I'm overcome with the urge to kiss him, but I'm also aware of the cameras mounted near the gate and people who might be watching from their windows. Despite how far we've already come, our love is still confined to hidden places, and today I'll have to pretend I've never even heard of Gaspar.

With one last longing look, I let go of his hand and square my shoulders. While Madame du Charbonneau was the one to come to me, I can't shake the feeling I'm the supplicant here. I need half a minute to work up the courage to press the doorbell, hyper-aware of how little I seem to fit into these surroundings. I'm just about to wish I'd worn my graduation outfit instead of my casual summer dress when the gate buzzes and starts to open.

The grounds are even more impressive when I walk down the cobbled pathway. From the street, half the house was hidden by the massive trees in front of it, but now the view is starting to clear, and I can't help but think of the house as cute—as cute as a three-story mansion can be. Its walls are whitewashed, with Greek-inspired elements on the edges. All the details and the roof are painted blue, which gives it a bit of a seaside charm, like a cottage—five sizes too big.

The Greek influence extends to the fountain, the centrepiece of which is a marble sculpture of a water nymph and a faun. I want to ask Gaspar whether it's an original art piece or a modern replication, but I don't dare give away his presence. Ahead of me under a columned canopy, a door opens, and Madame du Charbonneau steps out.

Even though she's at home, she's immaculately dressed and styled as before. She welcomes me with a big smile. "Mademoiselle Dubois, I'm so glad you found it. Come on in, let me get you some refreshments."

The foyer—yes, Gaspar's home has a foyer—is refreshingly cool. Two curved twin stairs lead to the second floor, with a wide staircase for the third floor. When I look up at the ceiling far above us, I notice a stunning chandelier that could've easily been hung in Versailles without anyone batting an eye. Its crystal ornaments send rainbow flickers of light across the paintings on the walls and polished marble floor. More Greek-inspired handiwork and bouquets of fresh flowers round off the first impression.

"We sometimes entertain people here," Madame du Charbonneau explains as she leads me through the double door between the two wings of stairs, pointing out a grand piano in the corner. "This is where Gaspar would play."

"Before I managed to put my foot down," he amends quickly.

"Do you have any pictures?" I ask before I can even think about whether it would be an appropriate request in this completely new line of work.

Madame du Charbonneau gives me a warm smile, not questioning my odd request at all. "I've collated a few for you. I also have videos—no recent ones, I'm afraid. As he got older, it became more and more difficult to convince him to let me take some. I had to contend with his social media account if I wanted to see him."

"Which was private for a reason!" Gaspar huffs. "I can't believe it. Probably sneaking into my follows with a fake profile."

I try my best to tune out his ranting as we enter a giant modern living room with a huge white sofa. Madame du Charbonneau has already prepared the table for us—there's white wine chilling in a bucket, two glasses, a platter of fruit and small bites, and most importantly, a tidy pile of folders and boxes containing everything she could find about her son.

Though I'm yearning to dig my fingers into the material, I let Madame du Charbonneau take the lead. We sit and sip at the wine as she explains, "My husband thinks I've lost my mind, reaching out to you like this. He doesn't believe in ghosts and thinks it's all a giant hoax, something to entertain the masses. He makes a lot of sense. If ghosts existed, why are we only learning about them now?"

"Sounds just like Papa." Gaspar is pacing the room in a half-hearted attempt at giving me some space. He stops here and there to look at a picture or sneer at a fancy vase.

Realising his mother yearns for my assurance, I smile. "It's hard to believe in ghosts when you can't see them, but there wouldn't be a whole arm of the police dedicated to them if they didn't exist." I'm not supposed to talk about GoPol, and they've done an admirable job at keeping their involvement as minimal as possible, but their name was dropped in my father's article and others have started to investigate them. "For me, ghosts have always been like real people. They may no longer be made of flesh and blood, but they're still out there—still thriving, still feeling."

Madame du Charbonneau hangs onto every word I say. "Gaspar is out there?"

"He is. We all become ghosts when we die."

For a moment, it looks as if there's tears in her eyes, but a polite smile, and they're all gone. "I guess, that means I'll see him some-day."

Gaspar groans, as if she's just revealed his worst nightmare.

"But that's hopefully still a long time away. Until then, I'd like to make contact with him." She picks up the first folder and opens it. "This is the obituary I had written for him."

"Look, she even paid someone else to write about me," Gaspar comments, "because she doesn't actually know me."

"Gaspar was a very bright child. Good manners, very talented at the piano. And he looked adorable in a suit." She shows me a picture of him as a seven-year-old. While I'd recognise those chocolatey eyes everywhere, it doesn't really look like him. Cute, yes, but devoid of all the personality that's jam-packed into the adult version.

I acknowledge the photo and flick through the rest of the folder. It has all kinds of records on his school life, reports from teachers, and even newspaper clippings from the times little Gaspar entered music recitals or sporting competitions.

"Fencing?" My gaze flicks to Gaspar, before I quickly lower my eyes.

He just snorts while his mother reports proudly, "Oh, yes. My husband is a passionate fencer, and he made sure Gaspar loved the sport as much as he did. He did very well."

She shows me another newspaper clipping which has Gaspar dressed in a white fencing uniform on a podium, mask under his arm. Despite winning the competition, he looks bored, chin raised in an affected manner. And once again, he's barely a teenager.

"Do you have anything from his later years? He died at twenty-two, didn't he?"

For once, Gaspar perks up and quips, "I've been dead to my parents since I turned fifteen."

The crude joke has me wincing, but I can't help but agree when all I'm presented with are pictures of a terribly accomplished childhood. One might think he was another of Charles Roubert's sons, if Charles had valued arts and culture. No wonder Sébastien and Gaspar found common ground through their childhood trauma.

"Oh, yes, of course." Slightly flustered, Madame du Charbonneau reaches for another folder. "I'm afraid he got a bit lost in his adolescent years—it's a fairly typical tale in our circles. Once he hit puberty, he developed a rebellious streak, talking back, dropping all his activities, and well... trying everything in the book to offend and embarrass us."

I blink at yet another description that doesn't fit Gaspar at all. "Sounds rough."

"Sounds overdramatic," Gaspar says. "I was just a normal teenager, finding ways to express myself—my *true* self."

Oblivious to Gaspar's argument, his mother nods. "Oh, yes, he stayed out late, to the point where I considered getting him a bodyguard. He went to illegal parties and probably took drugs." She sighs while Gaspar shakes his head in the background. "We often try to hide the ugly side, you know? It's not easy to talk about your child acting out, but I guess in this case, it's necessary so you get a full picture of the person he was."

Yet, I'm starting to believe I'm not going to get that here. Madame du Charbonneau's account's laced with prejudice and judgement. She tried so hard to raise the perfect little boy and was offended when he turned into his own person; one she had no control over.

"Could I see his room?" I ask, craving a real piece of Gaspar's past. Something that's truly him. "Ghosts often leave a spectral signature in the space they occupied," I fib. If they have, I've never been able to measure it.

"Of course." Madame du Charbonneau puts her glass down and stands. "I've tidied his room a little but mostly kept it as it was." Again, she looks close to tears. "I should really start throwing things out…" Suddenly, she frowns. "Or maybe not. Would it strengthen his memory if I kept it as it is?"

I don't see it making much difference if none of it represents Gaspar's soul, but I force myself to nod. "Potentially."

She lets out a big sigh of relief. "Good. I wouldn't know what to do with the room, anyway." A luxury only few people have.

We head back to the foyer and walk up to the third floor.

"My husband and I live mostly on the second floor, but Gaspar wanted to be close to the roof. If I'd known he'd use it to sneak out at night, I would've kept him closer." You'd think he'd died during one of his teenage excursions to the catacombs the way she's talking about it.

Gaspar points to the chestnut tree outside the house. "That one had perfect branches." He grimaces. "Do you see now why I had to get out as fast as I could?"

"He didn't live here when he died, did he?" I ask Madame du Charbonneau.

Another sigh. "No, he moved out the moment he turned eighteen. Occasionally, he'd come back for a weekend or the holidays, but he spent most of his time in the city centre. We wanted to buy him an apartment, but he was adamant on getting the full student experience. I don't have a key to his flat, but I managed to retrieve all his belongings. I think they've already rented out his room."

After all that time, they'd be stupid not to. Real estate space in Paris is worth gold.

"Well, here we are."

She opens the door to another grand room. It almost looks like a miniature apartment on its own, with a dedicated office space, his own living room, and a bed big enough to sleep four. The TV could fit four of Sébastien's in it, and I see every console I could think of, and a shelf full of games.

But it's all painfully tidy. No used clothes on the ground, no scribbles on the wall. It reminds me so much of Sébastien, which makes it impossible to wrap my head around. Sébastien's schedule was so full, he made it his entire personality as he grew up, but Gaspar rebelled. He'd yearned for ways to express himself, which makes seeing such a sanitised space—so beautiful you could hold a magazine photo shoot in here—feel just *wrong*. It's like all the wonderful edges and corners have been sanded off. If I didn't already know who I was supposed to be looking for, I'd be searching for some kind of rich prick with no personality.

"Ask for the room on the other side," Gaspar says once I've given this room a quick look, finding nothing of particular interest. "That one was my favourite. Unless she's cleared it all out to make space."

Obviously, I can't just walk into another room, so I pretend I'm looking for something in particular. "Is this where he spent most of the time?" Before she can even answer, I say, "I feel some energy from that room."

"That's the music room," she says, and although the whole energy thing is nonsense, I know if it were true I'd indeed find him there.

Madame du Charbonneau crosses the hallway and opens the door. "He was such a talented musician. If he hadn't quit piano early, he could've made a career out of it. Not that the arts provides many career options," she adds, which is an odd thing for an art curator to say. "My husband wanted him to study something of substance, so, naturally, Gaspar chose the course with the least profitable career prospects he could find." She rolls her eyes. "Social sciences—as if there's any money in that."

"I guess money isn't why people go into the arts."

"Oh, of course not." She looks a little embarrassed. "I didn't mean to offend. And I mean, you never know, right? You've certainly found your niche."

It takes everything in me not to grimace, and I can't help but think the Charbonneaus would've been happier meeting Hélène than they'd be with me—not that Gaspar will ever get to introduce me as his girlfriend.

We enter the room, and I immediately know I've found the heart of Gaspar, his refuge. There's another piano—why have one when you can have two?—but it's been moved into a corner and covered with a white sheet. Other instruments, including a drum set, fill almost every inch of the back half of the room. On the side, there's a shelf full of score sheets, but every other shelf or cupboard is filled with records, and the centrepiece is an old-fashioned record player next to a set of comfy armchairs.

"He collected these?" I ask, as I pull records at random, finding all kinds of different music styles from classic rock to techno, opera, and his favourite dubstep.

Gaspar lights up, telling me where his favourite albums are and which took the longest to hunt down or which odd corner of the world he found it in.

Madame du Charbonneau remains at the door, watching me with a tired look on her face. "Music was his everything. I didn't particularly like most of it—too loud and unmelodic if you ask me—"

"No one is," Gaspar jokes. "She doesn't have the ear for it."

I hide a chuckle behind a cough and study the album covers. Most of the artists are only familiar because Gaspar's introduced me to them before. The records mean little to him, but they were his whole world, his true passion.

"If it helps you find him, you can take some of his stuff," Madame du Charbonneau offers.

"Please take the record player," Gaspar says, and I nearly slap him. I'm not robbing his family. Besides, with the initial payment, I can buy him a new one.

I smile at his mother. "If you don't mind, I'll pick out a few records that speak to me." And by "speak to me", I mean his ghost literally recommending them.

After a while, I turn to his mother, my arms full of records. "Madame du Charbonneau, may I ask you a personal question?"

She tenses, telling me I'm walking on thin ice. "Sure, if it helps you find my son."

"What do you expect to find? Like, what would you tell him?"

It's unlikely Gaspar will ever agree to speak with her, but he's in the room now, able to hear her. Most importantly, I'm confused by what I've seen today. All this meaningless information feels more like a presentation on how great her son used to be and less about the Gaspar she's hoping to find.

For a moment, she simply stares, then something unexpected happens and the mask of polished politeness cracks wide open. A tear rolls down her cheek, and she takes a shaky breath. "I want to tell him that I love him, that he... That I miss him. So much." She clears her throat, while Gaspar groans. "As parents, you always think there's more time. Your child is young—they'll survive you—but then they don't, and everything you hoped for them never comes to pass." Once more, she takes a little break.

Gaspar shakes his head. "Oh no, imagine that. Spending twenty years on a project only to never see it completed. My heart's breaking."

I nearly smack him with my elbow. His mother is finally opening up, and he's twisting every word in her mouth.

"All the growing pains we go through only to end up with nothing. He's just gone, and I feel like I did it all wrong: that

I didn't love him enough or show him how much he meant to me—not the medals and certificates I showed you downstairs but him." Annoyed, she wipes her tears. "I'm afraid I wasn't a very good mother. I focused on all the wrong things when I should've just focused on him, listened to him when he told me about his dreams and his music, instead of dismissing them as fancies."

Gaspar's suddenly gone quiet. I glance at him, but he shakes his head.

"If you were to find him," Madame du Charbonneau says, taking a deep breath, "I want you to tell him that he was loved. And I'm proud he was my son. And I'm sad the world doesn't get to know him the way I did. Whatever he ended up doing, I know he would've been great at it, because he always led with passion. And that's the only thing that really makes a difference." Once more, she wipes her cheeks. "Look at me, a blubbering mess."

"It's okay," I say softly. "You lost someone important." He's terribly important to me, too.

She nods, still teary. "I guess I did. And if you find him... I just want to know if he's happy. If ghosts can be happy. I wouldn't really know, would I?"

"But I do," I assure her. "The afterlife is astounding—it's so much richer than you'd ever believe. Once he finds his place there, he'll be happy."

"The happiest I've ever been," Gaspar whispers. Since he can't take my hand, he gives me a light hug. "You're my home in the afterlife."

And while that's undoubtedly true, I feel like he's slowly thawing to his mother.

# Chapter 16

Though Gaspar's attitude towards his mother has mellowed ever so slightly, he refuses to make his presence known, so I leave the house with a bag full of photos and, most importantly, his favourite records. I promise to give his mother a semi-regular progress report, which I have no idea how to write yet. I hate lying to her. If I didn't full-heartedly believe this'll be beneficial for Gaspar, I would've called the whole thing off.

"Would it be the end of the world if you talked to her?" I ask him once we're several blocks down the street.

He's got his hands deep in his hoodie and shrugs. "Probably not."

"Her feelings are genuine. She loves you."

"Yeah, maybe." It doesn't sound very convincing. "But I've already told you it won't stop at one meeting, and she'll tout you around."

I grab his arm, forcing him to stop. "You don't know that."

There's a boy staring at us—or rather me—but I shoo him away with one stern look.

"I think I do—it's what she did to me. She loved me, alright, but she loved showing me off more. That's why she hated I studied social sciences. Makes it hard to brag about in front of her friends."

In my opinion, he's being unreasonably harsh. I don't want to invalidate his feelings, I'm sure he felt a lot of pressure growing up and it's not easy to find yourself when your parents look down on every choice you make, but his death changed everything. And maybe it's too late now, but with ghosts starting to become universally accepted, the door previously thought shut forever is only leant closed now.

"Believe me, the money is nice, but you don't want to be bound to her forever."

Alright, this has to stop. "Let's get two things straight: I don't care about the money. *You* told me to take it, and your mother practically forced me. You know I'd do these things for free." I've helped so many ghosts over the years without ever receiving anything for it.

"You shouldn't," Gaspar says adamantly. "I mean, you're awesome and all, and I know you're doing it because of what my father would call 'bleeding-heart syndrome'." He rolls his eyes heavily. "It's incomprehensible to him how anybody could help people from the goodness of their heart. Thing is: he's a little right. You deserve to be paid for an emotionally taxing and time-intensive task."

"It wouldn't be either if you just agreed to meet them." By the look of his hardening expression, we're just as far from that as before. "Alright, second thing: stop using your concern for me as a reason to refuse engaging with your parents. You're not worried about them 'sinking their talons into me'; you're scared for yourself, that you'll somehow get sucked into that life again, or that they'll be a bad influence on you, or maybe just that being with them will bring up all the hurt and pain from the past."

His bottom lip quivers in an effort to hold his protest in. "I'm happy with where I am," he says in a strangely tight voice.

"I know that. But it's not healthy to bury your past and lock it away. Not even for ghosts."

While I seem to be getting somewhere, he's clearly not ready to face it. Sniffling, he looks over his shoulder. "Hey, do you want to talk to Joséphine while we're here?"

I look at him, unimpressed. Maybe I'm pushing too hard. After all, he seems fine these days. Maybe this isn't a problem I need to solve.

I reach for his hand. "Let's do that."

The Chateau de Malmaison is practically around the corner from Gaspar's family home. It's a wide, beige building with two wings sitting at the end of a wide driveway lined by roses. These days it houses one of the many Napoleon museums, so I'm not surprised he often comes here to spend time with his wife. Since the museum is about to shut its doors for the day, we skip the exhibition and explore the grounds instead.

If music is Gaspar's passion, roses were Joséphine's. At one point, she collected over 250 different kinds in her garden and became quite the expert in botany and horticulture—no less than three roses were named after her in recognition of what she built here. Unfortunately, the house and gardens were ransacked when she died, and Napoleon exiled. With the chateau being turned into a museum, some roses were planted along the driveway, but it's hardly the beautiful collection it used to be.

Which is why my mouth drops open when we round a corner and find ourselves in a maze of multi-coloured roses filled with strolling ladies, laughing children, and animals—not just any kind of animals, but zebras, ostriches, and llamas, even...

"Is that a kangaroo?"

Someone looks at me weirdly and I do my usual pointing to my ear despite not wearing any earbuds.

Gaspar's eyes are wide. "I promise it didn't look like this when I lived here."

Of course not. When he lived here, he was blind to the ghost world. This is all ghost-made, an eerie replication of the past. A conspicuously powerful replication.

It doesn't take long for us to find the Empress—we just have to follow the trail of exotic animals. Joséphine's kneeling in front of a bed of roses, her dress covered by an apron, while a wide-brimmed hat protects her delicate skin from the sun—not that it'd burn if she didn't wear one. She's a pretty woman with long chestnut hair and hazel eyes, but not as stunning a beauty as you might imagine from Napoleon's infatuation—or the various powerful men she was involved with before him.

Sure enough, the familiar sight of one of Eiffel's resonators greets me. While she's probably powerful enough to pull the rose garden back into existence, no pictures of it have survived—there's not even a proper record of all her flowers, and the animals would definitely be gone. And yet, the grounds are as spectacular as they were at the height of her popularity.

The museum would kill for a picture of this for future restoration purposes.

Joséphine hears our steps and looks up, squinting against the sun. "May I help you?" While smiling, she keeps her mouth tightly shut. According to history, she had terrible teeth and was deeply ashamed of them; as if half the nobility didn't suffer from the same fate.

I quickly glance around to check for other visitors before I curtsy. "It's an honour to meet you, Your Majesty. My name's Alix Dubois, and this is my companion, Gaspar du Charbonneau."

Slowly, Josephine straightens, brushing dirt off her apron before removing her gardening gloves and throwing them into the basket at her side. "I've heard of you," she says with a silvery voice, then glances at Gaspar. "And I'm familiar with the Charbonneaus, of course."

I quickly tamper the spark of jealousy from Empress Joséphine's acknowledging my boyfriend as a peer.

He gives a half-hearted bow. "Hopefully, not too familiar."

Even when she laughs, she hides her teeth. Despite that, it's a bell-like sound that must've enchanted many men. "Honestly, they're no worse or better than any other family here." Her gaze lands on me again. "You, however, are different. My husband told me about you."

"Which one?" I ask, only to blush immediately, as if I've said something rude.

Joséphine snorts softly. "I only speak to one of them."

"Napoleon."

"The Emperor, yes. He said you were a very influential woman who might be the key to his Grand Campaign, and that if I ever met you, I should work my charms and convince you to join his side." She gives me a surprisingly cheeky smile. "Is it working yet?"

My stomach's been tightening more and more ever since she mentioned Napoleon. To hear he's actively enlisted her in wooing me makes it feel as if it's filled with concrete.

Joséphine cups one of the roses nearby. "Don't worry. I have no interest in that."

"You don't?"

"For two hundred years, he's dreamed of conquering the world, of making France the greatest nation in the world. But it's never enough, you know? There's always someone else to conquer, another battle to be fought. Death hasn't changed that one bit. If anything, it's made him more determined. If he can't rule the world of the living, he shall at least rule the world of the dead." She sighs heavily. "But what for? What's the point in conquering anything if you never pause to enjoy it?"

In my opinion, he should just leave people—and ghosts—alone. No need to conquer anything.

"It's not really a conquest, though, is it?" Surprisingly, it's Gaspar who speaks up. "It's a fight for autonomy. For freedom."

"Now doesn't that sound pretty?" Joséphine mocks, almost gently. "He was always good with coming up with reasons. First, France had to be defended—freedom was one of the big words touted around then. Once that was done, another threat arose, or a slight that demanded swift retribution. And then, of course, he was god-sent to rule the world."

Gaspar shuffles his feet. "It's different this time. This isn't about him, it's about the future of ghosts. It's about our dignity, but also our safety. Right now, we're completely at the mercy of the living."

I side-eye Gaspar, wondering what the hell he's talking about. Surely he doesn't mean to side with Napoleon?

"Are we?" Joséphine asks with endless patience. "I've found the living to be quite oblivious. Some are even appreciative—they've restored my house as best they could."

But not the garden.

Joséphine must've had the same thought, because she adds a little more matter-of-factly, "He promised my gardens a full return to glory. They may might be restored, but at what cost? The one that's here right now is pretty enough, I can always rely on my memory if I want to spend time with my roses." She pats the resonator next to her. "And with Monsieur Eiffel's wonderful invention, others can enjoy it, too. What do we need the living for? They'll join us soon enough as is."

"Not everyone's got a whole mansion and rose garden to themselves," Gaspar says, arms crossed.

I'm baffled by his confrontational nature. Why is he trying to pick a fight with Joséphine? Is this some relic from his family issues, his father who's always prided himself in the connection to the Empress? It's the only thing that would explain why he's rejecting her so thoroughly, even at the cost of aligning himself with Napoleon.

"Most other ghosts are quickly forgotten. Some are suffering." Gaspar finds my gaze, desperation shimmering in his eyes. "You're always talking about those poor souls in the catacombs, aren't you? How they're all squeezed into a tight space, disrespected and mutilated, while she has all this space for herself."

"I think you should go now," Joséphine says firmly.

Before I can even think about how to smooth the waves, I find myself walking out of Malmaison and down the street, Gaspar at my side, still fuming. I think I may have just been repelled by a powerful ghost.

"What was that about?" I ask, when I finally gain control of my feet again and will them to stop.

"It just annoys me so much," Gaspar says passionately. He looks so distraught, almost panicked. "People like Joséphine or my parents. They have so much, and instead of making sure everyone has enough, they spend all their energy in creating these picture-perfect environments only they and selected others can enjoy, while the rest of the world suffers. You'd think death would be the great equaliser, but it isn't—it's the same people at the top, the rich and famous, some of whom never did anything to deserve it."

I had no idea he felt that deeply about it. I thought I was the only one who truly cared about the cruel fate of the catacombs' ghosts—even my friends at the Panthéon would rather ignore their existence. The world of ghosts might be different in a lot of things, but it's far from perfect. Gaspar is right, and it's high time I acknowledged that. Still...

"What did you mean when you said this was a 'fight for freedom'?"

Gaspar swallows hard and buries his hands into his hoodie. "Just ghost rumours. Forget I said anything."

I narrow my eyes. "Gaspar, what's going on? What do you know?" It's ghost rumours we're specifically looking for.

"Nothing." His gaze briefly meets mine and he swallows again.

"I know stuff, though," another voice says.

I whirl around, coming face to face with my old catacombs tour guide. "Emily."

She gives me her usual derisive smile. "I found their headquarters." Then she looks over my shoulder at Gaspar. "Now, do you want to tell her, or should I?"

A terrible premonition strikes me, making me stumble away from Gaspar. "What does she mean?" My voice is nothing more than a breathless whisper.

Gaspar glares at Emily, but then his gaze falls on me, and I see guilt and misery flicker in his eyes. "I've known where it was for a while."

# CHAPTER 17

"You what?"

I contained my anger and disappointment until we made it back home, where I promptly told Sébastien and Dix. They're reacting with the same disbelief I felt. Dix just looks at Gaspar as if he's grown two extra heads, while Sébastien's fuming.

"You knew?" he asks, pacing the room. "You've known this whole time we've been looking?"

Gaspar looks tired but not exactly guilty. "Not the whole time." He sighs. "I knew you wouldn't understand."

Sébastien stops cold. "I don't. What on earth has possessed you to join the Chevalier's cause and sit there quietly while Alix and I agonise over trying to find out what's going on?"

"You're not ghosts. You don't get it," Gaspar answers sullenly.

"I'm a ghost—I don't get it, either," Dix says, snorting in contempt.

Trying to keep tempers from boiling too high, I reach out to Gaspar. "Why don't you explain it to us?" Despite my best intentions, my voice is tense.

He rolls his shoulders, clearly uncomfortable. "I don't know how. I haven't joined his *cause*, I just didn't do anything to put a stop to it. Call it curiosity."

"I'd call it betrayal," Dix snarls.

Gaspar glares. "This has nothing to do with you. I wanted to know what he was planning, what the endgame was; keep an open mind and such."

Sébastien nods. "So, what is it? What are they planning?"

To my dismay, Gaspar casts his gaze to the ground. "I can't tell you."

I look back at Sébastien and my heart breaks. This is so much bigger than Napoleon—he trusted Gaspar, believed in him, only to have it all explode back in his face. The hurt in his eyes is unbearable and I wish I could hug him—or failing that, make it all better. The three of us have been through so much already. I refuse to let this break us. Yes, Gaspar lied, but he must've had a good reason.

"Did he promise you something? He doesn't have a hold on you from the resurrection, does he?"

"I made my choice," Gaspar says unapologetically. "And no, I wasn't promised anything. Seriously, I'm not in the inner circle or something, I've just been hanging out in the catacombs, talking to ghosts, gauging the vibe."

"But not reporting on them," Sébastien surmises harshly.

Gaspar shakes his head. "Sorry, Séb. If I'd done that, I know you would've marched a battalion of salt slingers in there and destroyed them all."

Sébastien takes the words in, nostrils flaring. "Do I *need* to march a battalion of 'salt slingers' in there?"

Shrugging, Gaspar can't even meet his gaze. "Bézier would definitely order you."

"And you don't think that's concerning?"

It certainly concerns me.

"Oh, I think, Bézier is plenty concerning. He's just a nicer, less deranged version of your father; the same attitude without the layers of abuse."

He may as well have slapped Sébastien, throwing the abuse he's endured back in his face. Knuckles turning white, it seems to take Sébastien's entire training not to lash out. "And you think I'm the same?"

"Of course not," Gaspar says, but there's lingering doubt in his voice. "You're better, of course. I just don't know if you're... enough." He bites his lip, daring to glance at Sébastien.

"What's that supposed to mean?" I ask, outraged on Sébastien's behalf.

Gaspar grimaces. "Come on, you know it's never going to be enough. GoPol is conservative to a fault—ghosts will never be their priority. You've had so many good ideas, and you've brought them to GoPol time and time again, and Séb," he says pointedly, eager to make his case, "I know you mean well and you're trying your best, but it's just not enough. Unless there's a major shift, it can't be. It'll just be the same shit in a different colour. Like Bézier."

Something breaks in Sébastien. His eyes lose their light, and he seems to stare through Gaspar. In a toneless voice, he asks, "What about my agents? Are they alive?"

"I've only seen two," Gaspar says, a hint of empathy in his voice. "They... they joined the Chevalier."

Sébastien's still staring right through him. He's so pale I'm afraid he's going to bowl over. "I see." He nods sharply. "I can't do this anymore."

And with that, he marches out of the room. A moment later, I hear the front door close.

Gaspar sighs. "And there he goes, reporting back to his superiors."

"Can you blame him?" Dix explodes in his face. Where Sébastien withdrew, Dix goes into full-attack mode. "You went behind his back. You've just told him he'll never be enough for you and he deserves to be left in the dark. You lied to us—all of us! And for what? Some ghost pipe dream?"

Now, it's Gaspar whose eyes turn dead. "It's more than that."

"You broke his bloody heart! I hope it was worth it," Dix spits. Then he turns abruptly and runs after his older self.

Which leaves me and Gaspar. He raises his hands and flicks his wrist. "Come on, pile on me. I deserve it."

"You do," I say mercilessly. "That was a shitty move."

Even if he had good reasons, he handled this horribly, adding insult to injury. Have I misjudged him so much? Or is he still drifting, still desperately looking for a purpose?

"Why lie to us?"

He raises his gaze and gives me a sad, lopsided smile. "Because you'd already decided the Chevalier and Napoleon needed to be stopped. This whole time, you've been treating this like an active battlefield, as if the theft of Napoleon's bones were a declaration of war. You're so scared of his reputation, you've forgot the most important thing about him."

I raise my eyebrows. "And that would be?"

"He loves France. Napoleon's not the enemy; he's our hero."

While there's certainly something to be said for that perspective, I can't believe anybody in the twenty-first century would still fall for that. "He was a warmonger."

"It was a different time," Gaspar argues. "Everyone was at war all the time. The alliance attacked first! They hated the Republic and what it represented. Napoleon stepped in to defend our values."

"By crowning himself Emperor. How did that defend the values of the revolution?" I can't believe I'm arguing about history with Gaspar.

"He just realised France needed strong leadership. He still kept most of the changes."

"Oh, in that case, I'll proclaim myself Empress tomorrow."

Gaspar's gaze hits mine. "You should. You'd do so much good."

I scoff. "Don't be ridiculous."

"I'm not," he admits. "Like I said, it was a different time, but honestly, I'd vote for you or whatever. I wish we could just make *your* vision come true." Gaspar rolls his shoulders, uncomfortable, before meekly adding, "Well, Napoleon might be able to."

My head's swimming. I still can't believe this is truly happening—that Gaspar lied to us, letting us go on a wild goose chase, while he had all the answers. Or that he truly believes my vision is so good it's worth claiming it in blood. Or that he'd willingly hurt Sébastien like that. It's the last one which eats at me the hardest.

"Fine. Take me to him."

His eyes widen. "What?"

I cross my arms for added effect. "If you think he'd make my vision come true, then I should meet with him, right? Take me to the headquarters and let me decide for myself." It's not like I'm getting a proper explanation out of Gaspar tonight.

"It's too dangerous!"

"Why? The Chevalier wants me there. Napoleon wants me there."

"But not everyone does," Gaspar says, looking terribly dismayed. "Not all cataphiles—alive or dead—are... in favour of you. You wouldn't like it. I mean, this is a ghost movement for ghosts, and you're not one of us. What I mean is... it'd be much safer if you were already dead."

Anger is building in my chest, threatening to consume me. It really doesn't help he's babbling instead of giving me straight answers. "If it's so dangerous for me, why support it?"

He grimaces, then comes to me, trying to rub my arms. "Just trust me on this, please."

I don't plan to give him an inch. "After you just lied to us?"

"I'm sorry about that. It was dumb, I know. I should've trusted you'd understand, that Séb would get it. I know it's not really his fault GoPol is so shitty, and he can't change it in a day." He's giving me his best puppy eyes. "I messed up, okay? But please. The risk is way too high for you. That special interest... I don't know what the Chevalier wants you for, but he's determined to get his hands on you."

His words should scare me, but I've made up my mind. I'm done with sitting on the sidelines because everybody's decided I'd be safer somehow. What keeps me safe is information, and since no one else is willing to give me that, I need to go directly to the source.

Poking my finger into Gaspar's chest, I demand, "You're going to take me there."

"Alix…"

"You owe me!" Massively.

Gaspar winces. "Séb will salt me."

"Well, if you don't, *I* might." I'm almost angry enough to follow through. Judging by his paling face, he finally understands how royally he messed this all up. "You're going to take me, and you're going to do it now." Before Sébastien comes back and throws his weight in to stop me.

Gaspar swallows heavily, the fear in his eyes deepening. His gaze drops and he pulls up his shoulders. "If that's what you wish."

"I do."

# Chapter 18

An hour later, after I'd had some food and packed a backpack, Gaspar and I enter the catacombs through the basement of a derelict house I never would've considered if Gaspar hadn't told me it was safe. Trusting him might be stupid at the moment, but I truly believe he's got my best interests at heart.

I'm still angry with him. The haunted look in Sébastien's eyes won't leave my mind. I left him a note apologising for essentially going behind his back as well by taking this opportunity to explore the catacombs and the Chevalier's plans on my own. I promised to tell him everything, though. The least he deserves is to be able to make up his own mind, even if that means sending in the salt slingers, as Gaspar called them.

"You should've told us," I mutter as I climb through a long narrow tunnel behind Gaspar. It isn't a route I've taken before, but I roughly recognise it from the maps. If I remember correctly, it'll take us directly to the Banga—it just isn't a viable option for the way back.

For a moment, Gaspar hesitates, but then he admits, "I know."

"That's what I don't get," I continue. "Sure, Séb is still very GoPol-minded and I don't trust the Chevalier, but we... *We're* a team, aren't we? We could've talked this out."

He sighs. "Yeah, maybe."

Something's clearly bothering him. "What is it?" Another long, pregnant pause. "Gaspar, please talk to me." I thought we were all good now.

"Okay, okay. Well, it often feels like you and Séb make all the decisions. You discuss strategies, developments—"

"We didn't exclude you or anything." If anything, he always seemed a little bored.

"Not intentionally." He tries to look over the shoulder and catch my gaze, but the tunnel's far too narrow for that. "When you discuss these matters, it's often from a living perspective. Like I said, you'd already decided Napoleon had to be stopped, that there couldn't possibly be more to it."

I breathe through my nose so I won't blow up at him. With a strained voice that has little to do with the effort it takes to pull myself through the tunnel, I ask, "Did you forget the fact he tries to take over the world every decade or so?"

Gaspar snorts. "That's what the Panthéon says."

"Excuse me?"

Another heavy sigh. "Look, I like them, too, but you have to admit they're not exactly in touch with common ghosts. Sure, they have grand ideas about them, conceptually, but in a way, they're just like the Empress, content to be admired and respected for all of eternity, while the rest of us scramble for scraps."

"I'm all for the common ghost, you know that"—for the life of me, I wouldn't be able to choose between the Panthéon and Père Lachaise—"but don't you think they deserve that respect?"

"From the living, sure. But what have they done for the dead? Careful now. There's a hole here." And with that, Gaspar's already gone from my sight.

My heart races as I pull myself further along. The headlamp shows the tunnel narrowing up ahead, not an end in sight, but right in front of me is a hole I can easily climb over—or let myself drop in, down to the lower level. Which is where Gaspar is waiting. "Seriously?"

"It's easy," he tells me, when all he had to do was fall through the ceiling. "You can just poke your head through and dangle down for me to catch, or cross the hole first, drop the backpack, and go through backwards."

I guess I've found out why this path is rarely used to go the other way. Since the thought of going through upside down is too uncomfortable, I go with his second suggestion, pulling myself across while simultaneously undoing the straps of my backpack and letting it drop to my feet until I can give it enough of a shove to send it through the hole. Judging by the little *oomph*, Gaspar's caught it. Next, I shuffle backwards, doing some acrobatic bending of my limbs to somehow thread through the opening by touch alone. I scrape my knees as I wriggle around until the angle's enough for my legs to swing freely, the sudden weight nearly pulling the rest of me through. I escape the uncontrolled fall by frantically stretch my arms to block myself in, then slowly let my body down before my arms give way.

"The other way would've been easier," Gaspar says as he steadies me on the unstable ground. The floor of this chamber is covered in rubble—most of it stone, but some of it probably bone—tilting slightly towards a walkway.

I'm a little out of breath after the exercise and take a sip from my bottle. "It didn't feel safe."

Gaspar looks to the side but not before I catch the hurt in his eyes.

With a sigh, I hold my hand out. "I didn't mean it like that." It was the act of dangling upside down I feared, not his ability—or willingness—to catch me.

"You don't have to pretend. I messed up and now you don't trust me anymore. If you ever did."

"Ever? Really?"

He shuffles his feet, immediately apologetic. "Since you-know-what."

Oh, I know, but I'd thought we were past that. "Is that why you've kept this to yourself? Because you were afraid I'd judge you?"

"You *are* judging me."

"Because I don't understand. After everything the Chevalier did to you—"

"He didn't do anything." Gaspar leans against the wall, throwing up his hands. "I mean, yeah, he tried to bring me back to life, but it went wrong. And no, he didn't have the magic solution to fix it. I knew it was a risk when I asked him, so if anything, that's on me, not him. And while some of his methods are definitely unorthodox, he's doing it for the right reasons. Unlike your Panthéon ghosts, he actually cares for living and ghosts alike."

My Panthéon ghosts. For a short period, Gaspar was a guest at the Panthéon, but apparently, they made him so uncomfortable, he still holds a grudge.

"They care."

"They like to pretend they care, that they're the magnanimous leaders of ghostdom, chosen by the memory of the living world, but they do precious little to actually lead anyone."

"What do you want them to do? Create laws? Dictate people's afterlife? I thought you liked the fact ghosts simply existed in their necropolises." I shoulder my backpack, ready to get out of this room.

"I do!" Gaspar pushes off the wall and leads the way. "But it's not possible."

"What do you mean it's not possible?" We're walk down a corridor so narrow we need to keep our heads low. Rubble lines the ground, forcing me to place my feet carefully. "Ghosts have been around forever."

He snorts softly.

"What?"

"I didn't think you of all people would see them like that." He stops and throws me an apologetic glance. "Sorry. What I mean is just because ghosts have been that way for forever, doesn't mean they can't evolve, can't want more. The world's learnt about ghosts now, GoPol's scrambling to make plans to utilise us, people are arguing whether we're a threat or a resource. But they don't see us as people."

I can't help but wonder if I contributed to their plight. Are my visions of the future just as harmful? I've been trying to sell ghosts to the living by telling everyone how much they could offer us—like *resources*.

"It's not you," Gaspar says, much calmer. "You've always treated ghosts as humans, and you've advocated endlessly for us—now even publicly. Which is why I think you'd like this... from afar."

I'm so tired of his cagey responses. Why can't he be straight with me? "You mean I'd like it if I wasn't in personal danger from whatever's going on?"

"No, what..." He looks as if he's swallowed a frog. Shivering, he turns away and mumbles, "Something like that."

Soon, the waterlock of the Banga glistens in front of us, but we stop cold as he turns to me once more. "Listen, I think what the Chevalier's planning might ultimately be a good thing." Something's making him truly struggle with his words. It's as if he has to constantly rethink how to phrase things. "But it doesn't come without sacrifices. And I... I don't want you to become one of them."

I look into his eyes which are black as coal in the darkness, save for where my headlamp's light reflects in them. His words are laced with genuine worry. For all his lies, Gaspar truly cares for me. He just seems so... unstable. Maybe it's because he's still searching for his place in the afterlife.

"What's the Chevalier planning?" I whisper.

Gaspar takes my hand, casting me another desperate look. "I'll show you," he says, but the tone of his voice tells me he'd rather do anything but. Hanging his head in defeat, he leads me to the water. "It's not far now."

Surprised, I follow him onto the stones set into the water. Sébastien's agents have scoured the catacombs for weeks, going deeper and deeper, and the whole time the headquarters were barely past the Banga? Or apparently not even past it—inside it.

About two thirds to the other side, Gaspar veers off to the left. "Big step, that's it."

I'm amazed to find another hidden walkway under the water, leading to the flooded prison cells I've only ever caught the occasional glint of bent metal from before. Gaspar grabs hold of one of the bars and pulls me close.

"Just duck your head here, through this gap."

Everything inside me wants to run the other way. This is dangerous. I could get stuck between the bars, slowly drowning; I could slip and knock my head—again, drowning; I could—

Annoyed, I shake my head. If it weren't for Gaspar, I'd never even have thought to approach the bars, and that's when I recognise the ghostly power pushing me away, wanting me to turn away.

Gaspar's already through, still holding my hand. "You can still leave..."

Is he saying it out of concern or because the spectral willpower forces him to add his voice to the chorus in my head telling me to run? To go away and never come back.

It takes him tugging and an enormous amount of willpower to ignore all my instincts and duck through the gap in the bars. Nearly catching my hair in the corroded metal, I manage to keep my upper body away from the water's surface.

My feet find a step, and I pull myself up next to Gaspar, who regards me with immense relief. "You made it!"

Delirious laughter takes hold as I release the mental strain I had to exert to keep from running away. And suddenly, I slip, and then, I'm drowning.

# Chapter 19

Pure terror engulfs me as I'm dragged underwater. The cold seeps into my clothes at an alarming rate. I gasp for air, only for water to fill my mouth. Darkness sweeps me away, making me lose all sense of direction. Someone—I assume Gaspar—is pulling on my arm, nearly dislocating my shoulder, but I keep sinking like a stone into a bottomless pit of water.

My childhood drama drowns out thought and reason, and I know I'm dying, just as I was always meant to, at the bottom of the river.

Then someone grabs my other arm and I'm hauled onto the bank, beautiful stale air filling my lungs once more. Light flickers ahead, but I can't see clearly yet. Instead, my ears pop and suddenly, I hear people arguing.

"I don't care if you blame her for ruining your little venture!" The voice is vaguely familiar, though I'm sure I've never heard it hissing before. "We need her! And, most importantly, we want her here."

It's the Chevalier, furious on my behalf. But I still don't understand what happened. How did I start drowning in the Banga as if it were an endless hole in the ground. Surely, the entrance to this cave isn't underwater otherwise, the whole place would be flooded. And I slipped into the floods, didn't I?

"She deserved payback for selling me out," a deep voice growls.

My entire body freezes as the fear takes hold again. Unlike the drowning before, this threat is real. I thought I'd never hear that voice again, that we'd rid the world of his evil, but he's here: Jacques de Molay, the last grandmaster of the Knights Templar, and he's free.

"Breathe, Alix, please breathe…" Gaspar's tear-stricken voice reaches my ears, making me realise I'm not lying on some riverbank but in his arms. He's holding me tightly, as if he could protect me when he couldn't before. "I'm sorry, I'm so sorry."

I'm starting to see shapes in front of me. Jacques de Molay's hulking figure is uncanny. He's always been an imposing man, doubly so in his armour and with that giant sword on his back. The Chevalier's in front of him, his back turned to me. As at the World Fair, he's wearing his eerie ghost glasses, his swirling blue gaze hitting me when he looks over his shoulder.

"Is she okay?"

There's a third figure, smaller than the other two, and it takes me a moment to realise it must be Napoleon. "Stand up, soldier! The battle's not done yet."

I'm still wondering who he means when my body reacts to his command and takes a shuddering breath. My lungs hurt as if stung by a thousand bees as I claw myself back to the painful existence we call life. It's sheer wonder I don't create a whisper ghost right there and then.

Gaspar's grasp on me tightens painfully and a tear falls on my cheek from above. "I should've never brought you here. I couldn't tell you, but I wanted… I didn't want to bring you here."

"Nonsense," the Chevalier says, kneeling at my side. "It was high time Alix came to join us." He pushes up his glasses and grins. "Welcome to the Nexus Commune!"

My vision has finally cleared enough to take in my surroundings. We're in a cave that looks much more natural than the usually man-made corridors above. The ceiling hangs low, just high enough for people like Molay to stand tall, but it's uneven, creating large and small spaces that have been outfitted with furniture, carpets, and even ghostly plants, making it all surprisingly cosy. Everywhere I look, people are hanging out around fires, talking and laughing—even singing and dancing. Most of them are ghosts, of course, but I see more than one cataphile enjoying themselves. All this activity and excitement makes it seem like the world's darkest summer camp.

At least six different tunnels lead further into the catacombs, some of them lit, the others dark, leaving me to guess what other facilities there are. Instead, my gaze is drawn to the biggest open space, currently occupied by what looks like a small regiment. They're exercising under the command of a Napoleonic general—he's not one of my Panthéon ones, but there's something eerie about him, something disturbing I can't quite place my finger on. And then it hits me: he's alive.

Panicked, I whip my head round to stare at Molay, immediately regretting the movement when pain strikes me. It doesn't take long for my worst nightmare to be confirmed: Molay's also come back from the dead, while the Emperor beside him is still a ghost.

"Who?" I want to ask, but it's barely a whisper. Who would be mad enough to bind their life to the devil-worshipping Grandmaster of the Templars? After everything we went through to bring him down.

It's clear to me now the drowning I just experienced was in my head. My clothes are wet, but that's from wading through the Banga, not because I fell into the water. Though my brain's doing its best to reason the fear away, the fact this powerful ghost—*ex-ghost*—is back keeps my heart racing.

"You promised to disperse his bones."

"And I did," the Chevalier says in a casual manner. "But I kept the head. It would've been highly irresponsible of me to let all that arcane knowledge go to waste. It was ultimately the key to the resurrections and all the wonderful things yet to come. I owed him his own resurrection for all his help."

Basically, he's struck a deal with the devil. Gaining some strength, I sit up, Gaspar's arms still around me—not that he did anything to even remotely prepare me for this. Though, did he? He tried so hard to tell me but he couldn't, just as I couldn't breathe when it should've been the most natural thing to do.

"Molay put a spell on you?" I whisper.

Gaspar looks at me like a bedraggled puppy. "I tried."

I guess that at least partially explains why he kept all this quiet. A little louder, I ask, "Who's the poor sod you bonded to him?"

The Chevalier laughs softly. "I doubt he'd appreciate you calling him a poor sod, but Mathieu volunteered."

Of course he did. And he probably has no idea who Jacques de Molay was and why we had to take him down. Or maybe he does and just doesn't care.

"He's over there."

My gaze follows where the Chevalier's pointing, and I do another double take. Mathieu is at a table amid several ghosts as he chats to none other than Félice Humbert, the persistent reporter. Looks like she finally found a ghost whisperer willing to spill the beans—and by "beans" I mean highly curated, biased beans that'll only scratch the surface of what ghost whispering is truly about.

"He exchanged his whisper ghost for Molay?" I ask, trying to keep my voice neutral.

The Chevalier shakes his head. "On the contrary—I separated the two before we proceeded with the resurrection. It worked perfectly, by the way, so you can tell your other boyfriend to drop by and get the procedure done. Or I could do it for you."

"Never." There's not a single person whose resurrection would justify abandoning Petite Alix.

"Suit yourself." He rises and holds out his hand. "Come on. Let me show you around the commune."

I stare at the hand as if it's poisonous. He quickly withdraws it, and I get up with Gaspar's help instead. My ghost boyfriend's keeping uncharacteristically quiet, the guilt still etched onto his face. I get that he couldn't tell me about Molay's resurrection, but I still don't understand what he sees in the Chevalier to want to join him despite all the massive red flags. For now, I try to keep an open mind. At the very least, I can report to Sébastien. That is if they let me go.

The Chevalier leads me around the cave, Napoleon in tow, while Molay thankfully has more important, no doubt nefarious, things to do.

"I'm glad you could make it," the Chevalier says. "When Gaspar first came to us, I wanted to invite you, too, but he said you'd come on your own terms or not at all, so we didn't push... much."

He was probably protecting me from Molay, but since he couldn't tell us about him, he just kept quiet about everything, knowing Sébastien and I would've immediately come down here.

"You want me to join this?" I ask, not quite sure what "this" is yet.

Gaspar shuffles his feet a little. "I think it's ultimately a good thing."

*Ultimately*, meaning before it gets good, a lot of uncomfortable stuff is going to happen, courtesy of Molay—or Napoleon. Despite his fear for my life, I need to remember Gaspar somehow believed in whatever is going on down here. What did the Chevalier call it?

"The Nexus Commune. Hit me with the pitch."

The Chevalier grins. "Gladly. I mean, you already know the gist of it. I—just like everyone else down here"—he nods at a group of ghosts and cataphiles sitting around a table, drinking—"dream of a place to call our own. A place where people like us—outsiders, revenants, and ghosts—can live in harmony, undisturbed by the rigid views of society."

"So, your solution is..."

"A commune, right here in the catacombs, away from the hustle and bustle of the outside world. Ghosts and cataphiles together, working hard on making the catacombs autonomous." He shows me down a corridor which opens into another cave that seems stacked with cooking utensils, most of it spectral in nature. "Here's our kitchen. The ghosts don't have to eat, of course, but they still enjoy the act of sitting down for a meal, and our cooks love sharing recipes from all eras. Think of a historical meal, and we can probably cook it up."

I have to admit the energy in the kitchen is infections. Living chefs, dead housewives, and royal cooks mingle to create something new. It's exactly the kind of cooperation I dream off.

"Our sleeping quarters are mostly for the living," the Chevalier says as he opens the door to one of the other rooms. It's fairly functional, similar to the old bunker the Résistance met in until last year. "You'd be surprised how often we catch a ghost napping, though."

"And I'd be napping a lot better without your yapping," a grumpy old ghost yells.

Napoleon closes the door, commenting, "Many lesser ghosts lack the imagination to fill their days and nights. They nap because they don't know what else to do."

"Well, now they can do it in a bed," the Chevalier says in good humour.

Our next stop is the labs, which look bigger and more diverse than before. Most importantly, there are no dead animals in sight. Instead, I watch ghostly scientists working on chemical, physical, and spectral experiments, with two or three ghost whisperers desperately taking notes.

"This is the future, Alix, and you gave me the idea," the Chevalier says. "Isn't that what you wanted? Ghosts and living working together to create a better world."

"World?" I can't help glance at Napoleon, as if he's going to call for war at any given moment.

But he seems content—if a little bored—to let the Chevalier take the lead. "Well, a world below ground, free from all the rules and regulations society wants to shackle us with."

"It's a commune," Gaspar says, a burst of passion coming through. "A unique community made up of ghosts and living, all looking out for each other. No rulers, no class system, no haves and have-nots. Everyone here's equal, whether they're dead or alive."

It's getting harder and harder to ignore the excitement in the air. Yet, it all sounds a little too good. "If that's so, then why the need for such a strong military presence?" I can't help but notice the disproportionately large number of soldier ghosts. Most importantly, I can't get the picture of the exercising regiment and living generals out of my mind.

"It's not really without rulers, is it?" I throw a pointed glance at Napoleon.

Napoleon smirks, as if pleased I've called him out. "Of course, you need someone to take the reins."

"What he means is that in this delicate phase, we need some form of leadership," the Chevalier amends. "And sadly, we need protection." He regards me with a frown. "You know this as well as I do, but the living just can't leave well enough alone. How many GoPol agents have we had to divert over the last few weeks? And that's not even considering what the Quarry Department's done over the years."

"The Quarry Department?"

It's been a while since I thought about them. I'd briefly wondered if it was worth checking in with them to see if they could do something about the catacombs' ghosts, but despite the hints I found in GoPol's earliest records and changing public opinion, I still feel too self-conscious to rock up at a government agency and talk to them about ghosts.

The Chevalier continues down the corridors while he explains, "I followed up on your reports of tormented souls in the tourist part of the catacombs. You were absolutely right. What's been done to the ghosts there is horrific. They deserve so much better than this half existence."

Despite myself, the excitement bubbles up in me and I can barely stop myself from blurting out, "I know!" It should probably make me stop and think that my staunchest supporter in ghost rights is an anarchist necromancer.

"Unfortunately, the Quarry Department haven't really changed their ways since they took over the catacombs," the Chevalier continues. "They still see themselves as the authority on ghosts, the unsung heroes of the living. Rumour has it, they *want* to be unsung, just so their ghostly existence is as short as possible."

I pull a face. My head's swimming just thinking about the amount of effort one would have to put in to reduce their spectral footprint. Ideally, they'd have no relationships, no family, not even friendships, and of course no professional acknowledgement. An entirely unmemorable life. Why even live at all?

"Why would anyone want to cut their afterlife short?"

"Those people are religious fanatics who believe that what we call the afterlife is just some kind of purgatory before you move on to the *real* afterlife. Others are so anti-ghost, they don't want to become 'part of the problem', as they'd call it."

"But this life, this *afterlife,* is the one that matters," Napoleon says. "We've been put on this world, alive or dead, to fulfil our destiny. Running from your destiny just makes you a coward."

I guess I *am* a coward, because I'll run from Nostradamus' prophesied destiny for as long as I can. But when it comes to the afterlife, I hope I get to enjoy a long existence, just as I hope to live a long life before that. This world, whether the living or ghost part, is too beautiful to turn my back on.

"So, they see the whole existence of ghosts as a problem?"

The Chevalier rolls his eyes. "It's a common tale: we fear what we don't understand. But instead of furthering their understanding, the Quarry Department prefers to bury it. They're obsessed with something called the 'dead load'. You know the main task of the department is to stabilise the catacombs, right?"

I nod, trying to wrap my head around all this new information.

"Well, turns out it's not what you think it is. They're not talking about potential collapses—though they do that, too, on the side.

No, what they do is send their employees through the catacombs to measure the amount of spectral energy. If they find it's too high, they place little sigils on the walls to break it down. I've been removing these sigils for years, and ghosts now know to immediately abandon an area if they see someone measuring, causing lower readings."

That's a lot to process. I haven't met anyone from the Quarry Department yet, so I can't say if the Chevalier's assessment is right, but if all the ghosts are in on it... "What do you mean by 'breaking down the spectral energy'? What do they do to the ghosts?"

"Lower their power, destabilise them, make them forget a little more of themselves."

I think I'm going to be sick. "But why?"

"Some of them probably think they're helping, but as I said, it's mostly about the dead load, which is their heavily biased term for spectral power levels. They believe the weight of ghosts presses down on the living, leading to collapses and all sorts of metaphysical conditions." We reach another doorway but halt in front. "I'm not saying it's complete hogwash—there is such a thing as too many ghosts in a place." Napoleon clears his throat, and the Chevalier quickly amends, "Not here, of course. My point is we never talk about a 'living load', do we? All those heavy building in the upper world? The strain on the environment, on each other—that's a lot worse than anything ghosts do, and they're just merely existing."

If he's right, then the Quarry Department is deplorable for re-
ducing this so-called dead load, essentially eliminating ghosts, just
because they say so. Unsung heroes, my ass.

"Okay, but they've been at it for three hundred years. What's
that got to do with us... you, I mean?"

"I'm just one of the many victims of the authoritative regime
GoPol, and the Quarry Department run under the nose of every-
day Parisians. Together, they dictate who gets to be a ghost whisperer and what they do with their lives, and, apparently, when a
ghost has lasted long enough. Did you know there are plans to
weaken strongholds like the Panthéon and St. Denis?"

I know he's just trying to get into my head; he has to. If the
Quarry Department truly posed such a huge threat, my ghosts
would've told me. Then again, they don't think Napoleon is a
threat, either. "Do you have proof?"

"We've got Molay," he says softly. "What was done to him—"

"Happened for a very good reason." I'm not going to sympathise
with that devil-worshipping psychopath.

"And then you've got me," Napoleon says in a sombre voice. "I
was buried in seven sarcophagi, not to honour me—that was what
they told the king—but to contain me. To weaken me. For nearly
two hundred years, I was a prisoner in my own country, exiled right
there in the heart of Les Invalides."

He might feel this way, but that doesn't mean it wasn't warrant-
ed. Like Molay, the Quarry Department—or the Knights Hospi-

taller or whoever ordered it—might have had very good reason to seal away Napoleon.

"I heard you've been..."—how do I phrase this without invoking Napoleon's ire?—"...planning several campaigns over the years."

Gaspar squeezes my hand, acknowledging the risk I'm taking.

"Of course. I always plan my next move, my next campaign," Napoleon admits, not missing a single beat. "It's what I do, what I'm known for. Just as your writer friends still write and your philosophers still think, I plan and I plot. But it's hard to build momentum from behind a prison wall. I needed someone to break me out."

"Sounds like you two found each other," is out of my mouth faster than my fear can stop it.

Napoleon's face darkens, but the Chevalier grins. "Told you, she's quick-witted." He nods. "Yes, Alix, our partnership is mutually beneficial. My technology and his command might just be enough to secure this commune and make it a shining example for the future."

I lick my lips. "The future?"

"Well, we were hoping once people see the benefits, the concept might spread. I mean think of all the potential..." He suddenly grins, a hand on the door. "Actually, don't think, just look."

He opens the door and reveals a vaulted cave full of shelves and books. Scholars, from monks to modern researchers, are walking the aisles or sitting at the tables studying texts under blue spectral lights.

In wonder, I step among the tomes, trying to figure out which are real and which just spectral. Unable to help myself, I pick up a book of Molière's and flick through it. The text is hard to read, so it takes a moment to realise what it says. When I do, excitement rushes through me. "Wait! This is Molière's translation of Lucretius' *De Rerum Natura*. That text is lost."

"Is Molière lost?" the Chevalier asks, a hidden smile in his eyes.

No, Molière is one of the famous writers buried in Père Lachaise. "You mean he donated it to this place?" I'm not sure I could handle knowing he'd joined the commune.

The Chevalier shakes his hand. "No, this is one of the projects I'm the proudest of. I call it the Library of the Lost. The scholars here are working hard to recover lost volumes, burnt manuscripts, and banned books, using spectral memory."

My mouth drops open as I regard the tomes in front of me. There have been so many times in history when large amounts of books were accidentally or wilfully destroyed—when the people of the Great Revolution decided to get rid of tens of thousands of feudal texts, for example. It's the grand tragedy of history that we have such a limited corpus of surviving texts, unable to tell how much is missing. The chance of once more being able to read these books brings tears to my eyes.

"How?" I whisper.

The Chevalier moves in front of me, blocking my view. "I'll tell you another time; once you've made up your mind and joined the commune."

I swallow hard, reminded painfully that this is just a tour to win me over to the cause. Then again, how bad can a cause be if it helps reconstruct part of what was thought forever lost?

"In the Nexus Commune, we respect the past and welcome the future," the Chevalier says in a ceremonial voice. "We've already come so far. Now all we need is you."

"Me?" I stare, dread growing in my chest. "What could you ever need me for?"

The Chevalier smiles and points to Napoleon. "He's the tactician, the brawn that will secure the commune. I'm the brains of the operation, the man to make it happen. And you, my dear Alix, you're the heart. You're the one who'll capture the hearts of the ghosts, whom they'll rally around, and who'll give strength to our movement."

# Chapter 20

The meeting has me deeply confused. What the Chevalier showed me was a world of wonder, but I know in my heart there's more, that this commune can't stand without challenge. Napoleon's army will defend it, but will he be content once the catacombs belong to the ghosts and whisperers?

*It's an honour to finally meet the one who'll raise the dead and bring chaos and destruction to the world.*

The stupid prophecy's swirling through my mind again. My destiny. It's clear to me now it's about this moment, this decision. But how could I raise the dead and join the Chevalier if it'd bring so much sorrow to everyone?

My heart yearns for what the Chevalier promises, for that collaboration, for the lost texts, the hidden potential, but do I dare risk it? Do I dare tear it all down in the hopes of finding something better in the rubble? The Great Revolution did it, so why not me?

I snort. Yes, why shouldn't I decide the fate of millions of people? I clearly must be under another spell of Molay's to think my dream is worth that kind of risk and sacrifice.

"Just think about it," Gaspar says on the way back, hands deep in his hoodie—the Chevalier truly let us go. "We could set an example for the world as it learns to embrace ghosts. I mean, everyone becomes one eventually, so it's kind of stupid to disregard us completely. Ghosts need rights too, most of all, the right to exist."

"You're not seriously saying Molay should be running around free just because he's a ghost?" If only the grandmaster wasn't a part of the commune, I might actually consider it.

"Of course not! Look, I hate that, too, but I guess that's one of the sacrifices the Chevalier had to make to obtain the necessary knowledge."

Was it Molay's arcane knowledge that built the Library of the Lost?

"But don't worry, he's on our side..." Gaspar hesitates, clearly still struggling with the spells that prevented him from saying anything about Molay before. "If that's the side you choose."

I stop short and sigh. This whole trip—the whole day actually—has been a lot. I went from the emotional vulnerability of being in Gaspar's childhood home, to the surprising meeting with Empress Joséphine, to a devastating fight between my boyfriends, and that was all before I walked into the Chevalier's headquarters and learnt a million things and none.

"Do I have to choose?" Even before the words leave my lips, I already know the answer. The Chevalier and Napoleon will go through with their plan, whether I join them or not, so one day, sooner rather than later, I'll have to decide which side of history I want to be on. The thought makes the hairs stand up on my arms, and I hug myself, suddenly feeling terribly overwhelmed.

Gaspar walks back, rubs his hands over my upper arms, and pulls me into him, giving me a proper hug. "I'm sorry for putting you in that position."

Shaking my head, I try to muddle through my feelings and find the reason underneath. "No, I get it. Not, why you had to keep this from us, though I understand why you thought you had to"—he tenses slightly but doesn't pull back, for which I'm grateful—"but why this would excite you." He's always dreamed of helping underserved communities, and which community is more underserved than the ghosts no one even sees as humans anymore?

"Doesn't it excite you?" he asks, awe lacing his voice. Pulling back just enough to look into my eyes, he starts to paint a picture. "What if this city embraced the Nexus Commune? Just think of all the favours you've done for them over the years. You've tried to help so many, but if this commune becomes a reality, we can help all of them—or most of them. We can sort out that terrible mess in the tourist part, shut it down, and let the ghosts rest in peace. Instead of hunting and fearing ghosts, the cataphiles would respect and work with them. All those dreams you have, the potential… We can make it happen." His eyes are alight with fervour. "Victor can finally have his books written, and Rousseau can have his say on equity and equality. Marie Curie could revolutionise chemistry, physics, and metaphysics—again! And all the ghosts could live their afterlife in peace without the fear that one day a troop of GoPol officers will barge in there and remove all their memories; their very identity."

It's a beautiful image. And while I know it won't be that easy or that we'd all live happily ever after—and beyond—I've never felt so close to my dreams. All that stands between it are the very people I'm supposed to follow.

"With Napoleon, Molay, and the Chevalier at the helm, I'm afraid it'll be less Paris Commune and more Reign of Terror." As inspiring as the Great Revolution was, what followed was much worse than what it replaced. "How many people will have to die to make this dream a reality?" I whisper, shuddering as I wonder what it'd take to truly secure the catacombs.

But before he can answer, I pick up a whimper from the tunnel behind us. Head whipping around, my light beam splits the darkness and lands on the wide-eyed face of a boy, maybe eleven or twelve years old. My first thought is what a boy his age is doing in the catacombs, but then recognition trickles in. I've seen this face before. A number of times, actually. I vaguely remember seeing him on the grounds in front of Napoleon's tomb, or in the streets of Rueil-Malmaison. I think I even saw him running—or maybe hiding—in Joséphine's garden.

I open my mouth when the boy bolts. Quick as a snake, he dashes into a hidden crevice in the wall. Before I can react, Gaspar's after him, leaving me no choice but to follow.

The crevice is so tight, I worry about getting stuck several times before I stumble into an empty room, nearly falling to my death when I stumble over a hole. The stagnant flow of sewage moves deep under my feet. Panicked, I clutch the side of the walls, digging my fingers behind what feels like bones, and hold on for dear life until my heart rate slows. Once the static of my racing pulse quiets down, I pick up a cry further ahead.

"Leave me alone!" a high voice calls—the boy. "Or I'll call my whisperer, you stupid ghost!"

A whisper ghost. Carefully, I place my feet along the edge, circumventing the break-in above the sewage system, and push further, through a second narrow connective hallway into what looks like a dead-end. Gaspar has an iron grip on the boy's upper arm, refusing to let go, while he tears and pulls. Despite his threat, no whisperer comes to his aid.

"Why were you spying on us?" Gaspar says harshly. "Didn't your parents teach you that's bad manners?"

The boy bares his teeth and hisses, "I don't have parents!"

I wonder how old his whisperer is. Have they just turned recently? Or was his parental alienation the product of long years of death, tied to a man who no longer needs or may even value his parents?

The boy kicks then tries to bite Gaspar, leading the older ghost to forcefully push him into the wall. It's more reflex than intent, but the boy's eyes widen suddenly, and there's a fear in his eyes that twists my heart into a knot.

"Let go of him."

"If I do that, he'll vanish," Gaspar says, sounding not too happy himself. "He was spying on us."

"I know." There's no doubt about it when I consider how many times I've actually seen him now. "Still. You're hurting him."

"I'm not—" Gaspar starts to complain, but then he sighs, lets go of the boy's arm, and takes a step back. "Sorry."

Instead of vanishing, the feral little whisper ghost glares at Gaspar and rubs his arm. "Why'd you say sorry? I don't feel pain."

But he remembers it. The knot around my heart grows even tighter. I go down on one knee to be more on an even level with the boy and fish for a comforting smile. "What's your name?" I assume he's been following me because he wanted to speak to me, maybe even ask for a favour.

"I don't have to tell you my name, you dumb bitch!"

"Hey!" Gaspar snaps, taking another step towards the boy, which has him instantly flinching and half sinking into the wall behind him.

I reach out my hand to touch Gaspar's hip, the pressure intending to hold him back. "Don't."

Gaspar raises his hands. "I'm not going to hurt you," he tells him.

"I can't get hurt," he answers sullenly. "I'm dead."

"Since when?" I ask softly. If he doesn't want to tell me his name, it's fine. But I need to know why he's following me.

The boy glares at me, as if I'm the reason he died. "Longer than you've been alive."

A soft sigh escapes my lips. That would put his whisperer close to forty at the very least. No wonder his whisper ghost doesn't have parents anymore.

"Where's your whisperer?"

Is he another GoPol agent who completely disregarded his whisper ghost because he's of little use? I don't remember Sébastien or Dix telling me about another child whisper ghost, and this one's even younger than Dix and Lys. The thought his whisperer might've been indoctrinated by GoPol at such a young age makes me sick.

"None of your business, bi—" He breaks off after a quick glance in Gaspar's direction.

My ghost has crossed his arms, looking none too impressed. "If I were you, I'd start talking," he says in a low voice.

"And if I don't?" The words are defiant, but the trembling bottom lip belies the bravado. "You're just a simp anyway. Since you died again, you've been entirely useless."

So, this little whisper ghost knows what happened to Gaspar. If he died over twenty-five years ago, there's no way he'd know words like "simp", which tells me he picked it up from somewhere else. He's probably parroting what he's heard from his whisperer, and there's only one I can think of who's familiar with Gaspar's ill-fated resurrection and who'd call me a 'dumb bitch'. The age fits too. Sadly, this boy isn't here to ask a favour for himself; he's been sent to spy on us.

"Mathieu, is it?" I ask tiredly.

Gaspar tenses, while the boy wipes his nose with his elbow. "Mathy. I'm Mathy."

Though I don't feel like it, I smile once more. "Hello, Mathy."

Then I remember something. According to the Chevalier, Mathieu separated from his whisper ghost to bond with Molay instead. It doesn't surprise me he'd think less of a whisper ghost who's barely half his size—or little enough to replace him with a much stronger, more powerful ghost. To be honest, the only real surprise, the one that tells me even someone like Mathieu isn't a complete ass, is that he took care to separate properly from Mathy first. Unlike Ollie, who had no idea what would happen if Olivier agreed to bond to Louis XVI, Mathy gets to live as a normal ghost, no longer tied to his whisperer. Sadly for him, that also means his whisperer will never come to defend him.

"So, Mathieu sent you to spy on us?" Gaspar asks, still glowering.

"Her. You're unimportant."

I intensify my grip on Gaspar's hip and pull myself up again. "Why would he want to spy on me?"

Do I really need to ask? Mathieu and I hit it off immediately—and by "hitting it off" I mean hated each other at first sight. Of course, he doesn't trust me.

"Because you ruin everything!" he says with taught fervour. "You're a fucking liability and you should've been put down when we had the chance."

"Alright, that's enough!" Gaspar bellows, raising a hand.

The moment he does, Mathy flinches and hunches his shoulders. My heart bleeds, the knot tight. "Stop," I whisper, tears forming in my eyes.

Gaspar lowers his arms. "I wasn't going to hit him."

I know he wouldn't but someone did. Was it his father? Is that how Mathieu nearly died, almost beaten to death? I can't believe I feel sorry for the guy when he literally wishes me dead. Mathieu made his own bad choices but this boy still lives his past and that breaks my heart into a million jagged pieces.

"You're safe with us," I say as gently as I can.

"No one's safe as long as you're around," he says sullenly, but the learnt reply lacks Mathieu's viciousness.

"Is that so?" I sigh. "Is that why you're following me? To find out if I'm going to ruin your plans?"

Mathy pushes his bottom lip forward, shaking ever so slightly. "You will. You ruin everything. It's all your fault."

I cock my head, wondering if Mathieu has been blaming me or Mathy. "What is?"

"Everything," he blurts out. "That's why he had to do it. Why he had to get rid of me."

The shards of my broken heart pierce my lungs and I find it hard to breathe.

"But it's okay," Mathy says proudly, his voice gaining a bit of strength. "'Cause I'll still be useful to him, I'll prove myself. And if you dare double-cross him, he'll hear about it." And with that, Mathy fully sinks into the wall and vanishes.

Gaspar shakes his head. "What a nasty piece of work."

"Mathieu? Yes. Mathy? He's just confused." And angry. And hurt. Because maybe ghosts can't feel pain anymore, but that doesn't mean you can't cut them deep.

"He won't stop," Gaspar says, giving him a little more grace. "He'll just get better at hiding."

That's probably true. "Well, maybe he *wanted* to be found."

Part of me even wants him to continue, so I might have the chance at finding out what really drives Mathieu—or rather his poor, abandoned, and abused whisper ghost.

As if he's suddenly caught a whiff of how shattered my insides are, Gaspar reaches out to me and pulls me into a hug. "Let's go home."

# Chapter 21

By the time Gaspar and I make it back, it's the dead of night, yet when we quietly open the door and sneak inside, light is still burning in the living room. After I take off my waders and stow my shoes, I make my way over and poke my head in. Sure enough, Sébastien's at the dinner table, a laptop and some print-outs in front of him, while Dix is engrossed in watching the hedgehogs explore the potted plants.

Sébastien looks up and lets out a breath, as if he's been holding it all this time. "You're back."

"Sorry it got so late." I notice Gaspar hasn't followed me. The fight they had won't be cleared up tonight. "What is it, two?"

"Three thirty."

Wow, that *is* late. No wonder I'm exhausted. "Sorry."

"Where did you go?" Sébastien's voice sounds hollow, as if he's only following a reasonable protocol of questions.

I cross my arms and lean against the door frame. "I went into the catacombs."

"Of course you did." He gives me a quick look, as if only just registering the head lamp I'm holding. "And I assume you found what you were looking for?"

Dix looks up, then quickly lowers his head, pretending he's not listening.

A pang of guilt reverberates through me. I know Sébastien wanted to keep me safe, but after Gaspar dropped that bomb on us, I needed to know. "I did. It's not even that far in. They're definitely using ghost power to deter people they don't want to visit."

"Just as you thought." His voice still lacks emotion. Maybe it's the time of day, but something feels off.

"Well, I could've never dreamed up what I found." I move into the room and sit next to him, leaning forward as I allow some of the excitement bubble out. "It's a commune for the living and dead. Everyone's equal, everyone's looking out for each other, and they're working together to—"

Sébastien abruptly shuts his laptop, gets up, and walks out. A moment later, I hear the door to his room shut.

Dix looks at me apologetically. "He was worried sick about you. I had to physically restrain him from barging into the catacombs to find you, remind him he didn't even know where you'd gone."

The guilt intensifies and I look longingly at the wall between us. "I wrote him a note."

"And you think that made him worry less?" Dix throws up his hands. "Look, I don't blame you. If it were up to me, I'd have gone looking weeks ago. You did what you had to, and as I told him, you know how to handle yourself, and here you are—safe and sound."

Then why do I feel so raw?

"He'll be fine in the morning," Dix says. "Once he's gotten over his saviour complex, he'll realise it was the only way we'd ever get any information. And you got information, right? You won't keep it to yourself like that—"

"Don't be mean to Gaspar."

Dix grumbles a little, but he doesn't launch into a rant. "He hurt him."

"Yeah, I know. And he feels horrible about it." Otherwise, he'd be here, pretending everything was fine.

Dix snorts softly. "Séb really likes him," he whispers. "I thought he was cool, too."

"He's still figuring out who he wants to be as ghost." By ignoring everything he was. "Gaspar had a good reason—not for lying to us, but for seeking out the Chevalier. What they're planning... Well, the end result sounds nice. I think you'd like it."

Judging by the stubborn set of Dix's shoulders, that's another thing which won't get resolved tonight. Maybe I should just go to bed. But when I walk into the hallway, it's Sébastien's door I open.

He's lying in bed, turned away from me, yet way too quiet to be sound asleep. I tiptoe over and sit on the empty side, just in reach yet far away. For a few moments, I do nothing but listen to his strained breathing.

"I'm sorry I kept you up all night worrying." My words are met with stoic silence. "You told me to stay away from the Chevalier and I went anyway, taking a huge risk." Just because I was allowed to walk free doesn't mean it was a guarantee.

One more breath, deeper this time, then Sébastien turns. "But you're fine," he snaps, the first real emotion I've heard since I returned. "You're fine, because the Chevalier values you and Napoleon values you, and they all just want you to join them on their merry takeover, and *you* want it, too."

That's a whole lot of accusation to swallow, especially since none are entirely wrong. Well, except one. "There's no taking over anything."

He sits up, throwing the blanket off as far as my weight will allow, and turns on the bedside lamp, blinding me momentarily. "But that's what's going to happen, isn't it?"

Met with his anger, I answer a little sullenly, "No it's not. We didn't talk about any conquests." Though I'd have been stupid to ignore Napoleon's words about how he's always planning, always scheming. "We talked about the big plan, the endgame."

"Ah, right, ghost paradise."

His sarcasm cuts like a knife. For a moment, I look aside, unable to face him, but then my own anger rises and I turn on him. "And what's wrong with that? What's wrong with a place where ghosts and living can live together in peace? Where they can support each other, learn from each other, and improve both their worlds? What's wrong with a society where ghosts can contribute once more, where ghost whisperers can be more than GoPol agents or hunted?"

Where I could study in that Library of the Lost and learn the truth about what came before, uncover so many secret links and forgotten knowledge. My heart yearns for those spectral tomes like nothing before.

Sébastien stares. He opens his mouth and shuts it again, then all the tension goes out of him, and he hangs his head. "I'm sorry."

"About what?" I ask, more calmly now.

"If you say it's a good thing, I trust you. You know that." He looks up again, his blue gaze hitting mine. "I trust you a whole lot more than I trust myself." Swallowing, he adds, "For obvious reasons."

All I can do is stare at him, horrified. That's a whole lot of responsibility he's dumping on me.

Desperation creeps into his voice as he continues, "It's just I have a really bad feeling about this. You know they won't stick to the catacombs. With Napoleon at the helm, there will be violence, and with all the strange power that the Chevalier is accumulating—"

"—and Molay by his side," I add. When Sébastien's eyes widen, I shrug. "Mathieu bonded with him. He's *alive.*" Apparently, he didn't put a spell on me to keep his presence secret, which makes me think it was only kept secret, so I wouldn't be scared away. I'm not sure how I feel about that.

"Right," Sébastien says slowly, the worry barely hidden in his eyes. Well, the Chevalier, Napoleon, and *Molay*, that sounds like a recipe for disaster."—I wholeheartedly agree—"I get that this commune might be awesome for ghosts and cataphiles, but what about the rest of Paris? The living?"

Reflexively, I answer, "Why can't this be about ghosts? Don't get me wrong," I quickly amend when he opens his mouth. "I'm fully aware of how devious this combination is and if there's any kind of conquest or takeover, I want nothing to do with it, but what's wrong with creating a safe space for ghosts? A place where they can thrive? I don't see the living accommodating them anytime soon. Half the people still don't even believe in them." And the Quarry Department is apparently culling the ghost population without any kind of oversight.

Once more, Sébastien hangs his head, all the fight leaving him. "You're right."

"No, I'm not!" I don't know why, maybe I'm too tired, but tears of frustration are running down my cheeks.

Alarmed, he looks up. "Alix!" Moving in, he cups my face, rubbing his thumbs over my cheeks. "What's wrong? Why are you saying you're not right, when clearly you are?"

Now that they've started to fall, the tears won't stop. I'm crying about the ghosts, and I'm crying about Mathy and what he's been through, and how much Sébastien is like him, because he, too, was abused as a child to the point where he can't even trust his instincts, because they're so muddled with all the wrong he did when he didn't know better. Just like Mathy parrots Mathieu because he's the only one he could trust, even though he's not trustworthy at all—just like I can't be trusted either.

"I can't be your moral compass," I say through a whole lot of hiccups.

"But you are," Sébastien whispers, clearly overwhelmed by my emotional breakdown. "You're always right."

"No, I'm not! That's the whole point," I cry. "There is no right or wrong. Every path is right or none of them is. I mean, some are probably better than others, while some are definitely much worse. Some benefit the living and others benefit the ghosts, but that doesn't make either right."

I have to catch my breath and choke back some of the tears before I continue. "Decisions are complex. Each has repercussions beyond our wildest imagination."

If history's taught me anything then it's never just one thing, never just one issue that evokes change, but more like a perfect storm of innovation, initiative, and dissent. Nothing ever changed because everyone was happy.

"Look, Hélène often told me I don't care enough about the living and that's probably true, but then again, everyone else already cares about the living, but who, apart from me, cares about the ghosts?"

Sébastien casts his eyes down. "I'm trying to."

"Not enough." I hate I'm using Gaspar's words against him and quickly shake my head. "Which is fine! It doesn't make you wrong, nor does it make me right! Or the Chevalier right, or even the ghosts right!" Swallowing down some tears, I try to sort my thoughts. "What I've learnt from history is that if a group of people—be they women, people of colour, or in this case, ghosts—previously didn't have a voice or any sort of representation, they always have to carve out space for themselves first. And that process is messy. Sometimes it's violent, and it's almost always met with huge push-back, but that doesn't make the process wrong. Change is hard-won, no one knows that better than our country, right?"

His hands slip from my cheeks, and he nods. "You're right."

I almost want to strangle him, instead I answer with a hollow laugh. "But you're right, *too*. You're trained to see the conflicts, the dangers, all the bad things that could potentially happen to us and which we need to be protected from. That's your job, that's you. And there's nothing wrong about it. But I'm also not wrong when all I see is the potential, the good things that could come from it." My tears are drying up, and a real smile fights its way to the surface. I shuffle forward a little and grab his hands. "Neither of us are wrong or less valid—we just have different priorities and different approaches, and they're different again from Gaspar's."

"How?" he asks, barely concealing the hunger in his eyes.

"Because he's pro-ghost, obviously, and a lot of what you do—what you *have* to do—is anti-ghost, or not enough pro-ghost. And again, that doesn't make you wrong and him right. You both care deeply, about each other and others." I squeeze his hands tighter. "You're right to worry, to want to protect the living. There's nothing wrong with your priorities or your decision-making process. So, don't use me as a crutch for your morality. Just trust yourself, trust that you're doing the best you can, the best—"

Suddenly, Sébastien pulls me into him and presses his lips on mine, drinking me in as if he's wandered through a hot, merciless desert and I'm the first sip of water he's found in days. I lose myself in the feel of him, drowning in his love and devotion, in his eagerness to prove himself, to make up for all the wrongs in his past. And I hold him tight to let him know it's okay to have different opinions and different priorities, that I still support him, still value him, still love him.

This world we're living in is messy. It pulls us in a million different directions, constantly testing us, forcing us to draw lines in the sand, to take a stand. What things are worth fighting for? Dying for? There are as many answers as there are people, but so long as we respect each other, our actions don't actively hurt others, and we strive for compromise, we'll be alright.

At long last, Sébastien pulls away. His hand cups my face, while his forehead rests against mine. Deep shuddering breaths contrast the thunderous beats of our hearts. We might not always have the same opinion but we have a whole lot of love for each other, and if we look out for one another, we're good.

We shuffle around until we can both slip under the blanket. Sébastien puts an arm around my shoulders and pulls me against his chest, burying his nose in my hair. "So, what do we do now?"

"We gather more information, see where everyone stands. We need to know what the Chevalier is *really* planning and how he intends to make his vision come true." How he intends to secure his commune. "And then we decide what to do with that."

While I wholeheartedly believe something has to change, I'm not yet sold on this commune; not with those leaders at the top.

"So, you didn't join his commune?" Sébastien asks cautiously.

I shake my head slightly, not that I have much movement. Running my finger in a circle across Sébastien's naked chest, I tell him everything I saw and heard in the catacombs, finishing with, "He claims he wants and needs me, that I'm the heart of his project, the one to bring the ghosts together. You remember what Nostradamus said?"

"That you'll bring about France's darkest hour?"

I shudder, having forgotten about that particular add-on. "Yeah. What if it's this? What if it has to get really bad before it gets better?"

Despite the thought, I still can't see myself actively taking on the role of catalyst, not for all the promises the Chevalier showed me today.

"It's just a stupid prophecy," Sébastien says, sounding as if he's about to fall asleep. "The Chevalier doesn't even know about it."

"He still wants me."

"Yeah... Wait. You said Napoleon's still a ghost, right?" Forcing himself awake, he turns into me. When I nod, his eyes start to widen, pulling him away from the edge of sleep. "That's what he wants you for. Mathieu bonded with Molay, and others apparently bonded with his generals, but for the short guy, he wants someone special. Someone like you."

I stare at him as the realisation hits me. Right now, the resurrection is still limited to one ghost per ghost whisperer. Napoleon hasn't come alive yet, because he's still waiting. For me. His commanding power and my social network will create the perfect storm, the one that'll bring chaos and destruction.

"Never," I blurt out the moment I think of my actual whisper ghost. "I don't care what he offers—I won't abandon Petite Alix."

Sébastien pulls me against his chest, placing kisses on my head. "I know. And I'll die fighting before I let him do that to you."

More ominous words have never been spoken.

# CHAPTER 22

Despite what Gaspar has said about the Panthéon ghosts sitting in their ivory tower, not caring about common ghost issues, I sit them down after my shift to talk to them about what I found underground. I know Sébastien's opinion and I certainly know Gaspar's, but I haven't talked to many of the older ghosts yet, and I think I need their insight to get my head straight—channelling a little more "cautious protector" rather than "musical rebel" here.

"So, what do you think?" I look expectantly into my ghosts' faces.

After Sébastien's suggestion I might be the Chevalier's preferred choice of whisperer for Napoleon, when I saw her, I'd grabbed hold of Petite Alix and hugged her tight. Now she's sitting in my lap playing with Malou while the ghosts are gathered around.

"I don't trust this," Victor says with a grim face. "I wouldn't trust either of these men to lead a literature salon, much less a peaceful commune. If Napoleon's involved, it means war."

"As if you know what war is—you never fought in one," de Galles, one of the Napoleonic generals says. "Your father maybe, but it was the battles *we* fought that lifted your family up in the world and provided you with the opportunities you had."

"Or maybe the world changed and had a chance to breathe once the warmongers were gone," Victor retorts.

Next to de Galles, another military officer shakes his head. "Peace must be won."

"Well, it sure wasn't Napoleon who won it," Victor quips. "Or are we all forgetting he was defeated and exiled *twice*?"

"I still don't think this is going to go anywhere," Voltaire says, musing. "Napoleon has concocted many schemes over the years and failed every time. He has a certain charm, and as you can see, still has a hold over people—or maybe *people* are just bored, unequipped to do anything but wage war among themselves."

The military officers holler abuse and my stomach sinks a little. If this is how divided the Panthéon is, I have little hope for the rest of the ghosts. I notice Jean Lannes doesn't join in the chorus of his colleagues, watching the turmoil with a stony face. Of all the officers here, he knows Napoleon best, yet hasn't thrown his support in.

Since Napoleon is such a contested topic, I try to steer the conversation away. "What about the resurrection of Molay?"

"That right there," Victor says, "should tell you everything you need to know about this so-called commune. Molay is a monster, a dictator in his own right. He built Nexus—the ghost side of it—as an absolute dominion, a rule of terror and torture of the mind. I don't believe for a single moment that the Chevalier—or even Napoleon—will be able to control him once he's exerted that rule over the entire catacombs."

His words steer up dissent again with the generals proclaiming Napoleon can absolutely handle someone like Molay.

"Who even knows Molay's name these days? A bunch of so-called gamers?" de Galles shouts, then nods at me, "No insult to the historians, of course, but every person with a touch of education knows about Napoleon. He's vastly more powerful than this devil-worshipping wannabe grandmaster who single-handedly ruined the Templars."

That's not quite how it went down in history, but I guess he has a point—Napoleon and Molay aren't even in the same weight class when it comes to notoriety. Unless one little detail changes it all.

"But Molay's alive now. Napoleon isn't."

Jean Moulin, who's slowly pacing around the group, stops to say, "And we're still figuring out what it means to be resurrected. It's not alive as it used to be. Louis XVI lived too shortly to make any assumptions, whereas our only other case..." His face softens. "Well, even the Chevalier admitted the process was broken."

"Did he?" It's rare for Marie Curie to join these big discussions. She's usually busy in her lab. "I still remember his proud presentation. He didn't care about the heightened aggressiveness and touch of psychosis, then. In fact, as a fellow scientist, I'd say it was by design."

It's a chilling thought, considering it's Gaspar they're talking about. The Chevalier's always claimed it was due to the experimental nature of his resurrection, then subsequently assured me he'd ironed out those kinks, but, while Louis XVI's behaviour seemed pretty normal—despite maybe his wish for revenge—the whisperer he'd bonded to, Gaby's brother, completely lost it. The connection between whisperer and this new kind of ghost is still as broken as ever. I probably wouldn't even notice with Molay and Mathieu, though—they were both aggressive psychopaths before they were bonded.

"I still don't understand why anyone would *want* to be alive again," Rousseau muses. "Living is such a burden, so full of limits."

"You wouldn't understand anything, anyway," Voltaire shouts.

Victor strokes his chin, thoughtfully. "I quite enjoyed being alive—the food, the women, but most importantly the process of creating. The only thing that lasts in the afterlife is us. We can't create anything."

"So, you'd take the offer?" I know the Chevalier would salivate if he thought Victor Hugo would join his cause, and I'd much rather bond with him than Napoleon. If it weren't for the little girl sitting in my lap.

Almost all eyes are on Victor, most outraged. He immediately throws up his hands. "No, absolutely not. I believe in the order of things, and what makes living so enjoyable is we know it's fleeting. Besides, I have no wish to go through death again, however it would find me."

I let out a sigh of relief. "So, ignoring leadership, what do you guys think about the ghost commune?" In my opinion, it's a beautiful idea with lots of merit and potential—yes, I'm still lusting after those lost books.

Victor scoffs again. "If they're looking to emulate the Paris Commune from my time, they're nothing but romanticists."

"What's wrong with romanticists?" Émile Zola cries out.

"It was based on a lot of good ideas," Victor continues, not even getting into the dispute, "but reality was—excuse the language—a giant shit hole. No rules, just people screaming, calling everyone idiots, then murdering each other. Don't get me wrong. I wasn't a fan of the government in Versailles either, but the commune was not the way to go. While revolutions are rarely achieved without a fight, violence is no basis for government, and military officers shouldn't be the ones leading the way."

And cue another shouting match. While they talk over each other, Petite Alix turns her face up to me. "Why's everyone so mad?"

"They're not mad," I say, stroking her hair. "They're passionate."

I realise I won't find the answer here, because just like my boys, the ghosts all have different priorities. I understand those who won't accept slander against one of the greatest generals of all times, their former commander. And I understand Victor, Rousseau, and Voltaire, who hold military action in contempt, believing an advanced society should move beyond the tools of war.

But there's not a single period in time free of strife. Conflicts are inbred into the human condition, because we're all different. We all prioritise different things, and some of those are exclusive to each other, which is when it might get ugly. Realising that helps with my decision: the commune is a beautiful concept, but with a trio of ruthless megalomaniacs at the helm, it's bound to serve a nefarious purpose.

What we need is open conversation between the ghosts and living—not just a few select cataphiles—some kind of forum where all their voices can be heard. But how do I convince my fellow living to give the ghosts the time of day they deserve?

I'm still mulling over my thoughts when I pack up and leave the Panthéon. Since it's early July, it's still light outside, with people slowly gathering in the restaurants and coffees along the road. I'm about to text Gaby to see if she'd like to go out for dinner when a familiar figure waves at me. It's the British GoPol researcher.

Dread fills me as I run through the options for what might've brought her here. She's got the biggest smile plastered on her face and seems genuinely happy to see me, which makes me even more suspicious. Sure, she follows me online and comments on every single one of my ghost videos and Malou's posts, but instead of feeling flattered, I feel stalked.

Since she's waiting right next to the fence surrounding the Panthéon, I don't have a choice but to approach.

"So, this is it?" she says, looking up at the Panthéon with wonder. "You keep all your national heroes here in one place?"

"Yes." I open the gate, slip out, and lock it behind me.

Not minding my tight-lipped answer, Flo continues babbling. "I wanted to book your ghost tour, but they're all booked out way in advance. You wouldn't mind giving me a private tour, do you? Paid, of course."

"No, because it would be during my personal time."

Flo looks a little taken aback. "Oh, sorry, I didn't mean now. Just sometime? I'm sticking around for another week or two. Whenever suits you, really."

I unlock my bike, making no notion of inviting Flo along. "I don't do private tours."

Her face falls. "Sorry. Alistair often says I come on too strong."

I have no idea who Alistair is, but he's right. "What do you really want?" I ask with all the bluntness my nationality has blessed me with.

Flo's fingers are twitching and she's shuffling her feet. I'd feel sorry for her if I wasn't so bothered by her presence. Just because I've gone public doesn't mean everyone and their maman can stalk me now. When ghosts do it, I'm fine, but from the living it's just creepy.

"I was just hoping I could meet the heroes of your amazing videos, maybe chat to Marie Curie, catch a fight between Rousseau and Voltaire—the two of them are comedy gold—"

"They're esteemed philosophers, two of the brightest minds the world has ever seen," I snap. Sure, their squabbles can be entertaining but they don't deserve some Brit ridiculing them.

Flo pales and nearly takes a step back. The exuberant energy she came here with has completely evaporated. Still, she finds a half-smile in her. "You're protective of your ghosts. I get that. I'm protective of mine, too."

"I don't see any ghosts around you."

"Yeah... you know how it is. They struggle with leaving their haunting grounds, and most of the ones I hang with have never been to Paris. As for Al, he's helping the GoPol unit here. He's so busy I haven't seen him for two days."

I can't help it. I need to ask. "Who's Al?"

"Al's my brother's whisper ghost. Unlike my brother who's become a bit of a stuck-up ass, Al's still the warm, fuzzy guy he used to be." She smiles when she describes him. "He promised we'd do some fun stuff while we're in Paris, but it's all doom and gloom at the headquarters, so I'm on my own."

"Tell me about it."

I was trying so hard to blow her off, and there she goes and proves me wrong. The way she talks about Al and the rest of ghosts is exactly how I speak about mine. I assume Al's whisperer is the Alistair she mentioned before, the stuck-up GoPol agent who told his sister she was too much for people. The fact she seems more attached to his whisper ghost than the living version of him strangely endears her to me.

With a sigh, I lock the bike again. "Would you like to grab a crêpe from across the street? I'm starving."

Flo's eyes light up. "Yes, please! Gosh, I can't believe I haven't had a crêpe yet. What's the best topping? Should I go for something traditional or fancy?"

"You should go for one you like," I answer, laughing. "Sweet or savoury?" For me, it's a hearty crêpe with ham, spinach, and feta—my favourite.

We're in luck and manage to snatch up a small round table that's just been vacated. I order some wine before I help Flo decide from the many options available, laughing when she chooses both a savoury and sweet crêpe. "You're going to be so full."

"Oh, but they're thin."

"Not with all the toppings."

Flo shrugs and takes a deep sip of her wine, then leans back in her chair. "There's really something magical about this city, isn't there?"

"Well, it's full of ghosts."

She snorts. "So is London. Don't get me wrong, I love ghosts as much as the next girl, but I mean this right here—sitting outside, having dinner with a bunch of strangers around. I mean, the streets are packed. And just over there, the Eiffel Tower, alight." She grabs her phone to snap some pictures.

I smile at the tower, imagining Eiffel tinkering away in his workshop. "You're a researcher, right?"

Flo nods. "Yes. I mean, personally, I'd rather call myself an inventor, but the GRL isn't the greatest fan of my gadgets. Sometimes I can convince Alistair to try one out, and I believe he's still using the ghost tracker I built for him when he first started out, but he'll never admit it. As for the lab, they just want me to run test after test, which leaves me little time to work on my own projects."

Every word out of her mouth leaves me with a million other questions. I have a little more time to think when our plates arrive, all three so big, they completely cover the table.

"Oh, that looks so good!" Flo's eyes are wide with wonder and a little respect. "I didn't know they were going to be so big!"

I laugh. "They're just not folded up like the to-go ones." As we start eating, I tell her, "I hate to break it to you, but if you're an inventor, you would've loved being here in April. The ghosts put together a spectral World Fair, half of which were memories from the 19th century, the other half new ghost technology."

"Was that when you had those glitches? Where the ghosts became visible to everybody else?" Before I even have the chance to answer, she groans, "I *so* wish I could've been there. One, for the phenomenon itself. Two, because what I saw was amazing. So, it was a real fair?"

Between bites, I tell her how Eiffel put the whole thing together and what inventions I remember, leaving Flo bopping on her chair in excitement. "Ghost *puppies*?" she exclaims. "I want one."

"Same. I wish we could've taken one home. But we've already got two hedgehogs and Dix. Speaking of hedgehogs, I think this little lady is getting hungry."

While she'd been in Petite Alix's lap, Malou had napped, kept asleep by endless gentle strokes. Now, I hear her huffing and snuffling in her carry bag. I check whether the waiter is close-by, and when I can't see him, I quickly pull Malou out and put her on my lap, then proceed to feed her scraps from my plate.

"Is that…?" Flo's pitch grows higher as she shuffles her chair around a little to catch a peek. "Oh my god, she's even cuter than online. Can I… Could I take a picture later?"

Appreciating she won't disturb Malou while she's eating, I shrug. "Sure."

Flo continues cooing at Malou, nearly drawing the waiter's attention when he comes by to refill our wine glasses. As soon as he's gone, we catch a sneaky selfie with the lit-up Eiffel Tower in the background before I put Malou back in her bag.

"So, what are you working on at the moment? Not the GoPol stuff—your personal projects." Could Flo conceive something like the Library of the Lost, perhaps?

Impatiently, Flo swallows down the piece of crêpe she's just put in her mouth. "Right now, I'm this close to figuring out how to separate whisperers and whisper ghosts, without harming either."

My stomach falls. That's exactly what the Chevalier's been doing. I'd been carried away by her cheerfulness and exuberance, but she's just like him, without any boundaries, isn't she? "Why?"

"Alright, here's the thing. You know how when GoPol identifies a ghost whisperer, they destroy—" She stops herself, more serious now than before. "Yeah, that face you're making tells me you know exactly what I'm talking about. Now, I know why the number has to be regulated, or at least I sort of understand it, but I've always felt bad for the whisper ghosts. I mean, just imagine: you've just had a near-fatal accident, which is already hugely traumatizing, and then you're basically kidnapped, stuck into a tube and eviscerated. You haven't even realised you're dead yet, then salted from existence." She grimaces at her own wording. "Yes, they're ghosts, and they probably don't feel it, and you could argue they weren't even dead long enough to know any better, but they're still people, right? If someone was going to do that to Al, I would've beaten the shit out of them."

I've got tears in my eyes and they're not sad tears because of the horrible GoPol practices, but tears of joy, because someone else gets it. Someone else cares. Forget the Chevalier. If anyone's going to separate Dix and Sébastien to give Dix a full afterlife, we're going with Flo.

Distracted, she's looking past my shoulder. "Is that one of your ghosts?"

I still don't know how she can see ghosts when she doesn't have a whisper ghost, because sure enough, there's a ghost watching us from the opposite corner. Mathy.

"Excuse me a moment." I put my cutlery down, having mostly finished my crêpe. Then I quickly walk across the street.

Alarmed, Mathy takes a step back. Before I reach him, he flickers, seemingly ready to vanish, but then he stops and actually waits for me. "You didn't have to come over," he says, still in that forced grumpy voice.

"Well, I had to check. Were you spying on me or did you want something?"

"What could I want from someone like you?" he barks, but his bottom lip is quivering.

Well-aware of how this might look to any passers-by, I go down on one knee and ask gently, "Mathy? Are you okay?"

"I'm dead."

"Yes, I know that. Longer than I've been alive." I'm not saying he should be over it—Dix certainly isn't. "When was the last time you were alright?"

He doesn't answer immediately, a million emotions in his eyes. At last, he rolls his shoulders and looks past me. "I'm fine. I'll always be fine. Since I'm dead, you know, it doesn't matter."

"What doesn't matter?" I ask so softly I can barely hear my own words.

"What happens to me," Mathy answers sullenly. Then, after a pregnant pause, "I'm not disposable." For the first time, his anger isn't directed at me but the whisperer who abandoned him.

"No, you're not," I say, quite firmly. What Mathieu did to him is deplorable. I could never. Not like this.

Mathy shrugs. "Doesn't matter. I'm still his." An angry little fold appears between his eyes. "But I don't want to be. If he can get rid of me, why can't I?" His bottom lip is quivering again. "I shouldn't talk to you. He'll hate that."

Nothing binds Mathy to Mathieu anymore. If he wanted, he could strike out on his own, get as far away from him as he can. But he's never been alone. I'm starting to wonder if Mathieu continued to do to Mathy what his abuser did when they were alive. Or whether he was the abuser all along. I certainly wouldn't put it past him, angry and frustrated as he probably was with having such an annoyingly young whisper ghost.

"Listen, Mathy, I'm somewhat of a fairy godmother for ghosts." I probably deserve the critical eyebrow raise I get for that, but instead of amending my words, I smile at him. "Don't laugh. Ghosts come to me with favours—some want their grave site groomed, others want me to find family heirlooms so they won't get lost. I once had to find the fingerbone of a painter to bury it with him, so he could paint in the afterlife." The last one leaves the most impression. "Do you think you'd like me to grant you a favour?" If he asks me to help him get away from Mathieu, I'll do my damn hardest.

Mathy stares at the ground, shoulders drawn up. "You'd do anything?"

"If it's in my power to, then yes."

He shuffles his feet before mumbling something. I need to ask him to repeat it, before I catch what he wants me to do. "Can you help me go home? I want to see my parents."

I wipe an errant tear from my cheek before smiling. "Yes. It might take a while, but yes, I can probably find them."

Mathy raises his chin, doing a valiant attempt of looking unaffected. "Then, that's what I want. If you're really a fairy godmother, prove it. If you're lying..." He never says what terrible things he'll do to me, he just shoots me a glare and vanishes.

More tears make it down my cheeks now he's gone. Looks like I was right about Mathieu being the actual abuser here. What an asshole.

"Wow!"

I whirl around to see Flo behind me, my bag hanging over her arm. She must've paid for our meal before following me. Now she's regarding me with awe.

"I've never seen anyone deal with ghosts that way." She grins at me. "You should talk more about that on your channel, show everyone what you do for them."

"As if anyone cares." My voice is a little stuffy and I clear my throat.

Flo takes my answer in a stride. "Well, I do, and your fans do. But I get what you mean." She smiles. "You need to keep going, though, because I believe that right there, that kind of empathy... that's exactly what the world needs. I might tinker with futuristic gadgets, but you, Alix, you *are* the future."

# CHAPTER 23

While classes have finished for the year, Gaby and I are back at the Sorbonne to collect our results. In the end, Gaby took all her exams one way or the other and she's feeling a lot better.

"I can't believe I passed the industrialisation paper! Last year was so bad," Gaby exclaims.

"I told you."

"Thanks to you!" Gaby hugs me tight, the happiest she's been for ages.

We're walking down the corridor when I see Félice-freak-ing-Humbert coming out of the admin office. "Quick, hide me." I pull Gaby behind a shelf, but it's too late.

"Mademoiselle Dubois!" Félice calls out. "What a surprise!"

Gaby throws me a concerned look, while I grimace. "Is it?"

"Oh yes, I was trying to get some soundbites from your lecturers, but they said they don't do interviews, which is obviously bullshit." Félice positions herself so she's blocking Gaby and me in the corner I was trying to hide in. "But I'm glad I met you. I was hoping for another interview." Leaning in, she says, "A juicier one."

"Juicier?" Gaby asks. "I thought you were a serious journalist." She's quickly picked up who Félice is.

Félice shrugs. "I just want the inside scoop, and juicy sells. Not that I have to explain myself to you. I just need to talk to Alix."

Gaby crosses her arms, half stepping in front of me. "You can't just stalk people and force them to talk to you."

"Besides," I add, "Don't you already have all the inside scoop you need? I saw you cosying up to Mathieu in the catacombs."

"Ew." Gaby pulls a face. "Isn't that the creep who hates you for no reason?"

If Félice is bothered by this, she doesn't show. "Mathieu was very talkative, true!" Her eyes lit up. "And he told me a lot about you, which I could print, of course, but I thought I'd give you a chance to tell your side of the story."

She's bordering on blackmail—again—and I think we all know it. Time to call her bluff. "I'm sure he had nothing but nice things to say about me."

"He called you some kind of stupid ghost activist," Félice spills without missing a beat, "and judging by your new online presence that seems to hit the mark. So, I want to know. Why ghosts? Why are you so passionate about them? Is it just from a historical point of view? Because, apparently, the department thinks it's all hogwash and no professor will debase themselves publicly coming out in favour of ghosts. I assume—"

"Way too much!" Gaby cuts in. "She doesn't want to talk to you, so take the hint and leave her alone!"

Félice raises an eyebrow before crossing her arms and sneering at me. "Fine, you want to do this the hard way: give me a good story or I'll make sure everyone knows about your ghost boyfriend, most importantly his parents. From everything I've read about the du Charbonneaus lately, I don't think they'll appreciate you defiling their only son's memory."

She knows Gaspar's identity. Of course she does. The Chevalier knows, which means Mathieu probably knows as well, and of course he'd have all kinds of feelings about me *dating* a ghost.

"Aren't you worried about losing every ounce of credibility?" Gaby asks, while I'm too stunned to speak. "That won't even be good enough for gossip rags."

"It wouldn't be good for Alix here, either," Félice says promptly.

Just then, someone clears their throat behind her. "Do I need to call security, or will you leave the campus on your own, Mademoiselle Humbert?" I've never heard Madame Canet address someone so sharply. "We don't appreciate the press hounding our students." She looks past Félice at us and nods towards her office. "Mademoiselles Dubois and Lemel, if I could have a chat with you in my office?"

"Gladly." Gaby and I jostle Félice aside, who still won't budge, and rush down the corridor.

"You've got three days to get back to me, or I'll go to the du Charbonneaus!" she calls after me.

I'm amazed she's giving me any time at all. I don't know if Félice was always so asinine or if hanging with Mathieu has turned her attitude up a notch, but I need to talk to my father to see if there's anything he can do before she ruins my life.

"Du Charbonneau?" Madame Canet asks as she ushers us into her office. "Isn't that the family of the sociology student who died last year?"

Exhausted, I drop into one of the chairs in front of her desk. "Yes. He's... a friend."

She grabs a pot of coffee from a mini kitchen and three cups before settling in her chair. "I'm sorry. I didn't know you two were acquainted."

"Oh, no, we weren't. I met him as a ghost."

"Right," she says, her voice a little tense. "How is he?" Shaking her head, she laughs a little. "Is that even something you ask?"

Gaby smiles warmly at her. "It definitely is. And as for Gaspar, well..." I throw Gaby a panicked look and she giggles. "He's good. In fact, he was lucky to have Alix at his side to help him transition. These days, he's happily hanging with the Panthéon ghosts or exploring the catacombs." Now she throws me a look, letting me fill the gaps with what else Gaspar is doing these days.

I fight down the blush and sink a little deeper into the chair. "A lot has happened since he died."

Madame Canet pours some coffee and hands us the cups. "Well, I'll let campus security know to keep an eye out on this so-called journalist. We may be on holiday now, but we can't have reporters harassing students and staff. You might want to think about taking legal action."

I definitely will if this continues—between my father and Sébastien's GoPol contacts, we can probably get her blackballed pretty quickly. While that might prevent a PR nightmare, it won't prevent her from going to Gaspar's parents and upsetting them greatly with her half-truths. There's only one thing that'll help in that regard, and that's for me to come clean before she does so.

"Anyway, let's put Madame Humbert aside for now," Madame Canet says. She leans over her table on her elbows. "I've actually been watching your videos since we last spoke and I'm obsessed."

Gaby grins wildly. "Told you."

"Obsessed?" I ask nervously.

Madame Canet nods, a twinkle in her eyes. "I've already learnt so much about ghosts from them, and of course, the Panthéon videos are a historian's dream."

"So, you believe me?"

"Well, I believed you last time, but yes. I mean, if you made all that up, I'd still give you credit, because you've got those peers down to a notch. And I know you're a bright student, Alix, but I don't think you're an expert at philosophy with a chemistry degree and creative writing course under your belt."

I laugh out loud when she puts it like that. While I've certainly picked up a lot through my interactions with the Panthéon ghosts, I'm in no way an expert, especially for anything that comes out of Marie Curie's mouth.

"This is all very exciting," Madame Canet continues. "There has to be some kind of verification process, but being able to talk to primary sources will turn the whole world of history upside down."

"I know, right!" Gaby exclaims excitedly. "We can solve so many mysteries, right old wrongs, and open up completely new perspectives. No more history will be written by the winners."

"It'll still be written by them, but it could be annotated by the losers in the future," I muse.

Madame Canet chuckles. "That's a good one. I like it." She picks up her coffee cup and leans back in her chair. "Now, I was actually planning to call you in, so good you're here anyway. As I said, I've been devouring all your content and can't wait for the next videos, and it got me thinking about everything you've said—and wrote last year. So, I started reaching out to people to see if I could find out who'd be able to take a look at the catacombs' situation. I can't promise anything, but I might at least get you in front of a decision maker to plead your case. It'll probably be a lengthy process, so don't expect results soon, but maybe as awareness grows, we'll be able to shut them down."

I sit in my chair with awe, completely forgetting the warm cup in my hand and nearly telling Madame Canet I want to marry her. In the end, I go with the slightly less creepy, "You're officially my favourite teacher."

She laughs. "I expect to be in the acknowledgements of your master's thesis. In fact, I actually expect to be on the title page as your supervisor. We could work something out with the catacombs and give you a scientific leg to stand on. If that's something you're interested in."

Gaby looks as if she's nearly exploding with glee, while I can't fight off the grin. I open my mouth, but Gaby bursts out first, "Yes! Yes, she wants to do that. One hundred per cent."

Guess I just found my master's thesis.

# CHAPTER 24

My head is buzzing with ideas for my master's thesis proposal. There's nothing I'd love to do more than spend the rest of the afternoon working out a killer project and dream about how much ghost stuff I can get away with. Madame Canet's support means everything to me. She's always been one of my favourite teachers since she values out-of-the-box thinking and new perspectives and isn't afraid to shake up the world a little—or a lot in this case.

Unfortunately, there are more pressing matters to deal with, and my thesis has to wait. Félice's visit has rattled me more than I wish to admit. She probably doesn't have much of a leg to stand on, but that doesn't mean she can't make life harder for me—if that's even possible.

As soon as I get off the bike, I call my father and tell him what happened. "That's illegal," he says before I'm halfway through my tale. "You can't use blackmail to extort information." He groans and I know he's rubbing his face in frustration. "See, that's why I don't like this woman—the job is all about building relationships, not stalking and blackmailing people until they give you a sound-bite. If she publishes anything, you can sue her."

"Well, she built *one* relationship." I tell him all about her and Mathieu as I take the stairs to the apartment. Holding the phone between my shoulder and my cheek, I search for my keys and open the door. "Can't you do something about it? Like blackball her?"

"Not until she's actually published something. I mean, you could try the police, see if you can get a restraining order…"

I snort. "As if that'll magically keep her away."

"Or you could tell Séb and see if GoPol wants to put a block out. They should, since she's threatening to blow your NDA wide open. Plus, they actually have the power to do these things."

"It feels a little overkill"—I kick off my shoes and drop my bag on the drawers—"like I'm cheating or something."

Papa snorts. "She's been *threatening* you!"

"Who's threatening you?" Gaspar appears in front of me so suddenly, I give a little start.

I hold up a finger and end the call. "Fine, fine, I'll mention it to Séb. Thanks, Papa."

Gaspar grimaces at the mention of Sébastien, and I suppress a sigh. Though I've made up with both, they haven't forgiven each other yet, not even after I told Sébastien about Molay's spell.

Stowing the phone away, I lean forward to give him a quick kiss before I explain. "Félice Humbert has been bothering me again. Apparently, Mathieu told her about us, and now she's found out who you really are and is threatening to tell your parents if I don't give her another candid interview."

"That's all she's got? There's nothing wrong with our relationship." He slips his arms around my waist and pulls me to him.

"I'd say it's pretty unconventional, but…"—I miss a breath when he kisses my neck—"it's not wrong, I agree."

"Good." Gaspar purrs, sending little vibrations across my skin.

I put my hands on his chest to gain a little distance and try to remember what I was talking about. It comes back fairly quickly. "However, do you really want your parents to find out from Félice?"

"They wouldn't believe her."

"Wouldn't they?" I somehow doubt his mum wouldn't at least question it after hiring me to find her son. He leans in to resume his kisses, but I put a finger on his lips. "Think about it. Imagine Félice telling your parents. How would they feel about it? What would they do?"

Gaspar leans his forehead on my collar bone and groans softly. "They'd come after you. Sue you or some bullshit." Looking up, he falls into a rant, "Which they won't win, because the world is still very sceptical about ghosts, and neither they nor Félice have any evidence. So, it's a moot point."

He's probably right about that. I don't see any judge ruling in their favour. Heck, there are no ghost laws, so how could I have broken any? "It's probably better if I return the money. Just tell your maman I can't find you." I haven't touched a single cent yet because of how dirty it makes me feel.

Gaspar frowns at me. "No! You deserve that money."

"For what?"

"You found me," he quips. "Nine months ago." Cheekily, he steals another kiss.

I swoon a little and wrap my arms around him, pulling him closer. For a few precious moments, we put all thoughts of Félice and his parents aside and just revel in the intimacy. He found me as much as I found him.

Then, Gaspar pulls away, frowning again. "Let's get it over with."

"Let's get it—" My eyes widen. "Wait! Do you mean...?"

"Yes, let's tell them you've found me. We have a quick chat and then we get the hell out of there and never deal with them again."

I don't think it's going to be that quick and easy, but it's a start. I lean in for another kiss when the door opens and Sébastien walks in. Looking over my shoulder, I see him hesitate for a moment, but then he lowers his gaze and walks past us, as if we aren't standing right there in the middle of the hallway. I watch him enter the bathroom and lock the door behind him. A moment later, the shower runs, signalling he won't be out for a while.

"Can't you two make up already?" I sigh. Their quarrel's hurting me in a way I never thought possible. Gaspar took such great care of Sébastien when he got hurt and during recovery. They love each other, if not exactly the same way the way they love me. "Maybe if you apologised…" It was him who got us all in this mess, after all.

"He wouldn't accept it," Gaspar says, which isn't quite the same as outright refusing to do so.

"It'd be a start." I look deep into his eyes, trying to warm his heart a little. "Please."

When Gaspar looks away, I know the rift is even deeper than I thought. Heartbroken, I hug him tight and try to hold back the tears building in my eyes. *Small wins*, I tell myself. *Let's repair one relationship first before we tackle the next.*

When I told Gaspar's mother I'd found him, she wanted to come by immediately. It would've been too much too soon, so I talked her into meeting at her place the next day. But judging by Gaspar's face now, he wishes he could take his consent back, but it's too late; he'd never leave me high and dry. I squeeze his hand to show him I'll be with him every step of the way, then let go and ring the doorbell.

Within seconds, the door's ripped open. "Gaspar?" Madame du Charbonneau is always so well put together that the wild eyes and heavy breathing make her look like an entirely different person. There're even stray hairs falling into her face, as if she's run to the door.

Gaspar squares his shoulders and steps inside. "Hello, Maman."

"He's here," I say, vaguely gesturing in his direction.

Madame du Charbonneau squints, but I know no matter how hard she tries, she won't see him. Disappointment washes over her face moments before she plasters a fake smile on. "Sorry, I'm forgetting my manners. Hello, Mademoiselle Dubois. Would you like to come inside? I've got coffee prepared."

"Of course."

Gaspar looks longingly at the door when it closes behind me. Then, hands buried in his hoodie, he follows his mother to the living room.

"I was surprised when you texted last night," Madame du Charbonneau says. "I didn't expect you to yield results this fast, but I guess you really *are* the expert."

"He was easy enough to find... given all the information," I add hastily.

To my surprise, Madame du Charbonneau isn't alone today. When we enter the living room, a harsh-looking, balding man stands near the coffee table, adjusting the cuffs on his immaculate suit. He sneers at me the moment I enter his space. Gaspar tenses and for a moment it looks as if he's going to bolt.

"May I introduce you to my father?" he says with a scathing tone.

"Monsieur du Charbonneau, I assume?" I try for a smile, but it dries up the moment his contemptuous gaze hits my outstretched hand.

His wife puts herself between us, with enough smiles for all of us. "Oh, yes. This is Gaspar's father. When I told him you found our son, he wanted to be here. Even cancelled an important meeting."

"What a fucking honour," Gaspar says, a reply I'll keep to myself.

"I'm just here so I can look this fraud in the eyes and tell her to stop fucking with my family." Looks like I've found out where Gaspar's angry potty mouth comes from. This is going to be fun. "Using people's grief to make cash is something only the most deplorable people will do."

"Henri, please!" Madame du Charbonneau pleads. "I did my research. Mademoiselle Dubois is no impostor."

Then why have I been riddled with impostor syndrome's ever since she turned up on my doorstep?

Monsieur du Charbonneau snorts derisively. "How would we know? Anyone can claim to talk to ghosts. She's just another of these Gen-Z influencers, trying to make quick money by hopping on trends and exploiting other people."

"Look, if it's about the money, I was planning on returning it anyway—"

"See!" Monsieur du Charbonneau flings a hand in my direction. "Now that she's caught, she's backpedalling."

I clap my hands over my mouth, startling, when Gaspar walks up to his father and punches him straight in the face. "Gaspar!"

Fortunately—or unfortunately—his punch goes through his father's body without even upsetting a single remaining hair on his head. All it achieves is his parents are now staring at me in confusion.

"Oh, is that's how it's going to be?" Monsieur du Charbonneau says. "You're going to put on a little act?"

Horrified, I stare at him. "No! I... I just..." I can't really tell him his dead son just tried to punch him on my behalf.

Meanwhile, Gaspar's shouting, "You shut your damn mouth! It was Maman who sought Alix out, not the other way around."

In a display of absurd ignorance, Madame du Charbonneau has moved to the coffee table and is pouring coffee into the three waiting cups. An assortment of treats have been laid out. "How about we hold off the accusations and sit down to chat? She's found him, Henri," she says in such blissful relief.

Monsieur du Charbonneau huffs. "Of course she has. And so fast!" His face turns into an angry grimace. "Because she's fucking making it up!" Surprisingly, his voice softens, "Sophie, I know you wish this were true. We both grieve for Gaspar."

"Yeah, sure you do," Gaspar shoots back. Useless arms crossed, he's resorted to glowering.

"But talking to hacks like this won't bring him back. There's no such thing as ghosts, and there's certainly no such thing as a ghost *whisperer*. Can't you see how she's scamming you?"

I wish they'd had this talk before I got here. I'm trying really hard to be sympathetic—of course, not everyone will believe me. I probably wouldn't believe myself either—but that doesn't mean it doesn't hurt being accused of tricking a poor grieving woman out of her money. The money she paid me is *so* going back. "Maybe, I should just go," I say softly.

Monsieur du Charbonneau whirls around, immediately flying off the handle again. "Yes, maybe you *should*! Or maybe I should call the police and inform them about your little scheme."

"You'd be surprised about the police's response," I can't help but say.

"What was that?"

"Oh, that was good," Gaspar applauds. "Get Sébastien here and let him handle this guy."

As happy as it makes me to hear him thoughtlessly turning to Sébastien for help, I don't think it'll help my situation. I try to project calm instead. "Monsieur du Charbonneau, I understand how hard this is to believe. For the longest time, even I thought it was all in my head, but it's not. Ghosts are real, and I can truly see them, and right now, your son is standing over there, ready to talk to you."

"You think I'd tell them anything?" Gaspar asks, laughing in disbelief.

Madame du Charbonneau's eyes are growing big. The desire to speak with her son is practically oozing from her eyes. She believes me, not because I've proven myself trustworthy, but because she *needs* this to work. And even though, I haven't lied to her, apart from the bit about not knowing Gaspar, I feel bad.

"Please sit," she begs.

Her husband is shaking his head. "No. No, I won't let you pull wool over our eyes. You think you're so clever with your little acting chops and that platform you've built, but we're not falling for it. And if my son really were a ghost, he'd do anything to stay away from this place. I know him. He'd rather run off to a party or one of his illegal concerts than take responsibility."

"Responsibility?" Gaspar repeats, outraged. "Now, it was my responsibility to stay alive, or what? Oh, fuck this, I'm going." He strides off before I even get another word in.

"Gaspar, wait!"

Not minding his parents, I run after Gaspar as he strides into the corridor. Instead of walking out the door, he heads upstairs, and I know exactly where he's going. Half a minute later, I join him in the music room, where he swipes his arm across the pile of scoresheets on top of the piano. Only the top piece of paper gently sails down to the floor.

"I hate him!" he exclaims loudly. "I fucking *hate* that man!" Tears of anger—and maybe something else—are gathering in his eyes. "He has no right to talk to you like that! And of course, I'm the horrible son who won't ever come visit his parents." He throws his hands in the air, a terribly desperate smile on his face. "I mean he's right—I didn't want to come here. I never wanted to see him again." Angrily, he wipes tears from his cheeks. "It's like I can never do anything right, even in death. I'm still the enfant terrible, the traitor son, the black sheep, just because I don't buy into their performative bullshit. I—"

Unable to listen to him any longer, I rush over and sling my arms around his middle, hugging him tight, while tears run down my face. "I'm sorry I brought you here," I whisper. "You said over and over again how you didn't want to come. I just thought it would help you and maybe your mother—I'm sorry. I should've listened to you."

Giving into his tears, Gaspar returns the hug and buries his face in my heart, soaking in my presence.

Just then, I hear someone clearing their throat behind me. Alarmed, I tear away from Gaspar and find myself face to face with his mother.

Madame du Charbonneau is in the doorway, holding onto it as if she'd fall otherwise. Her face looks more ghostly than Gaspar ever did. "What's going on here?"

# Chapter 25

My heart's pounding in my chest as I follow Madame du Charbonneau back downstairs. I have no idea how to explain this. It's just so weird. I mean, these are Gaspar's parents, and they can't even hear it from him. If it were me, I'd throw myself out, too.

Gaspar stays by my side and this time he won't let go of my hand, determined to prove his presence to his parents. "Just tell them the truth," he says. "If they get it, fine. If not, you don't have to see them ever again."

But I'd still be the one dealing with the fallout.

We return to the living room where his father is on the couch at last, drinking his coffee. Madame du Charbonneau takes a seat next to him and puts her hand on his thigh in order to stay him. I awkwardly sit opposite them, while Gaspar takes place on the armrest of my chair, watching his father sullenly. Nervously, I reach for the coffee and take a sip.

"What is she still doing here?" Monsieur du Charbonneau asks, his aggressiveness dialled down a little but not by much.

"I believe her," his wife says. Grief no longer controls her features, and her voice won't allow any protest. "I saw her with him."

He raises an eyebrow. "You *saw* Gaspar?"

Madame du Charbonneau tucks a strand behind her ear. "No, of course not, but I saw her interacting with him in a way you simply can't do on your own."

"What's *that* supposed to mean?" her husband asks, now even more suspicious. I can't blame him. That made it sound way worse than what we did.

"We hugged," I tell him before he gets the wrong idea—to be fair, we've done the wrong idea and more, but hopefully I won't have to confess to that today.

Gaspar rubs my back. "Do you want me to lift up your hair or something like that to prove my presence?"

I shake my head and take a deep breath. "Alright, I think it's time for me to come clean."

"High time," Monsieur du Charbonneau says.

"I didn't want to take this job. It's not something I normally do, because messages from the beyond are rarely well-received." Case in point. "But also, because I already knew Gaspar. In fact, he was right beside me when you first came to my apartment." My hands are shaking I'm that nervous. "It felt wrong to take the money—and you can have it back, really. I don't want it. Gaspar insisted I take it, but it just doesn't feel right."

"Damn right it doesn't," his father growls, but his mother intensifies her grip on his leg.

Sharply, she demands, "Let her speak."

I rub my hands together, then push them between my knees to keep them still. "I met your son the day he died. I wasn't very good at recognising ghosts then—I mean, some are obvious, others not so much."

"I didn't even realise I was dead myself," Gaspar adds.

"He says, he didn't really realise he was dead, either. It takes some time to wrap your head around it. Anyway, to cut a long story short, we hit it off, hung out a bit—eventually, I found out he was a ghost—and here we are. Friends. We're friends."

"Ouch," he says, but I hear from his voice he's not being serious.

Madame du Charbonneau nods, her face still stony. "You said upstairs he didn't want to come today." It's almost impossible to detect the hurt in her voice.

Deflating, I throw a forlorn glance at Gaspar. "He didn't. I thought it'd be good for him to reconnect with you, but there's a lot of... hurt."

Laughing softly, Monsieur du Charbonneau shakes his head. "This is ridiculous. You not only admit to taking advantage of us, but now you're adding insult to injury? What's going on in that sick mind of yours?"

Gaspar glares at him before dictating to me what he wants me to tell his father. "You hadn't seen Gaspar for six months before his death. The last time was at the dinner you threw for his birthday. It was cut short, because the two of you got into a fight about Gaspar's studies. You'd come across a great job that would've seen him earning good money within five years, you'd used your connections to all but guarantee the position for him, all he had to do was give up his stupid little degree."

"Did you tell her that?" Monsieur du Charbonneau asks his wife, still angry, but a little unsettled by the detail.

While Madame du Charbonneau shakes her head, I say, "No, she didn't, because"—I hate this, but I stay true to Gaspar's whispers—"she likes to hide the ugly things. I only heard about all the successes and great things he did before he rebelled—and by the way, no, he never took drugs."

His mother lets out a funny little sigh of relief, but then the pain returns to her face and I'm aware I've put it there.

"I'm not usually in the business of calling out people. Every family has their problems and this one's no business of mine. I'm just repeating what Gaspar's saying."

"And I'm sorry I'm making you go through this, but it's the only way to get through to these thickheads. Sometimes you have to play a little dirty to unearth the real issues," Gaspar murmurs.

"I know." With a deep sigh I continue. "Test me if you must. I don't have skin in this game, but Gaspar does. And I think you have this amazing chance to reconnect and reevaluate your relationship. If you're open to that, I'm happy to help. For free."

Gaspar snorts. "They should pay you."

"No, it wouldn't be right."

"Okay, I admit it, you're good," Monsieur du Charbonneau says. He crosses his arms and sits back, regarding me with a frown. "You mentioned his birthday party. What did I tell him before he left?"

Expectantly, I look up to Gaspar. He seems a bit lost, staring at his father. Then he swallows. "Does he really want me to repeat that?"

"What was it?"

"That if I don't take this job, if I embarrass him in front of his friend just to continue with a social degree, I shouldn't bother re-turning home. That I'm not his son anymore." His voice is shaking slightly in the end. "I shouldn't have come."

I put my hand on his to keep him here, sensing—or rather *hoping*—there's more to this line of questioning. Maybe it's some sort of self-punishment. As I repeat Gaspar's words, I feel them cut into my own skin. Even if it was in the heat of the moment, you should never tell a child something like that.

Madame du Charbonneau stares at her husband, as if she's seeing him for the first time. "You didn't," she whispers.

His father folds his hands in front of his face and looks inward. All that aggressiveness has left for good. After a long while, he nods. "Yeah, I did." Rubbing his eyes, he takes a deep, shuddering breath before vaguely looking in my direction. "I'm sorry. I... There's no excuse for what I said. Or did. I should've never tried to jump that offer on you."

Gaspar stares at him for the longest time. Then some of the tension goes out of him and he makes me relay, "It's okay. I was never going to work in either field, anyway."

Though I feel tempted to edit his words to take some of the sting out, I can't. He's putting his trust in me.

"Well, for what it's worth," his father says, "I'd rather have you alive and well than in a job you'd hate. It's not worth it. None of it is worth it." He rubs his face, looking up to the ceiling, which is about as emotional as he'll likely ever allow himself to get.

Madame du Charbonneau takes his hand and squeezes it, before addressing me. "It hurts to realise you've done everything wrong and there's no chance to right it. Or maybe there is?" she adds, hopeful, while tears gather in her eyes.

Gaspar looks quite overwhelmed, as well. He's let go of this wall he'd built, and there's a hunger in his eyes, the yearning for an actual heart-to-heart without me as the in-between, for one last hug, one last "I love you".

"That's the beautiful thing about the ghosts," I say softly. "They're not really gone. As long as we remember them, they'll be here, and they see us and hear us. They'll know." I throw another glance at Gaspar, who has tears running down his cheeks now. "He knows you love him, I promise."

A ravaging sob tears from his mother's throat, and she clamps down on her mouth to stifle it, while his father grimaces, as if in pain.

I feel so sorry for them, so ill-equipped to truly foster this connection between parents and son, so inadequate for this task. And yet, I'm all they'll ever have of Gaspar again, and I promise myself I'll cherish this task and help grow this connection for as long as they live.

Everyone's feelings are too raw that day, but I tell them a little about what Gaspar's doing with his afterlife—which is considerably hard without mentioning his temporary resurrection, the Chevalier, or what's going on with Napoleon—and agree to come back some other time for more stories. It wasn't a terribly long meeting, but I feel mentally exhausted when we leave the house.

And so does Gaspar. I see him rubbing his face several times before I decide to gently nudge him. "You okay?"

"Yeah... Surprisingly, I think I am."

My heart flows out to him and I hug him, ignoring the fact we're out on the street. "I'm glad you gave it a shot."

He puts an arm around my shoulders and kisses my head. "I'm glad you pushed me. You were right. I needed that... A little. Maybe a lot. We'll see."

Smiling up at him, I give him another hug before letting go. "They're both flawed, but they *do* love and miss you."

"Yeah," he says with a big sigh. "I guess I'm not perfect, either."

"To me, you are."

Gaspar laughs and it's like watching the sun dawn on his face. Some of the darkness that's kept a hold on him ever since he returned to me has lifted. "You don't count. You see the best in everyone." Swallowing, he adds, "Dead or alive."

I shrug. "Not everyone. I can't support the commune."

As wondrous as it was to see ghosts and living come together to rebuild the past and create something new, I can't ignore the underlying threat.

He sobers immediately and nods. "I know. I don't think I can, either."

My eyes widen. "Really?"

"It's too good to be true," he says, with a tortured grimace. "I got carried away by the future the Chevalier promised and the energy down there, but Séb... I guess he's right. I mean, I know he is. They're planning more than a peaceful commune. I was so focused on the dream I ignored what it'll likely take to get there. We both know the Chevalier and Napoleon—and certainly Molay—will do whatever it takes to achieve their goals. I don't want anyone to get hurt—dead or living. I'm not a monster." His voice shakes on the last word. "Not anymore."

I squeeze his hands and stare into his eyes, making sure I hold him there. "You're not a monster, you just yearn for a better world. I'm the same. It just... It just takes time, I guess. Making the world better won't happen in a day. Every change in history was part of a longer process—that's why you never really know when you've lived through a historic event until you've also lived through the consequences."

"So, you're saying, we're just impatient?"

Throwing my head back, I laugh out loud. "Oh, yes, very much so. I mean, come on, world, it can't take that long to accept ghosts and completely restructure everything."

Gaspar grins. "Seriously, what's up with that?"

Our merriment is interrupted when my phone rings with the tune I've assigned to Sébastien. Usually, we text throughout the day, so for him to ring, it must be important. "What's up?" I greet, while Gaspar shuffles his feet.

"I've found Mathieu," Sébastien says. "Meaning, I've found out who he is, and who his parents are, and where they live. Or rather, where one lives, and where the other's buried."

# CHAPTER 26

I never considered one of Mathieu's parents might be dead. I wonder if he even knows. According to Sébastien's sleuthing, Mathieu had a troubled childhood. He found the accident that made him a ghost whisperer and it's exactly as gut-churning as I feared: beaten within an inch of his life by an abusive father. His mother left him initially, but after his release—he was given ridiculously little time—she took him back. Abuse is complex and I'm trying not to blame her. Who knows what hold he had over her? Mathieu, however, didn't last long. At fifteen, he ran away and eventually found himself in the catacombs. There are no further records of him. As for his mother? She took one too many sleeping pills a few years later.

It sucks his father is still alive to abuse others—he's even got a new family these days—just as it sucks that instead of getting help, Mathieu continued the cycle of abuse by becoming an absolute shithead and taking it out on his little whisper ghost, only to abandon him for an even bigger abuser when the time came.

But today, we get to make a little magic happen, the kind only the ghost world is capable of.

Luckily for me, Mathieu's mother's buried on Père Lachaise where she's been welcomed with open arms; she escaped in death what she couldn't escape in life. I'm in no way saying suicide is the solution—it's really not—but with the afterlife being what it is, people get a second chance. She's found a supportive tribe, one that allowed her to move on and heal and build a whole new life. There's only one thing missing.

"My maman died?" Mathy asks, in a strange mix of horror and hope. "She's here?"

I get it. It's not easy to hear a relative has died, but this allows me to do more than I'd promised. Instead of helping him see his parents, he gets to actually reunite with one.

Sébastien and Dix have come along to see the result of their excellent sleuthing. Sébastien got the data, and Dix checked Père Lachaise and prepared Mathy's maman for his visit. I came straight from Gaspar's parents, which means he's with me, too. Despite having changed his opinion about the Chevalier's dream, he hasn't yet hashed it out with Sébastien, and there's this weird tension between them. They both talk to me but completely ignore each other. Dix looks about as over the whole thing as I feel.

Mathy seems concerned. We're still standing at the gates of Père Lachaise, where I summoned him. His bottom lip is quivering. "Does she even want to see me?"

He probably doesn't have many memories of her choosing him over his father. As an adult, I know she was a victim, too, but to little Mathy, the pain of doubt will always be there. Especially after having been conditioned to believe he doesn't deserve her love by his older self.

"Oh, yes," Dix says. "When I told her, she started crying immediately, then she pleaded to lead her to you. Your mother wants you."

It's nearly undetectable, but I know my broken boys well, and there's pain in Dix's response. His mother never truly cared for him, least of all his whisper ghost side.

Mathy throws a fearful glance at me. "Will you come?"

I smile. "Of course. Look! You've got all four of us here with you. If at any point you feel like calling it off, that's okay, too. We won't judge. We're here for you." I wonder if I should offer to hold his hand, but he'd probably scoff.

He nods decisively. "Alright. Let's go see her."

My grandmother and Beatrice are waiting not too far down the path, falling into step with me as we start walking. "It's a wonderful thing you're doing, love. Clarice has been running around telling everyone her son is coming to visit today. I don't think I've ever seen her this happy, not even at poker night when she won the whole pot."

"What kind of pot?" I ask, amused. I've noticed Mathy's listening intently, hungry for any information about his mother, while I just want to know what ghosts have to gamble.

Beatrice cackles. "Flowers. She's getting all the grave flowers for a whole month. Her grave will look more decked out than Jim Morrison's."

"She rarely gets flowers, so I can't be mad about it," my grandmother says. I mentally make a notice to occasionally place flowers on Clarice's grave in the future. "But that bluff. Damn it, that hurt. What a poker face."

Mathy giggles, a sound I haven't heard from him before. He's such a tough little guy, but beneath that hard exterior, he's just a boy, yearning and deserving of love.

I catch Sébastien's gaze and see he's moved as well. This case probably hits home in a different way for him. Let's make sure we give Mathy the happy ending Sébastien and Dix never got.

More and more ghosts line the paths, pointing at Mathy and whispering to the point where his face sours. "What are they looking at?"

"They're excited to see you."

"Why?" he asks, incredulous, as if it'd never occurred to him *anyone* would be happy to see *him*.

"Because we've heard so much about Clarice's sweet little boy," my grandmother says with a big smile. "Your mother loves you so much."

Mathy stops short, the tremor of his bottom lip spreading to his whole body. "No, she doesn't. She doesn't care about me. She never did."

I put my hands on his shoulder and crouch to look into his eyes. "That's a lie, Mathy. You were told lies. If she didn't care, do you think everyone here would be so happy to see you? Your maman loves you, even if she wasn't strong enough to protect you back then. She might not be strong enough now, either, but *you* are."

Tears run down his face through the cracks in his mask. "I'm not strong, either. If I were, he wouldn't have replaced me."

"That's because he's an idiot," Dix says bluntly. "Whisperers can be idiots sometimes."

"Yeah, because whisper ghosts are always *so* mature," Sébastien mutters, eliciting a snort from Gaspar. If Sébastien notices, he doesn't let it show.

Mathy, however, has found a smile. "He's a pretty big idiot for letting me go."

"Oh yes, the biggest idiot," I agree full-heartedly, then offer him my hand. "Shall we go meet your maman now?"

Mathy looks at my hand as if considering all the traps I might've laid for him. I half-expect him to shrug it off, but then he grabs it, though he looks away embarrassed.

I don't comment, just hold his hand with enough pressure to let him know I'm there. We continue our way, climbing up the hill now, when a cry rises out of the crowd ahead of us.

"Mathy!" A woman with flowing blond hair and a flower crown bursts onto the path.

And just like that, Mathy lets go of my hand and runs towards her. Throwing himself in her arms, he cries even harder. All the feelings he's held in for so many decades come pouring out as his mother swirls him around, laughing and crying at the same time.

Next to me, I hear Sébastien take a shuddering breath. A tear's running down his face as well, and I grab his hand and lean against his shoulder, quite moved myself. Though I see ghosts reunite all the time, it always hits the same. How anyone can say the dead no longer feel anything is beyond me.

Mathy and his mother look like they're never going to let go of each other again. When he's eventually stopped crying, he rattles down everything he ever did in a big messed-up jumble, while his mother listens patiently, repeatedly stroking his hair or kissing his face. Then she turns and introduces him to her cemetery friends, who are all delighted to meet him. There's so much love pouring at him, Mathy won't ever feel unloved again.

"Do you think he can stay here?" Sébastien asks softly. "At Père Lachaise?"

"I don't see why not," Dix says. "Mathieu might be a horrible guy, but he did one good thing for the boy. He could've left him to rot, like what happened to Ollie. Instead, he's given Mathy his freedom."

There's a big pause after that, and I know even though Dix may not have intended it, it's hurting Sébastien. So much so, he says at last, "If you want, we can still go to the Chevalier."

"No!" Dix scoffs. "Absolutely not. You're not going to get rid of me that easily."

"You just said—"

"There may be another way," I interrupt before they can fight about it. "Flo told me she's working on an ethical way of separating whisper ghosts from their whisperers."

Sébastien arches an eyebrow. "Flo? Ah, Florence, Alistair's little sister. He told me she's a bit of a genius."

"Maybe he should tell her that sometimes," I say pointedly. It figures Sébastien's dealt with Alistair. Flo mentioned he and his whisper ghost had been kept busy, just like Sébastien and Dix. "Anyway, we were talking about her research plans, and that was one of them. You might get your freedom, Dix, without endangering Séb or yourself."

"I don't want..." Dix mumbles so much I can only guess the rest of the sentence. He absolutely wants his freedom—and to last longer than Sébastien's lifespan.

"That's good!" Suddenly, Mathy appears in front of us again. His mother's behind him, holding his shoulders while softly smiling down at him. Mathy, however, looks serious. "You can't go to the Chevalier for a separation. Once you're down there, he'll bind you to another of Napoleon's generals. That's what he's been doing to the GoPol officers they caught. But he doesn't always bother to separate them properly first, only if he thinks they make a better bargaining chip."

I feel the blood drain from my face and freeze in my veins as I hear his chilling words. When I saw the two resurrected generals, I figured the GoPol agents had been tempted to join the Chevalier, not that they'd been forcefully separated from their counterparts.

"What happens with the whisperers afterwards?" Sébastien asks, his voice not betraying a single emotion.

"He keeps them locked up in his lab for further experiments," Mathy says with the kind of coldness he's acquired over the years at Mathieu's side. He nods. "If you want, I'll tell you everything I know."

Looks like Mathieu really *was* an idiot when he replaced his whisper ghost with Molay.

# CHAPTER 27

Mathy's information sends everyone into a frenzy. Not only did he confirm the Chevalier's been *kidnapping* and separating whisperers from their whisper ghosts by force, but he's also told us he's conspiring with Napoleon and Molay to raise an army of the dead and march on the Places of Power in order to secure his commune. GoPol is ready to go to war, and thanks to my earlier visit to the Chevalier's headquarters, I get to lead the charge—or at least, I'm invited to the strategy meeting.

Sébastien warned me there'd be many important people at the meeting, people I should have no business meeting. I walk into the room at his side and feel immediately intimidated by the amount of middle-aged, mostly male, suit-bearing decision makers. The only one I recognise is Thomas Bézier, who acknowledges me with a nod. The rest are the defence minister, some military officers, city admin, and the police chief, as well as several senior GoPol agents. They all blur into one after a while.

Then, to my surprise, the door opens, and Flo slips in together with an older man, whom I assume is her big brother. Or rather her big brothers.

She waves at me and immediately drags the dead brother along to sit by me, leaving the living one to trail them. "Salut, Alix!" She kisses my cheeks before introducing the whisper ghost. "This is my brother, Al. The other one's my brother too, but this one's my favourite."

"We're literally the same person," Alistair complains before greeting Sébastien.

"Debatable," Flo says, while Al grins. He's about Dix's age, and by the looks of it, he's got the same boyish charm, exacerbated by a mop of red hair and wild smattering of freckles, just like his sister.

After introducing Gaspar—they obviously already know Dix and Sébastien—I say, "I'm surprised you're a part of this. Are researchers usually invited to strategy meetings?" Never mind they're not GoPol France, either.

"I asked Alistair and Al to join us to add their experience," Sébastien explains. "They dealt with a necromancer in London."

Flo grins. "And I get to come because I built some stellar ghost traps."

Al shudders. "They're so annoying."

"Al helped me test them." Flo laughs and runs her hand through his hair. Then she notices my shocked face. "He wasn't a big fan, but I swear, they're harmless. No ghosts were harmed during testing."

"Tell that to my dignity," Al mutters.

I notice Alistair looks slightly annoyed, as if he's embarrassed by how his younger self and sister are conducting themselves in this serious setting, but I appreciate the breath of fresh air they're bringing. And I'm glad I'm not the only civilian in the room, though talk of ghost traps makes me nervous, because in my mind all I see is Petite Alix locked in a tube.

The meeting starts with Sébastien giving a presentation on what we know about the Chevalier from his own meagre reconnaissance, my direct report, and Mathy's insider knowledge. I know pretty much all of this, which is probably why I get distracted by how sexy he is when he's practically oozing confidence. At least half the room have little to no knowledge of ghosts, but where they would've raised their eyebrows if I'd been the one conveying this information, they all nod and frown at Sébastien—not in confusion but with appropriate concern.

"Right now, Coullier has no idea how much we know. He's probably aware we know of his location when he let Mademoiselle Dubois go"—his icy, confident gaze hits me, and I've never been happier to be called so formally by him before—"but he never divulged the sensitive parts of his plans to her."

"Does he trust her?" Bézier asks, and I know what he's asking: they're going to send me in as bait to distract the Chevalier and his ghostly conspirators while GoPol launch their attack.

Sébastien and I share a look and his eyes widen slightly, as if he's had the same thought. "It's more complicated than that. Coullier knows about her connection to GoPol,"—aka my connection to him—"so, no, he knows he can't trust her. He's trying to woo Mademoiselle Dubois because of her wide and varied connections to other ghosts he'd love to add to his army. Furthermore, we believe he's chosen her to bring back Napoleon."

Everyone in the room cranes their necks to take a look, probably wondering why Napoleon would choose someone like me as his whisper partner. Chilling as the thought is, I can't quite imagine it myself. And wouldn't he have tried to charm me more? The first time I met him, he kept the meeting brief and was fairly hostile, not exactly a good base for a life-long partnership. Even at the headquarters, he showed very little interest in me. Either he only sees me as a tool unworthy of affection or Sébastien is wrong.

Gaspar puts a hand on my thigh when the whispers arise. They're wondering if I'm a threat, if the Chevalier has already bought me with his promises.

Sébastien notices the shift and quickly continues with his summary. "We're facing two specific threats here: one, Coullier is preparing a big ritual with enough fanfare to befit an emperor. All he needs is Mademoiselle Dubois. Two, Molay is planning to raise an army of the dead. We know there's not enough ghost whisperers to do it Coullier's way. Even if they were to catch all our ghost whisperers, he'd only have a few dozen. Instead, they're reserving our agents for the officers and powerful ghosts they wish to reward, while using a combination of dark magic and science to imbue their chosen army with powers that could make them effective against the living."

The skin on my arms prickles as I imagine this army of the dead spilling out of the catacombs. Will they be like zombies? Skeletons? Or will they look alive and be able to touch and harm the living, but impervious to death themselves, like ghosts everyone can see? Whatever it is, with Molay behind the wheel, I know it's going to be horrible. For all we know, the attack could just target our minds. I shudder, thinking of his powerful hallucinations, and Gaspar's grip intensifies.

"We'll stop them," he whispers.

I give him a quick smile before focusing on Sébastien again, who's moved on to the actual plan.

"Right now, we have the advantage. Coullier isn't ready to move his plan along just yet—he thinks he has time. His location may've been leaked, but we haven't even been able to confirm he's taken our agents yet. When we didn't attack right after Mademoiselle Dubois' return, he must've figured we'd keep observing. We have the information and we have the timing. Question is, do we have the numbers?"

Bézier takes over, and for the next half hour they talking troop movements and manoeuvres that go straight over my head. The overall consensus is they don't want to attract the public's attention by responding to this threat with a large military or police presence. It wouldn't work in the catacombs, anyway—you can't exactly send an army down there, not with that many bottle necks and narrow corridors.

"We'll need a special task force for this," Bézier surmises. "Police will guard the entrances and exits. Any cataphiles will be arrested and questioned. Most will be harmless and may be released, but we want to keep anyone working with Coullier or the ghosts. This has to be stomped out completely."

They're actually going to clean out the catacombs. Memories flash in my mind of the police raid that ended my first date with Gaspar. This'll be like that, only a hundred times bigger.

"GoPol will lead the main attack on Coullier's headquarters, intercept the rituals and secure the ghosts—or whatever this Molay is at the moment—responsible. All other ghosts will be salted."

"What?"

Everyone stares at me. Heat crawls up my face and I fight the urge to sink into my chair. After a few shaky breaths that feel as if they last minutes, I speak up more calmly. "Why are we salting *all* the ghosts?"

"Because that's what GoPol does," Gaspar mutters, catching a glare from Sébastien.

Bézier raises an eyebrow, then has the audacity to misinterpret my question and present an answer to the important people in the room. "Salting is one of the few weapons against ghosts at our disposal. It doesn't kill them, though it can temporarily create a similar effect. Most importantly, it resets their minds. They'd revert to their original state, before they were charmed and lured in by Coullier. In short, they'd forget all about their riot aspirations."

The appreciative murmurs and nods make me sick. They all think this is a fantastic, maybe even *humane,* way to deal with the ghosts, when it's everything but.

"That seems unnecessarily cruel," Flo whispers. "Are all the ghosts down there in league with Coullier?"

Alistair scoffs. "Of course they are. Who do you think will make up that army he wants to raise? It's not like there are ghost prisons we could put them in."

He's right. There's precious little else we can do to bring ghosts to justice. I'm just not convinced we have the authority to judge them. To just throw a blanket condemnation of every ghost who doesn't hightail it out of the catacombs when GoPol comes through seems shortsighted and, as Florence said, cruel. Maybe some of the ghosts deserve this treatment if they truly stand behind the Chevalier's plan, but I already know this'll hit hundreds of innocent ghosts who were just dreaming of a better future. It seems like a good way to harbour more animosity between the living and the dead instead of resolving the situation.

"Now, we need someone to lead this task force, someone who knows the catacombs and the Chevalier well enough." Bézier's gaze lands on Sébastien. "How's your arm, Roubert?"

Alarmed, I look at him. As far as I know, the cast isn't supposed to come off until next week, but Sébastien has that look in his eyes, the one he has before he does something really noble and stupid. "The doctor said, if necessary, I can have the cast removed now, but I need to be careful to avoid re-fracturing my arm."

"Will you be well enough to lead this mission?"

I want to shake my head and scream at him, maybe plead, but I've already lost my temper once in this room, and Sébastien is purposefully ignoring the anguish in my eyes. "Absolutely."

"You won't even get into the headquarters," Gaspar says, losing his shit in my place. "Sure, you know where he is, but Molay's guarding the entrance. Unless he wants you to enter, you may as well stand in front of a brick wall."

Sébastien's jaw clenches, but he simply pretends he hasn't heard him. Despite everything going down, the two are still at odds, and it's giving me major anxiety.

"What about Molay?" I hiss at him. Stubborn or not, Gaspar is right. People look at me, so I clear my throat and explain louder, "When I approached the headquarters, everything inside me screamed to look away, to go somewhere else. That kind of repelling is something powerful ghosts can do. It's how the Chevalier... Coullier avoided detection for so long. Even though we know exactly where he is, we likely won't get through the barrier."

"I'm not so sure about that," Sébastien says, unable to ignore me this time. "You withstood it and got through."

"With Gaspar's help!"

Once again, he avoids looking at Gaspar. "Our agents were turned away when they didn't know what they were looking for. I believe knowing *exactly* where to go will be a game changer."

"C-Trente was extremely determined to enter the Panthéon, and he still couldn't." I wish we didn't have to do this in front of everyone, but I can hardly ask them to take a break while I knock some sense into my boyfriend. "The agents were turned away then, too."

He flicks me a quick gaze, clearly begging me to let it rest. "That was the Panthéon, which has dozens of powerful ghosts. Coullier has two, maybe a few generals in addition to that. And you're forgetting the most important thing."

"Which is?"

"Coullier's looking for more ghost whisperers. The majority of our agents weren't turned away; they were sucked in."

I gasp. "You can't possibly be serious!"

"Oh, he is," Gaspar says, snorting derisively. "He finally gets to do what he's been training for all his life, hunt down ghosts."

My head whips around to Gaspar just as Dix snarls. "What are you gonna do? Run to the Chevalier and betray us all again? You shouldn't even be here."

"Dix!" I hiss, drawing further frowns.

Sébastien ignores the ghosts and confidently declares, "We're the bait. We'll get through."

I think I'm going to be sick. It doesn't matter how experienced he is or how prepared they are, or even how many fancy ghost traps Flo equips him with. He's walking into the lion's den, risking not just himself but his bond with Dix. Not that his whisper ghost seems to mind. He's got his arms crossed, jaw as clenched as his older counterpart.

"I'm happy to join the task force," Alistair offers, as do some of the senior agents.

Flo takes a shaky breath before raising her hand. "I think I should come, too. Once we get inside, I might be able to disable some of Coullier's installations or manipulate them to our advantage."

If everyone's going, I sure won't be left behind. "Fine, I'll play bait, too."

Sébastien's professional mask breaks at last. "No!"

He's being ridiculous. Why does he—and everyone else—gets to sacrifice themselves, while I have to sit back and twiddle my thumbs, worrying? "I found the headquarters. I was in there, *and* I know the Chevalier, Napoleon, and Molay."

"And they know you," Bézier says. Several of the other men nod. "We've just established Coullier's waiting for you to join him."

"Maybe she should be secured in the meantime," one grey-haired man suggests. "Minimise the risk."

Now I'm getting arrested? "I'm not going to *join* him!"

"That won't be necessary," Sébastien says, then whispers, "You can't go. You know what he wants."

Napoleon. He wants me to bring Napoleon back to life and bind me to him.

"I appreciate your offer, Mademoiselle Dubois," Bézier says, "truly. But in this situation, sending you in there is an unnecessary risk. You did your part when you brought us this information."

An unnecessary risk—compared to the *necessary* risk of sending an injured agent to lead this mission.

"Sorry, Alix," Dix mouths. "The Chevalier, Napoleon, *and* Molay are already singularly interested in you. We're not going to deliver you on a silver platter."

I cross my arms, fighting tears of frustration. "Whatever."

Gaspar reaches out to rub my arm. "Don't worry, I'll stay with you."

"Damn right you are," Sébastien growls through clenched teeth. I can't tell whether that's because he still doesn't trust him or whether he's decided Gaspar will have to guard and protect me from doing something stupid—the pretty way of *securing* me. Probably both.

"What about Molay?" I ask loudly, trying to drown out their stupid fight. "How are you planning to fight off his hallucinations?"

Bézier smiles. "Glad you asked." He nods at an agent near the door. "You may bring in Monsieur Laugier now."

*Laugier.* Surprised, I watch as Marie's Uncle Paul enters, his arms full of medieval-looking contraptions and scrolls.

Bézier introduces him and says, "The Knights Hospitallers are experienced in countering the dark arts, of the kind this particular ghost employs. They've bound him once; they'll bind him again."

# Chapter 28

As soon as the meeting ends, everyone bustles off to make important calls, raid the armoury—there's a need for copious amounts of salt and whatever special equipment Paul and Flo need—and rally the troops. I stay behind, still fuming, Gaspar by my side. Sébastien gets up but only to close the door.

Dix watches him. "This isn't an occasion where I'd rather be downstairs, is it?" He meets Sébastien's dark gaze and grimaces. "You know what? I'll head downstairs either way." He runs off, straight through the door.

Silence stretches. I could've told Dix this wouldn't be one of those times—I'm too angry to even consider it, and I doubt it's on Sébastien's mind, either. He's looking at me like a beaten puppy.

"I'm sorry, Alix," he says softly, then crouches next to my chair, looking up at me.

"Whatever." I continue staring at the empty screen.

"You know I trust you," he continues. "Just—"

"Not enough to hold my own."

His eyes widen. "That's not what I was going to say. I'm *worried* about you. I'd be worried sick if I knew you were down there."

I turn to him. "And you think I don't worry? That I won't be worried when you intend to be the vanguard, leading a tiny team against two of the most horrible military leaders the world has ever seen and a ruthless scientist?"

He winces and lowers his eyes. "It's part of my job."

"Oh, right. The job you couldn't leave behind." I know I'm being unfair. Sébastien continuing as a GoPol agent when GoPol's brought him so much personal pain is nothing but noble. He's in it for the right reasons, to make it better. I just don't see how this suicide mission will help anyone. "Besides, you're injured."

He hides the pain over my words and focuses on my last argument. "It's mostly healed. If I don't use it too much, I should be fine."

"You're going to crawl through the catacombs with one arm?"

"Yeah, sure, if there's a ghost threat to stop," Gaspar muses.

Sébastien's face hardens immediately. "You don't think this is a threat worth stopping?"

Gaspar leans past me, eyes flashing. "You just held a whole meeting about fighting, capturing, and *salting* ghosts and a few errant cataphiles, and you never once stopped to wonder if maybe, *maybe*, there's another way to go about it or if any of the ghosts are worth saving. No one in the entire room cared about *why* this is even happening, why they might be following the Chevalier, because no one ever cares about ghosts. And you don't either."

I lean back in, feeling very much in the middle, not just physically, but emotionally, too. Gaspar's right about the blatant disregard of every ghost, and the readiness with which GoPol were planning on wiping their collective minds. On the other hand, I believe the threat posed by the Chevalier, Molay, and Napoleon is real and needs to be dealt with sooner than later. Once again, I wish we had more time. I haven't even talked to the ghosts who so readily want to follow Napoleon, just Gaspar, and he changed his mind easily enough.

Sébastien glares across my lap. "It's all a game for you—start a little rebellion here, have a little conquest there. Anything to pass the time. It's not like you have anything to lose. But what the Chevalier is doing is endangering *living* people. People could die!"

"Oh, the horror!" Gaspar says sarcastically. "It'd be the end of the world if anyone else became a ghost."

"See!" Sébastien says to me, throwing his hand out at Gaspar. "Who doesn't care now?"

"I don't care?" Gaspar shouts back. "If I didn't care, I'd be down there! I'd be marching with Napoleon, and I'd tell Alix to join us, too."

Sébastien shakes his head with a mirthless little laugh. "Because that's what you really want, the two of you living your best ghost life, damn anyone still alive."

"Hey! Leave me out of this!" I'm not planning on becoming a ghost anytime soon.

Immediately, Sébastien folds. "I'm sorry." He lowers his gaze, resting his forehead on my thigh, still crouching. "You told me I should trust my instincts, and my instincts tell me we need to stop this rebellion now, before it grows into something much bigger."

"It's a commune, not a rebellion," Gaspar mutters.

"It's anarchy," I say softly, "full of potential, unhindered by laws and rules, but with no security—for anyone."

Sébastien looks up, and I realise he's still more inclined to trust me than his own judgement. With the right words, I could probably sway him to sit this one out, but it'd be the end of him and his career at GoPol, and I liked the confident guy I saw today, the one who was so sure of himself and held his own in a room of very important and powerful people. As much as I hate to see him taking such a huge risk, I know he wouldn't be able to live with himself if he stayed home and did nothing while the Chevalier, Molay, and Napoleon cooked up horrors, the likes of which we've likely never seen before.

I drop my crossed arms and gently run my hand over his short blond hair, savouring the feel, as if it's the last time I'll get to touch it. "You need to save your agents." That's what this is all about. The living people he feels responsible for. "And the city."

He lets go of a shuddering breath, his whole body trembling under the release. "I promise I'll use my salt gun sparingly." He stands and bends over to kiss my cheek. "I'll see you again—one way or another."

My stomach is twisted into a painful knot so tight I can't breathe until he's left, and even then, the breath I take is shallow and stingy. I have to sit with the pain for five minutes before I trust my body enough to get up. The entire time Gaspar's been angrily muttering to himself, but to be honest, I haven't heard a single word.

I leave the GoPol building in a haze of worry, frustration, and doubt. I still don't know what the right thing to do is or if there even is a "right thing". I don't even know if I should worry about Sébastien, Dix, and Flo, or about the ghosts who'll suffer simply because they chose to make the catacombs their home.

We're halfway down the street when Gaspar's ranting finally penetrates the vacuum of shock around me. "Honestly, if they could find a way to eliminate all of us, they totally would. They *hate* we have this invisible community, thinking it's some big conspiracy instead of just normal afterlife. And yes, I know Séb isn't like that, but he can't separate himself from that thinking either. It's so deeply ingrained in him." He pauses, but only for half a second. "Well, I guess, if he dies on this stupid mission, he'll finally understand what an impossible existence being a ghost is in this world.”

“Are you *hoping* he dies?”

Gaspar throws his hands up in the air. “I’m just saying that if he does, he might finally get it.”

I stare at him in disbelief.

Slowly, what he’s just said dawns on him, and the anger gives way first to frustration then dismay. “Sorry. That was a terrible thing to say. I don’t want him to die—for one, because that would take out Dix, and secondly because dying is awful and he deserves a long happy life.” He wraps his arms around me. “Just like you.”

I let myself breathe in his intimacy, finding solace in his embrace. “I want you to have a happy afterlife, too.”

“It is what it is.”

“But it could be so much better.”

Gaspar leans his forehead against mine, looking into my eyes, then gently kisses my lips. “Mine’s better than most. At least I have someone who listens to me. Two people actually,” he says with a pained smile. “Do you think it’s my fault? Did I push him in this direction?”

“I don’t think so. You know Séb—he’s always trying to make right by everyone. He needs to prove he’s better than his father.”

“He already is,” Gaspar says, adamantly. “He’s so much better.”

“I know that, you do, too, but he has to prove it to himself every single day.”

"Fucking Séb," Gaspar mutters. "Always the hero."

"And now he's walking straight into a trap." I know GoPol has a fancy plan to deal with the Chevalier and Molay, but I don't think they understand nearly enough of their dark arts to counter them. "What if it's not me he wants for Napoleon? What if it's him?" With everything I know about Napoleon, I don't see how he'd want to bond with someone like me over Sébastien.

Gaspar's eyes widen. "Of course! That's why he let you get away with that information. He knew Séb wouldn't be able to hold back. He wants you, too, but not for that—the Chevalier wants you as a partner; he wants Séb as a tool and bargaining chip to assure your loyalty."

It's all starting to make terrible sense. The Chevalier charmed Gaspar so he could use him to lure me in, and to force my hand and guarantee my loyalty, he'll force-bind Sébastien to Napoleon's life. I can only hope he intends to keep Dix separate as another bargaining chip, knowing how much he means to both me and Sébastien.

"You have to go after him. Warn him. Protect him."

Gaspar regards me with a pained expression. "Do you think he'd listen to me? Even want me there? He was pretty clear in that meeting."

I put my hands on Gaspar's face. "Sébastien loves you. That's why he's so mad at you, because you hurt him when you went behind his back. Deeply. And I know you love him, too. Even when you think he's too stubborn to listen. I can't lose him." My voice breaks off, and I blink back tears.

Gaspar swallows. "I don't want to lose him, either—not to the Chevalier, not to Napoleon, not to anyone." He kisses me on the forehead. "I don't know what good I'll be against someone like Molay, but I'll watch out for him. I promise."

For a minute longer, we hold each other, then Gaspar gives me a quick kiss and runs back into the GoPol building. The knot inside twists even tighter. Now all my boys are going into the catacombs, ready to face unspeakable horrors.

"You're not really going to sit back and watch it all come tumbling down, are you?"

I look around to find Emily, the dearly departed tour guide. "What's it to you?"

She shrugs. "Nothing. Just never took you for a coward."

"I'm not."

I may not be an experienced fighter like Sébastien, or a ghost with little to lose like Gaspar, but I've held my own through some equally tough challenges. It still grates on me I was banned to sit on the sidelines when I have so much to bring to the battle. Not experience nor bravado, and definitely not fighting prowess, but I've got something they won't even consider: my ghosts.

As soon as the meeting ends, everyone bustles off to make important calls, raid the armoury—there's a need for copious amounts of salt and whatever special equipment Paul and Flo need—and rally the troops. I stay behind, still fuming, Gaspar by my side. Sébastien gets up but only to close the door.

Dix watches him. "This isn't an occasion where I'd rather be downstairs, is it?" He meets Sébastien's dark gaze and grimaces. "You know what? I'll head downstairs either way." He runs off, straight through the door.

Silence stretches. I could've told Dix this wouldn't be one of those times—I'm too angry to even consider it, and I doubt it's on Sébastien's mind, either. He's looking at me like a beaten puppy.

"I'm sorry, Alix," he says softly, then crouches next to my chair, looking up at me.

"Whatever." I continue staring at the empty screen.

"You know I trust you," he continues. "Just—"

"Not enough to hold my own."

His eyes widen. "That's not what I was going to say. I'm *worried* about you. I'd be worried sick if I knew you were down there."

I turn to him. "And you think I don't worry? That I won't be worried when you intend to be the vanguard, leading a tiny team against two of the most horrible military leaders the world has ever seen and a ruthless scientist?"

He winces and lowers his eyes. "It's part of my job."

"Oh, right. The job you couldn't leave behind." I know I'm being unfair. Sébastien continuing as a GoPol agent when GoPol's brought him so much personal pain is nothing but noble. He's in it for the right reasons, to make it better. I just don't see how this suicide mission will help anyone. "Besides, you're injured."

He hides the pain over my words and focuses on my last argument. "It's mostly healed. If I don't use it too much, I should be fine."

"You're going to crawl through the catacombs with one arm?"

"Yeah, sure, if there's a ghost threat to stop," Gaspar muses.

Sébastien's face hardens immediately. "You don't think this is a threat worth stopping?"

Gaspar leans past me, eyes flashing. "You just held a whole meeting about fighting, capturing, and *salting* ghosts and a few errant cataphiles, and you never once stopped to wonder if maybe, *maybe*, there's another way to go about it or if any of the ghosts are worth saving. No one in the entire room cared about *why* this is even happening, why they might be following the Chevalier, because no one ever cares about ghosts. And you don't either."

I lean back in, feeling very much in the middle, not just physically, but emotionally, too. Gaspar's right about the blatant disregard of every ghost, and the readiness with which GoPol were planning on wiping their collective minds. On the other hand, I believe the threat posed by the Chevalier, Molay, and Napoleon is real and needs to be dealt with sooner than later. Once again, I wish we had more time. I haven't even talked to the ghosts who so readily want to follow Napoleon, just Gaspar, and he changed his mind easily enough.

Sébastien glares across my lap. "It's all a game for you—start a little rebellion here, have a little conquest there. Anything to pass the time. It's not like you have anything to lose. But what the Chevalier is doing is endangering *living* people. People could die!"

"Oh, the horror!" Gaspar says sarcastically. "It'd be the end of the world if anyone else became a ghost."

"See!" Sébastien says to me, throwing his hand out at Gaspar. "Who doesn't care now?"

"I don't care?" Gaspar shouts back. "If I didn't care, I'd be down there! I'd be marching with Napoleon, and I'd tell Alix to join us, too."

Sébastien shakes his head with a mirthless little laugh. "Because that's what you really want, the two of you living your best ghost life, damn anyone still alive."

"Hey! Leave me out of this!" I'm not planning on becoming a ghost anytime soon.

Immediately, Sébastien folds. "I'm sorry." He lowers his gaze, resting his forehead on my thigh, still crouching. "You told me I should trust my instincts, and my instincts tell me we need to stop this rebellion now, before it grows into something much bigger."

"It's a commune, not a rebellion," Gaspar mutters.

"It's anarchy," I say softly, "full of potential, unhindered by laws and rules, but with no security—for anyone."

Sébastien looks up, and I realise he's still more inclined to trust me than his own judgement. With the right words, I could probably sway him to sit this one out, but it'd be the end of him and his career at GoPol, and I liked the confident guy I saw today, the one who was so sure of himself and held his own in a room of very important and powerful people. As much as I hate to see him taking such a huge risk, I know he wouldn't be able to live with himself if he stayed home and did nothing while the Chevalier, Molay, and Napoleon cooked up horrors, the likes of which we've likely never seen before.

I drop my crossed arms and gently run my hand over his short blond hair, savouring the feel, as if it's the last time I'll get to touch it. "You need to save your agents." That's what this is all about. The living people he feels responsible for. "And the city."

He lets go of a shuddering breath, his whole body trembling under the release. "I promise I'll use my salt gun sparingly." He stands and bends over to kiss my cheek. "I'll see you again—one way or another."

My stomach is twisted into a painful knot so tight I can't breathe until he's left, and even then, the breath I take is shallow and stingy. I have to sit with the pain for five minutes before I trust my body enough to get up. The entire time Gaspar's been angrily muttering to himself, but to be honest, I haven't heard a single word.

I leave the GoPol building in a haze of worry, frustration, and doubt. I still don't know what the right thing to do is or if there even is a "right thing". I don't even know if I should worry about Sébastien, Dix, and Flo, or about the ghosts who'll suffer simply because they chose to make the catacombs their home.

We're halfway down the street when Gaspar's ranting finally penetrates the vacuum of shock around me. "Honestly, if they could find a way to eliminate all of us, they totally would. They *hate* we have this invisible community, thinking it's some big conspiracy instead of just normal afterlife. And yes, I know Séb isn't like that, but he can't separate himself from that thinking either. It's so deeply ingrained in him." He pauses, but only for half a second. "Well, I guess, if he dies on this stupid mission, he'll finally understand what an impossible existence being a ghost is in this world."

"Are you *hoping* he dies?"

Gaspar throws his hands up in the air. "I'm just saying that if he does, he might finally get it."

I stare at him in disbelief.

Slowly, what he's just said dawns on him, and the anger gives way first to frustration then dismay. "Sorry. That was a terrible thing to say. I don't want him to die—for one, because that would take out Dix, and secondly because dying is awful and he deserves a long happy life." He wraps his arms around me. "Just like you."

I let myself breathe in his intimacy, finding solace in his embrace. "I want you to have a happy afterlife, too."

"It is what it is."

"But it could be so much better."

Gaspar leans his forehead against mine, looking into my eyes, then gently kisses my lips. "Mine's better than most. At least I have someone who listens to me. Two people actually," he says with a pained smile. "Do you think it's my fault? Did I push him in this direction?"

"I don't think so. You know Séb—he's always trying to make right by everyone. He needs to prove he's better than his father."

"He already is," Gaspar says, adamantly. "He's so much better."

"I know that, you do, too, but he has to prove it to himself every single day."

"Fucking Séb," Gaspar mutters. "Always the hero."

"And now he's walking straight into a trap." I know GoPol has a fancy plan to deal with the Chevalier and Molay, but I don't think they understand nearly enough of their dark arts to counter them. "What if it's not me he wants for Napoleon? What if it's him?" With everything I know about Napoleon, I don't see how he'd want to bond with someone like me over Sébastien.

Gaspar's eyes widen. "Of course! That's why he let you get away with that information. He knew Séb wouldn't be able to hold back. He wants you, too, but not for that—the Chevalier wants you as a partner; he wants Séb as a tool and bargaining chip to assure your loyalty."

It's all starting to make terrible sense. The Chevalier charmed Gaspar so he could use him to lure me in, and to force my hand and guarantee my loyalty, he'll force-bind Sébastien to Napoleon's life. I can only hope he intends to keep Dix separate as another bargaining chip, knowing how much he means to both me and Sébastien.

"You have to go after him. Warn him. Protect him."

Gaspar regards me with a pained expression. "Do you think he'd listen to me? Even want me there? He was pretty clear in that meeting."

I put my hands on Gaspar's face. "Sébastien loves you. That's why he's so mad at you, because you hurt him when you went behind his back. Deeply. And I know you love him, too. Even when you think he's too stubborn to listen. I can't lose him." My voice breaks off, and I blink back tears.

Gaspar swallows. "I don't want to lose him, either—not to the Chevalier, not to Napoleon, not to anyone." He kisses me on the forehead. "I don't know what good I'll be against someone like Molay, but I'll watch out for him. I promise."

For a minute longer, we hold each other, then Gaspar gives me a quick kiss and runs back into the GoPol building. The knot inside twists even tighter. Now all my boys are going into the catacombs, ready to face unspeakable horrors.

"You're not really going to sit back and watch it all come tumbling down, are you?"

I look around to find Emily, the dearly departed tour guide. "What's it to you?"

She shrugs. "Nothing. Just never took you for a coward."

"I'm not."

I may not be an experienced fighter like Sébastien, or a ghost with little to lose like Gaspar, but I've held my own through some equally tough challenges. It still grates on me I was banned to sit on the sidelines when I have so much to bring to the battle. Not experience nor bravado, and definitely not fighting prowess, but I've got something they won't even consider: my ghosts.

#

A few hours later, I'm back on Père Lachaise for my very own strategy meeting. At first, I thought about holding it at the Panthéon, but that's still open to the public, and I've had enough of making an ass out of myself in front of people for one day—besides, I wanted a space where *all* my ghost friends are welcome. The Panthéon ghosts weren't too happy at first, but as soon as they got to bask in the admiration of the other ghosts their egos were sufficiently stroked.

Now we're in the sunshine around Abelard and Héloïse's crypt. For the occasional visitor, I'm just resting my feet or waiting for a friend, maybe a date. What they don't see are the crowds of ghosts gathered around the grave. Jean Moulin's leading the meeting, currently talking to Mathy to get a fresh overview. Half the Panthéon ghosts have made it, among them Victor, Voltaire, Rousseau, and Jean Lannes, who looks on darkly but determined. Emily is there, grinning from ear to ear, as if this is all just an exciting adventure, and of course, my grandmother, Beatrice, and Alexandre de Beauharnais are also there. The last strides up and down the rows of ghosts, counting and strategizing in his head.

No one tells me I should stay away, because they're all of the same opinion: the Chevalier, Napoleon, and Molay need to be stopped at all costs before they can get their hands on Sébastien or any other ghost whisperers currently on GoPol's task force—and before they can raise their army of the dead.

Jean Moulin finishes talking to Mathy, who looks positively excited. This might be the first time in his afterlife he's actually been valued for his insight. He looks like he still can't believe how many ghosts have welcomed him with open arms. He returns to his mother, who immediately pulls him close and kisses his head.

Now, Jean Moulin is calling Alexandre, Lannes, and the other generals from the Panthéon and surrounding necropolises together. None of the other ghosts protest, which is a first—especially for my Panthéon ghosts. Apparently, they respect lived experience. This is a matter of war, so it's only fair the dead military officers decide on strategy.

I sit between my grandmother and Victor Hugo while we wait for the generals to come up with a plan.

"Nasty business," my grandmother mutters. "What's it with men always waging war to get what they want?"

Victor sighs. "That's a good question I've written many a book about."

"Did you write down the answer?" my grandmother asks, an eyebrow raised.

"That's for the reader to decide."

"So, you didn't."

I can't help but snort. It helps a little with the stomach pains I'm still having because of Sébastien, and now Gaspar as well. I know they have their own preparations to go through, so hopefully, they're not in the catacombs yet, but with each passing hour, my anxiety grows. Battling Molay in the Boutique of Psychosis was bad enough—I still have nightmares about it sometimes. Now he's not just back to life but has teamed up with the Chevalier and making use of his extensive resources. And to top it all off, Napoleon's waiting in the wings, ready to lead the army they're raising for him.

Back when Molay was still in power, no living could withstand his terror. Sébastien was completely incapacitated, reliving the nightmare of his murder—not that I knew what was happening to him back then. Even the Chevalier was knocked out cold, though I never learnt what images haunted him. And I was drowning, just as I'd drowned once more in the Banga. The only reason we came out alive was because I managed to summon Alexandre, Jean, and the other generals to my aid. They're the ones who subdued Molay, holding him captive until we were able to disperse his bones—or so I'd thought.

That's why it's so wild to me ghosts weren't even a factor in GoPol's meeting. Bézier only sees them as a threat, something to be eliminated, but never an asset, and Sébastien went along with it because he's so used to GoPol and their whisper ghosts handling every crisis. It tells me we still have a long way to go in this living-dead relationship.

At last, the generals turn, and Alexandre and Jean Lannes prepare to lay out their plan. I shuffle forward, eager to hear what they've concocted, and even more eager to leave and follow Sébastien and Gaspar into the dark.

Alexandre is about to start when a commotion at the back of the crowd draws everyone's attention. People are making space, some of whom are gasping, while others bow. Curiously, I crane my neck, hoping to catch a glimpse of what's going on.

"Oh dear," Victor mutters. "Here we go."

And then I see them. Three women in elaborate dresses that have never seen the inside of the catacombs and yet they're here, demanding everyone's respect and attention. It's the Triad of Queens: Constance d'Arles, Catherine de Medici, and Marie Antoinette.

Catherine looks dignified and a little scary, Marie Antoinette gives me an excited little wave, and Constance is repeatedly hitting her palm with a clunky piece of wood, her eyes gleaming. "We heard there was a fight?"

# CHAPTER 29

The police are blocking off all the entrances into the catacombs I know of. Emily tells me she knows a few further afield they definitely couldn't have found, but I go with the Triad's method of phasing through stone like a ghost instead. When they summoned me from the middle of the catacombs straight to St. Denis, it was an excruciating experience. All that pressure on my living body almost killed me, but that was over a prolonged period. Today, it's merely a matter of phasing through a few metres below my feet.

The headache has barely enough time to make an appearance before my feet hit the ground and I'm in open space again—or as open as a sewage canal can be.

"It stinks!" Marie Antoinette complains, holding her dress scandalously high to avoid dragging it through the filth. "Why did those naughty men have to hide below like dirty rats? Oh dear,

I hope we don't come across rats. Are there rats here, Madame Dubois?"

"If there's a rat, we'll squash it," Constance says with unmistakable glee. "Man or animal."

Jean Lannes has a seriously concerned look on his face when he shuffles past the queens to lead our little troupe. Not all the ghosts are joining me, most are planning on descending straight on the headquarters when I call them. This little vanguard consists of the queens, who are there to get me through any obstacle—man or stone—Emily, who'll guide me, and Jean and Alexandre, who are acting as my personal bodyguards. Oh, and Victor, who's waxing poetic about the sewer system.

"Hidden in the dark lies the conscience of the city. The stink is reflective of the darkness and suffering of the underclass, of the hidden injustices just beneath the surface of society. Its muck is symbolic of the sins of our past, clinging to our feet as we drag ourselves to a brighter future."

If he continues like this, I'll be begging Molay for a swift death, and then Sébastien for a full round of salt.

With Emily's knowledge and the queens' help, we make surprisingly fast passage through the catacombs. On the other hand, I have no idea where I am and how to get back. At one point, Jean hushes Victor, because he hears voices up ahead. The ghosts hide me in a little nook. I hear a group of three or four cataphiles clambering by.

"Don't tell me they've closed down Richelieu as well," one complains. "Maybe we should just find a camping spot and wait until they're gone."

"I've got work tomorrow!" one of his friends cries out, then the tunnels swallow their voices again.

I highly doubt those cataphiles are part of the Chevalier's group and I feel sorry they're caught in the middle. Normally, the police wouldn't care so long as they have reasonable equipment, but knowing what awaits them today, I really hope they stay underground until it's all over.

We're getting closer to the Banga when I hear sounds like a stampede running towards us. Suddenly, a flurry of ghosts press down the tunnel, leaving me nowhere to escape. They're screaming and crying or calling out for their friends. Some run into the walls, but too many stay on the paths. Any second now, they're going to trample or squash me.

I scramble backwards, hoping to make it back to the bigger cavern we passed not too long ago, when my backpack catches on something protruding from the ceiling. Panicked, I stare into the eyes of the ghost in front of me.

"Calm yourselves!" Catherine orders, her voice like a cracking whip. Even I straighten and would've knocked my head on the ceiling if Alexandre hadn't quickly put his hand over me.

"Thanks," I mouth.

The ghosts stop. They stare at Catherine and the other queens, and then they flee the other way. Can't say I blame them.

"I guess we're going the right way?" I ask breathlessly.

Emily scoffs. "Would I lead you astray?"

I spare everyone my answer, tug my backpack free, and continue down the corridor until it becomes so narrow I have to squeeze through sideways, dragging my backpack with my feet. I pop out of a crevice into a wider corridor I would've never even considered a viable path and take several deep breaths.

Ahead, I hear liquid dripping into a larger body of water. We must be near the Banga now, though I still don't recognise the spot. "Where are we?"

Emily puts her finger on her lips and whispers, "Close now. The Banga's through that wall."

"Are we going to phase again?" I mentally prepare myself for the inevitable pressure.

"Yes, but we're going through here," she points at the ground in front. "Don't want to get caught up in Molay's defences."

It takes me a moment to realise what she's saying. The head-quarters aren't ahead, they're below us. We've arrived.

"I hear the battle," Constance says blissfully.

My own heartbeat was too loud in my ears to catch it before, but now I hear the noise below my feet. The occasional shot's fired and people are shouting, though I only hear muffled sounds through the rock.

"Let's go!" If there's a fight already, my boys could be in danger.

"Wait!" Victor says. "I'll call the others now. You wait ten seconds before you follow."

Constance rolls her eyes. "Want all the glory to yourself, don't you?"

Victor ignores her and nods at Jean and Alexandre. "Keep our girl safe, that's all I ask." And then he steps into the floor, sinking as though he's on a spectral elevator. Ghosts gathering around, sinking with him, and my heartbeat quickens with anticipation.

Ten seconds have never felt so long. I'm only at eight when Constance has had enough. "Let's go!"

And before I can take another breath, I lurch forward and fall through the floor, straight into mayhem.

# Chapter 30

My landing is anything but gentle. For a moment, all the breath is knocked out of me. A salt bullet whizzes over my head, hitting a ghost I know from Père Lachaise merely two metres away.

I want to raise my head, but Alexandre pushes me down. "Stay low! Watch!"

"Behind here!" Jean calls, and they drag me behind an overturned table, now acting as a barricade. From there, I take a moment to figure out what the hell is going on.

The good news is Sébastien's plan has worked, and the ghost whisperers made it through Molay's mental barrier. Now, though, they're in his hellish nightmare. While there's a whole battalion of ghosts ready to fight, Molay's in the middle of the room, looming over everyone like a puppeteer. A GoPol agent in riot gear shoots their salt gun at him, which bounces off Molay's armour without effect. In return, Molay slices off their arm with that massive sword of his, then throws out a hand and brings down another agent by simply projecting whatever they fear most into their mind. I see them flailing their arms, as if endlessly falling, until they lose their footing and crash to the ground, still grasping for the air.

Somewhere in the back, Napoleon directs his troops, reacting to the flood of new ghosts who have entered with Victor Hugo. I see old-fashioned guns, rapiers, swords, and even a cannon or two as different eras clash in ghostly mayhem. The ghosts buy the small bunch of ghost whisperers some time, and I see Alistair driving back a ghostly general, until suddenly, a blue light emits from the ground and the ghost freezes—one of Flo's ghost traps, I assume.

I duck behind the table when a cannon ball flies over my head. Next to me, Jean groans. His leg is flickering, switching between healthy and well to crushed and bleeding. The sight makes me shiver and I quickly turn my face back to the battle, eagerly searching the crowds once more.

"They're not here."

"Who?" Alexandre asks.

"Sébastien, Dix, and Gaspar."

Did Gaspar manage to get through to Sébastien and convince him it was a bad idea to climb into the catacombs? Does he have that kind of power over him? Could my boys safe?

"The Chevalier's missing, too," Jean muses. "And Napoleon looks ready to retreat."

"He does?" To me, it looks like he's perfectly happy in his vantage point, secured by two rows of loyal men. When the queens make their way over, all he does is bark orders.

Jean nods. "He's stalling. This battle's a distraction."

My stomach turns. Has the Chevalier managed to lure Sébastien into a trap and is preparing Napoleon's resurrection? Is he currently cutting Dix from him, while Gaspar does nothing but watch?

"Eyes on the prize, Alix," Alexandre says. "We need to stop Molay first."

Emily catches my gaze. Unlike the other ghosts, she doesn't look keen to engage in battle. "I'll find them." Then she's gone. Hopefully, she'll keep that promise instead of using it as an excuse to escape.

"How do we stop Molay?" It's not like I have a giant broadsword to hand or would know how to use it if I did.

"Believe in us," Alexandre suggests, "and summon as many friends to your aid as you can."

I'm glad I don't have to join the fray just yet. Instead, I mentally go through all the battle-experienced ghosts I know and try to summon them to the cave. As is, there's already way too many people here. I see one GoPol agent lowering their weapon, staring around in confusion, not sure who to even shoot. A man walks up and claps their shoulder hard, upon which, they simply fire at every ghost they see. Surprised, I realise Bézier's joined the team despite being unable to see ghosts.

One of the Panthéon generals turns and knocks the gun from the GoPol agent before swiping their rifle across their head, knocking them out cold. Bézier stares at the downed agent, and I see fear washing across his face. It must be pure hell to know you're in a room full of hostile people but unable to see any of them.

"You were able to best Molay last time," Jean says to Alexandre. "Maybe you should go repeat the feat."

"He's alive now. Besides, my job is here. With Alix."

Jean looks as if he wants to argue but simply nods and returns to his watchful stance. I can tell he wants to bellow orders and resume his duties as the marshal he once was, instead of sitting behind this table, making sure I don't come to harm. As if I'm what's important here.

"If you can defeat him—"

Suddenly, Flo cries out. She braces herself and then somehow manages to throw her body backwards, as if she's been hit by one of the cannon balls. At the last moment, Al slips behind her, cushioning her fall before she crashes into the wall. Barely acknowledging him, she scrambles up, desperately shouting Alistair's name.

Her brother, who's in a one-on-one battle with one of Napoleon's officers, glances over his shoulder. Suddenly, he lurches forward when his opponent uses his distraction to sink his rapier into Alistair's guts or leg—it's hard to see from here. Immediately, three ghosts from Père Lachaise force the general back, while a dead nurse swiftly tends to Alistair who can only stare in disbelief. He's probably never been helped like this before.

Meanwhile, Flo's still crying her heart out, and now she looks as if she's performing CPR on the naked stone. Al's crouching next to her, trying to get her attention, while endlessly repeating, "I'm here. It's alright. I'm here. I'm still here."

I realise then what's happening. She must be reliving the accident which temporarily took Alistair's life—the birth of his whisper ghost. Flo must've been present when it happened, and sure enough now there's blood running down her face, though she never hit her head.

"I've got to help her," I tell my bodyguards and leave the safety of my table.

"Alix!" Alexandre and Jean scramble after me. Jean loosens some shots from his rifle in defence.

Keeping my head low, I slide across the floor, nearly knocking Al away. "Flo! Listen to me!" To her brother, I say, "It's psychosis."

"What?" Al looks confused. "What are you even doing here?"

"I—"

Suddenly, water fills my mouth, and the ground liquefies beneath me. Before I can hold onto another thought, I plunge into the cold waters of the Seine. It's so dark! My lungs screaming with the need for air, while stars dance in front of my eyes.

Then I'm suddenly outside on the street, a street I recognise as the Rue de Sèvres, near the Sorbonne. A cyclist's coming towards me, floppy brown hair flying in the wind. Just as I recognise him, a white van pulls up beside him.

"Gaspar! Don't!"

But it all happens too fast, the van turns without blinking, wheels skid across the asphalt, brakes scream, and then there's a bone-crunching thunk, and suddenly, it's me who's hurled across the handlebars, face aiming for the hard, unforgiving concrete.

Pain erupts in my body as I'm hurled into another vision. Now, I'm standing in a clear-glass tube, like the ones beneath GoPol. In front of me, Charles is securing Dix on a table. No, not Dix—seventeen-year-old Sébastien. Sébastien has his eyes turned to the ceiling, staring into nothingness, while his father attaches an electric wire to his chest. His eyes widen slightly, and I see him swallowing, but he doesn't even try to get out of his restraints.

I hammer against the walls of my prison, begging Charles to stop, to not do this to his son, but he's single-minded, and when the jolt hits Sébastien, it's my own heart that stops.

The tube fills with water, but I can't even bring myself to care. At least if I drown this time, it'll all be over. The waves crash over my head as I sink into the deep, the bright circle of light that's the lab light or maybe the sun growing more and more distant. A shadow covers it.

Suddenly, someone grabs me and pulls me out of the deep. At first, he looks like Gaspar, but when I come to, sputtering and gasping, it's Victor's arms which are wrapped around me. He's swaying me back and forth, pressing my head against his chest and kissing my head as he whispers my name. No, not my name.

"Leopoldine." The daughter he lost to the floods.

I realise now he's crying; *the* Victor Hugo is crying over me.

"She's alright, Victor," Voltaire says, surprisingly mellow. "She's back with us."

When Victor finally let's go and clears his throat, as if he never lost it, I find myself back behind the barricade. But this time Flo and even Alistair are here with me. By the looks of it, my ghosts managed to pull Flo out of her psychotic attack as well. She's still crying, but she's no longer bleeding.

"How does he even do that?" she asks, still distraught.

"Beats me," Al answers, "but it only seems to work on the living."

Alistair turns to look at me. "What are you doing here? Weren't you supposed to stay out of this?" He's holding his side which sports a spectral bandage.

"She brought the ghosts," Flo says. "The ones on our side." She wipes her face, then grabs her bag and starts upending it. From the random parts falling on the ground, she starts assembling something. "Molay's surrounded by some sort of force field. He's impervious to salt—obviously—and he's evaded every normal bullet.

No ghost can get closer than five metres while he picks off our agents one by one. He's got to have a weakness."

"Mathieu," I say. "They're connected now, so—"

"If we kill him, we kill Molay," Alistair says darkly.

I didn't want to go quite that far, but essentially that'd do the trick. I glance at Victor. "Have you seen Mathieu?"

He nods but looks unhappy. "He's well-protected—Molay's sealed him neatly in a ritual circle. Nothing, neither ghost nor living, can penetrate it." He points across the room. "It's over there, behind Napoleon."

So, he's protected by magic, Napoleon, and all the troops between us.

"I'll get him," Alistair says, and tries to pull himself up, only to realise he's hurt worse than he thought.

"You took a sword to the side!" Flo hisses as she drags her brother back down, then dabs his perspiring face. "You're out of commission."

"Speaking of out of commission." My voice nearly breaks. "Sébastien stayed home, didn't he?"

Alistair looks at me as if I'm crazy. "Why would he—? No, he led us here. The Chevalier fled down one of those tunnels, the one Napoleon's guarding. Roubert went after him."

I nearly faint when he confirms my worst fears. *Please let Sébastien be okay, please.*

Flo looks at the ghosts around us. "We need a distraction. Can you pull Napoleon's troops away so Alix and I can slip through? I think I might have something to get through that defence around Mathieu."

"Are you mad?" Alistair asks.

"I've had basic training. And you're injured."

Al puts a hand on her shoulder. "I'll take care of her."

"Just like you took care of her when Molay attacked?" Alistair looks out of his mind, but he has precious little choice today because he's not going anywhere without help.

"We might be able to turn the tide," Voltaire muses. "With the queens' help, we can draw Napoleon's and Molay's attention away." He locks gazes with Victor. "You up for it, old friend?"

Victor shrugs. "Might as well do some field research for my next novel." He nods at Alexandre and Jean. "You stay with the girls. Make sure they get across the room safely."

Alexandre's hand closes around my shoulder. "She won't leave my sight. Again."

But Jean groans, looking deeply tortured. "You need… I know Napoleon. I know how he thinks. Let me take charge of the troops."

Victor and Voltaire exchange a glance. "I thought you didn't want to fight him," Victor says at last.

Ashamed, Jean looks to his feet. "But I do want to fight Molay. What he's doing is unnatural. He needs to be stopped."

Voltaire nods. "In that case... Alexandre, are you good watching her by yourself?"

"He won't have to do it alone," Al declares. "I'm going with them, too."

Alexandre smiles wanly. "Then we should be fine."

Before he can slip away, I throw my arms around Victor and hug him tight. "Thanks for saving me."

He clears his throat, then puts his arm around me. "Anytime. Just stay alive, kid."

Easier said than done.

# Chapter 31

Nothing about this fight makes any sense. Adding ghosts to the mix is a surreal experience. They can't really die, but they still remember what it's like to be hit, although those who have been stumble around confused, wondering what they're even doing here. Skirmishes are fought with weapons as much as they're fought with will power—it's the only way to explain why Marie Antoinette is beating a World War I soldier's ass with her freaking fan.

When Catherine de Medici orders people around, half the ones on the other side respond, eagerly prostrating themselves, even if the majority have never lived in a monarchy. And of course, Constance d'Arles is having the time of her afterlife, bashing people left and right.

As the majority of the Panthéon ghosts are gathered on the far side, even Napoleon is drawn that way. I don't pay much attention to anything happening after that, because it's time for the four of us to move out. Heads kept low, Flo and I use the wall to round the cave, while Alexandre and Al guard us. Flo's carrying her make-shift device, which looks a bit like a bazooka with a pointy end. When I ask her what it's supposed to do, she answers, "Disperse spectral energy, hopefully."

"A ghost bomb?"

She winces. "If you want to call it that."

I don't have time to worry how this'll affect any of the ghosts around me. Right now, the mission is to get to Mathieu and... make him stop, I guess—by whatever means necessary.

We make it across the cave and sure enough, Mathieu's in a circle of arcane symbols, looking terribly bored. When he locks gazes with me, his eyes widen, and he scrambles to his feet. Somehow, he looks... happy? "You're here."

"Um, duh." Why would Mathieu be happy to see me?

"We thought you weren't going to come when your boyfriends showed up alone." He gives me an ugly grin. "But you couldn't stay away, right?" He notices Flo. "Who's that? A new friend?"

"No need to sound so jealous. I know it's tough for you to make friends."

Mathieu snorts, still strangely amused. "I think I've made a very powerful friend."

"Oh yeah, another psychopath. Suits you."

Flo ignores our back and forth and kneels at the edge of the ritual circle to take a closer look. I leave her to test the boundaries and find a way through while I distract Mathieu.

"I met Mathy."

He rolls his eyes. "'Course you did. He's a horrible spy."

"At least he's not a horrible human being like you."

Mathieu sneers. "We're the same person."

I raise an eyebrow. "Hardly. You haven't been the same person for decades. Unlike him, you grew up and became another version of your father."

The mention of his father wipes the smirk off his face. He snarls and hisses, "I'm nothing like my father."

"Sure, if that helps you sleep at night." I'm not usually in the business of throwing people's childhood trauma back into their faces, but in this case, I can only think of innocent little Mathy, who's finally free of his abuser, yet still craves and fears his attention. "Was it so hard to treat him any better than you were treated?"

"Shut up, bitch! You know nothing." He makes a movement, as if to step out of his circle and strangle me, but then thinks better of it and quickly steps back.

*Interesting.*

"I actually know a lot. Thanks to Mathy, I know how you turned out so shitty and why you're hiding in the catacombs, as well as why you're so incapable of valuing anything else but power. I know you got Mathy from your Papa." I feel bile crawling up my throat even as I try to skirt around the actual nature of what was done to him.

His face darkens as every word cuts a little deeper. "What did he tell you?"

"Tell me?" I don't want to rat Mathy out. Not like this. "He didn't need to tell me anything. It was written all over his face, in the way he flinched." My throat tightens, but I force myself to continue. "The longing for human connection in his voice. It's in you, too, isn't it? Under all that spite and anger, you're still just a little boy."

"I'm going to kill you," Mathieu growls. "I don't care if they want you, you're nothing special." So, they still want me for something.

The temptation to tell him to come and get me is high, but I don't want to alert him to the fact I know why he's been hidden in this circle. I need to trust that Flo can figure out a way to disrupt it. So far, she and Al, who's helping, don't seem to have made any progress.

"Is that what you wanted to be? Special?" I force a pitying smile on my lips. "Maman's special little boy?"

"Don't you dare talk about my mother!"

There really is a little broken boy in Mathieu, a tiny part that hasn't been extinguished by all that hatred yet. A weakness, but also a shred of humanity. "I've met her."

A vein pulses at his temple and his eyes blaze. Oh, how he wishes he could leave his circle and make me stop talking. "No, you didn't."

"She died, you know? Quite a long time ago, actually."

"What?" For a tiny moment, Mathieu lets me look behind that anger. I assume he didn't know.

My smile's a little more genuine this time. "She's buried in Père Lachaise. You should've seen her face when I brought Mathy to her, and his. They were so happy to have each other." When was the last time Mathieu was happy?

But the moment of sympathy is over and he's back to sneering. "How nice for them." He snorts, then spits across the line, hitting neither me nor Flo. "Of course that little weakling would run back to her. As if she ever did shit for him. She's the reason he exists in the first place. Her inaction, her *weakness*, is why *he* got away with so much. That woman took him back, for ghosts' sake!" Clearly, we're no longer talking about Mathy.

"She was a victim, too," I say softly, feeling an annoying pang of pity for Mathieu. It's washed away by a sickly, slimy feeling I can't quite place. Something behind me.

I'm vaguely aware of Alexandre engaging in a fight, but don't dare glance over my shoulder. I feel like I'm this short of a breakthrough.

"Oh, give me a break," Mathieu shouts. "She had one job. One job!"

"To love you?"

He stares at me as if I've just declared my love for platypus eggs. "You think I care about her *love*?" he says at last, though with a strangely broken voice.

"Because she *does* love you. She made mistakes, yes, and maybe she wasn't strong enough to protect you, but she's always loved you. And if you want—"

"Watch out!" Al shouts, at the same time pushing his sister behind him.

I have zero time to react to his warning or Mathieu's sudden grin. Before I can do so much as turn my head, an armoured arm wraps around my waist, the metal digging into my stomach as I'm lifted off my feet and thrown over my attacker's shoulder. Squashed between a medieval shoulder plate and arm guard, I can barely breathe. And that's before I get that awful feeling of water filling my mouth again.

Jacques de Molay isn't fully plunging me into another nightmare vision, just holding me at the edge of it, like a threat. "Time to meet your destiny."

*Destiny. Like the one where I bring chaos and destruction.* My head swirls as I fight down the panic, rising in equal parts thanks to his words and the vision he's tormenting me with. "Let me go!"

As useless as it is, I hammer my fists against his armour and kick his breastplate, trying to wriggle out of his painful grip, all to no avail. I'm as helpless in his hands as a puppy.

"Alexandre!" I shout instead.

"That one will take a while to regenerate."

Sure enough, I see my beloved general on the ground, cut into freaking pieces. My heart nearly jumps out of my chest, and a strangled sob bursts from my lips. "What... What did you do to him?"

Instead of answering, Molay carries me down one of the tunnels—the one Napoleon was guarding before. I scream, as if that'd help me now I realise what's going to happen, why Molay isn't killing or incapacitating me but taking me away from the battlefield, why I can't see Napoleon anymore.

"Jean!" I cry, then quickly rattle off every ghosts' name I know. One by one, they appear at the mouth of the tunnel, but an invisible barrier keeps them from following, much less saving me.

Just then, someone barrels through the gathered ghosts. Mathieu! "Wait!" he shouts, his eyes wild. "What did my maman say? I need to know. I need to—"

He's knocked sideways by a rudimentary club. Spattered in blood from head to toe, Constance d'Arles beats him to a pulp.

My stomach lurches and with it my entire body as Molay sinks to his knees, groaning. His grip loosens and I tumble to the stone floor, wincing in pain. Blood appears on his temple, but he snarls and forces the injury away with the power of his will. Still, he flickers in and out of injury, just as Olivier had.

"Alix!" Flo shouts and rolls something down the corridor. Her ghost bomb.

Pure instinct has me lunging for it. I have no idea if I need to pull a trigger or stab him with the pointy end, so I take a page out of Constance's playbook and smash the bulky end across Molay's unprotected head. Blood sprays across my face and suddenly a sulphuric smell in the air makes me gag.

Molay tilts to the side, groaning, but then he shakes his head and pulls my leg out from under me. Somehow, I manage to retain one of the lessons Sébastien taught me and catch my fall, using the momentum to twist out of Molay's grip and, this time, ram the makeshift weapon into Molay's throat.

Visions of drowning, electric shocks, and vehicle impacts try to pull me under, but they're like butterfly wings, fragile and fleeting. Whatever Flo put in her weapon, it's messing with Molay's ghost powers.

Suddenly, there's Bézier and Paul. The former pushes me away while Paul slaps some runes on Molay's face and chest, before wrapping iron chains around his body, all the while singing in Latin. Before my eyes, the living body decomposes, erasing all trace of the wounds I caused. All that's left is the charred skeleton.

Paul wipes the sweat from his brow. Apparently, it cost him a lot. "Never thought I'd live through one of those."

Bézier gives me a long look, his eyebrows crawling up. "I vaguely remember telling you to stay home, Mademoiselle Dubois." Then his face breaks into a grin. "But I suppose I have to thank you for taking down this monster and bringing us all this support. Not bad for a ghost-consultant-slash-history-student."

As much as I appreciate his begrudging praise, I'm still too shaky on my feet to do much more than nod. And then, my ghosts are here, Victor hugging me tight, as if he'll never let me go again. "You did it. You survived."

By the looks of it, everything crumbled with Molay's death. The ghosts I brought excitedly chat among themselves as they disperse, returning to their haunting grounds. The commune itself is slowly falling apart without the ghosts or Molay's spells to uphold them, the spectral spaces they created dissolving. My heart aches for the Library of the Lost which will be lost again.

The few unhurt GoPol agents take care of the injured ones. Some people have been cuffed—the Chevalier's supporters and some of the historic figures who came back to life by bonding with one of the kidnapped ghost whisperers. They've been located and freed, too, and I see more than one overjoyed reunion.

The battle is won; Molay has been neutralised. I should be happy. Instead, dread fills me the more I watch the scene in front of me, and it's not because of the commune's unfulfilled potential. Something's missing. Something vital.

"I need to find Sébastien!" He never returned from the tunnels.

Bézier nods then quickly calls a few whisperers over. "We need to locate Roubert—and Coullier. You two take that tunnel, you take this one. Dubois, you're with me."

I appreciate he's not telling me to stay back this time but lets me be part of the search. Together with the ghosts, we race down the corridor Molay tried to carry me down, only to arrive at a crossing two minutes later. It seems to be the start of a confusing maze, and I can feel my heart sink.

"Damn it!" Bézier grunts. "We don't have the manpower to explore all these tunnels."

"Sure, we do." When he frowns, I explain, "There's still a lot of ghosts here. Your Majesties? You take these three. Victor, you take the sewer. Voltaire..." One by one, I send my ghost friends down the tunnels, until all but Jean Lannes is gone.

Bézier nods at me appreciatively. "Remind me to hire you as soon as we're back. I'll take this one." And with that, he, too, vanishes into the darkness.

Jean looks at me. "Shall we take this one, then?" He offers the last remaining tunnel.

"Don't!" Suddenly, Emily's back. Or maybe she was there the whole time, waiting for Bézier to leave.

"Did you find them?" I'd almost forgotten about her promise.

"Yes, and you need to come quick. But not down there." Instead, she faces a stone wall and points to a dark hole near the ceiling I would've totally missed if she hadn't pointed it out. "Take this one, instead. It's safer."

I stare at the dark void, swallowing. "If it leads me to Séb and Gaspar, I don't care about safe. Let's go."

# CHAPTER 32

"I know you're there."

The Chevalier's voice is muffled by the layer of stone that separates us. Emily's secret passageway has had me crawling at an excruciating pace for close to half an hour. It's more like an air duct than a tunnel, and I try not to think about the fact I haven't come across a place where I could turn around yet. If I need to leave via this route, I'll have to crawl backwards.

My muscles are cramping, and I feel the exhaustion of the battle deep in my bones. If it hadn't been for my boys at the end, I would've given up already. As is, I keep pushing forward, following Emily's lead, while Jean brings up the rear. At last, however, we seem to be getting somewhere.

"I know you've been worried about Napoleon's resurrection," the Chevalier says.

I can't tell if he's talking to someone else or if he knows I'm somewhere in the walls above or maybe below him. It's really hard to tell when there's nothing but stone around me. The earth shakes, and the rumbling motion goes through my body, setting me on edge. We must be close to a Métro line. But which one? I've lost all orientation in the dark.

"But you don't have to be. We're not going to bring him back to life."

That's good news for once, but then why do I feel so sick?

"That was never the plan. What's the point in bringing people back to life when they can just die again?"

I wonder if he's heard about Molay's demise yet. He must have.

"The goal is to transcend life and death, to get the best of both existences. Why should people stop mattering just because they're dead? Why should we lose all the geniuses, the thinkers, and the heroes, just because their bodies gave out? You know how much ghosts still have to offer the world. How much *better* our world would be if it was led by people like Hugo, Voltaire... and Napoleon."

One thing's not like the other. I can't pretend I'm entirely unaffected by this vision the Chevalier's painting; many of the arguments are close to my own heart. It's the solution and consequences that scare the shit out of me.

Yes, I want the world to hear the wisdom of Voltaire once more, or to benefit from Marie Curie, Gustave Eiffel, and all the other scientists and inventors who left their mark on the world. I want people to read Victor's newest novel or groan over his collection of sewer poetry, but I don't want to disenfranchise those who haven't made a name for themselves yet and establish some kind of undead republic. Life and death are separate for a reason and to mess with it is just wrong.

My leg cramps and I bite on my cheek to avoid betraying my position. It's becoming clearer and clearer the Chevalier's talking to me.

"Look, you went behind my back and betrayed me; I went behind your back and betrayed you. I think we're even. No hard feelings."

Yeah, it's definitely me, and in my opinion, we're so far from even it's not even funny.

"You and I, we're the same," the Chevalier continues, his voice growing stronger now, as if there's less stone separating us. "We both want a world where ghosts and the living coexist."

There's a huge difference between co-existence and conquest, but who am I to interrupt?

"GoPol won't give you that. The government won't."

I hear him laughing softly. We must be so close now.

"Big changes require big sacrifices. That's why we had a revolution—many of them. That's how we were able to build an empire spanning most of Europe. It's all about sacrifice. You know this."

If this were a history class, I could write an essay on the hypothesis. He's not entirely wrong, but it's a tired argument—just a prettier way of saying the end justifies the means. Sacrifices sound so noble until you realise it's never the leaders who sacrifice anything but the common people who die en masse.

The tunnel widens in front of me. I can't see it, but I feel the space, and I nearly gasp in relief.

"I need you, Alix." His voice is even clearer now, the barrier between us thinning. "Your connection to the ghosts of Paris is so unique it left traces in your spectral signature. Look, I'd rather have you join me willingly, but I *will* have you, one way or another."

And that's about the end of me joining anything willingly.

"Careful now," Emily whispers. Then she points to a thin sliver of light in front of me. It's not much, just a small hole in the wall where the stone has crumbled. The light itself comes from a flickering candle, but it allows me to peer into a room slightly below me and just off to the right. My hole must be below average eye-height in a wall at the back of the room. Someone's blocking most of my view, but when they move, my heart drops into my stomach.

The Chevalier's on the other side of the room, his gaze turned towards the ceiling, and Napoleon's on a makeshift throne, looking bored. There are four or five others—living people—dressed in dark colours. Two are holding Sébastien down, his face in the dirt, his broken arm twisted on his back. Blood cakes his blond hair and a third person's holding a gun to his head, finger on the trigger. And then there's Gaspar, caught in another ritual circle, only this one seems to be keeping him in. Another man's behind him, weapon aimed at his back. No doubt it's filled with salt.

"I know you're close, Alix. Have you seen them yet?" the Chevalier asks. "If not, I've got your lover boys here. Don't make me take them from you."

"Just go." It's the first time someone else has spoken, and it takes a moment to realise the raspy sound came from Sébastien's lips.

The man holding a gun to his head presses the nuzzle deeper, as if he could stab him with it. "Shut up," he hisses.

The Chevalier raises his hand. "Don't be rude. Roubert Junior here just wants to play the hero."

He must've given a sign because suddenly Sébastien cries out in pain as the man holding his broken arm twists it further. The one with the gun kicks his face, making him cough up blood. I clamp my hands around my mouth to keep my cries in but can't stop the tears running down my cheeks.

"What were you going to say, Séb?" the Chevalier asks.

It takes Sébastien a moment to gather enough breath to speak again. At first, it's just a mumble, but then he repeats himself, "So, kill me. I'd gladly die for her."

"So eager to become a ghost, huh?"

No. No, no, no. This can't be happening. This is not how this day is going to end.

"I guess, he's right, Alix. Killing him will only turn him into a ghost, and you've already proven you don't mind your lovers a little less corporeal."

I hate him, I hate him so much it hurts.

"So, how about the other one? Shall I fill his chest with salt? Replace all those sweet memories with nothing? After everything you've been through already…"

"It's okay, Alix," Gaspar calls out. "He can take the memories from me—I'll just fall in love with you all over again."

"Ah, he's gone through the Roubert school of self-sacrifice. How sweet."

One of the men chortles, making me wish I could punch his teeth in.

"Now, now, Alix," the Chevalier says, turning around, still searching for me. "I know you won't let anything happen to these boys. Haven't they already suffered enough? Just to be clear: I won't let Gaspar go after one round of salt. I'll have him salted time and time again, until it's not just his memory that frays but his entire being. As for your precious Sébastien, we still have unfinished business. You know what his father did to me. I'll do that to him, and then some. He'll suffer a lot more before he dies. Or maybe I'll kill him now and bring him back the old way—you know, the one that taints his soul. Would you like that?" His voice hardens suddenly. "Or will you finally come out of hiding and do what you're destined for?"

"If you want to get out," Emily whispers, "Jean could send you through the stone. He's powerful enough."

Jean looks as if he'd rather salt his soul than send me into the lion's den.

"Don't." There's a new voice in the tunnel, right in front of me. I squint, trying to make out anything in the darkness. When I finally do, I nearly cry out. It's Dix, crouching in front of me, drawing circles in the dust. "Just leave, Alix."

I shake my head, but he won't have it. "He'll take the suffering, they both will, but you can't work with the Chevalier. He'll use you to release unspeakable evil on the world. Séb... Séb would rather die and go through hell than allow that."

But Dix, beautiful, broken Dix would cease to exist. The Chevalier won't separate them, not anymore. Leaving Sébastien means saying goodbye to Dix.

"You need to think of everyone else," he continues, "of all the innocents."

Why do I have to do that? Why can't I be selfish and save my boys? Aren't they just as innocent?

Dix crawls forward until he can cup my tear-stained face. "Thank you for making my existence infinitely lighter to bear. You're a ray of hope for every ghost in the dark. Live, Alix. Leave now and never turn back. You can do this." He kisses my forehead and gives me a lopsided smile, then locks gazes with Jean. "Take her home."

Jean looks at me, compassion written all over his face.

"I'm growing impatient," the Chevalier calls out. "Shall we fire that first round of salt? How much do you think Gaspar can take before he's forgotten all about you?"

"Please," Dix begs.

My eyelids flutter shut as I try not to pass out. Leaving my boys to certain death and worse... I'm not sure I can survive this. The decision is mine and it might just break my heart—and my mind—either way.

I return Jean's gaze. "Take me out of here."

# Chapter 33

My soul shatters into a million pieces as Jean swiftly carries me through the tunnels and caves of the catacombs. A volatile mixture of unbearable pain, grief, anger, and hate for the Chevalier, but most importantly myself for leaving the boys eats me alive. I can't believe I did that, that I saw them in distress and turned my back on them. The world seems so meaningless without them. Why should I save a world in which those beautiful souls won't exist?

I want to scream and beg Jean to turn around, to carry me back, to let me submit to whatever evil the Chevalier has planned. Whatever it is, it can't be worse than what'll happen to my boys now. I'd gladly die for them, be tied to Napoleon for the rest of my worthless life, or endure every torture in the Chevalier's sick mind. But I can't.

Somewhere buried beneath all the shame and pain, the cruelty of my own conscience stubbornly defends my decision. Giving myself to the Chevalier might save Sébastien, Dix, and Gaspar, but it'd condemn the rest of Paris—of France. Nostradamus once said I'd bring about France's darkest hour, but today, I defy his prophecy. I reject my destiny, even though it costs me my heart, mind, and soul.

Sébastien wouldn't have it any other way. Choosing him over anyone else is something he'd never forgive himself for. He'd be grateful and he'd be understanding, but it'd slowly eat him alive until there was nothing left but an empty shell, and whenever I looked into his steel-blue eyes, I'd see nothing but torment.

Of course, Dix would be the first to suffer. I still have his face burnt into my brain—that quiet martyrdom when he accepted he was done for, that his existence had come to an end after less than ten years. He pretended he'd made his peace with it, that he's the dedicated special agent his older self is, but I know him better. I know that, inside, he's raging against the world that created him after a terrible betrayal, treated him like less than a person for the better part of his existence, and will forget him as soon as Sébastien takes his place. He never chose this, never had enough agency to strike out on his own, to leave it all behind. He deserves better, and I know his loss will forever weigh on mine and Sébastien's heart.

And Gaspar... My sweet, sweet hedgehog boy. How defiantly he declared his love for me. He's already clawed his way back to the light once. He was healing at last, only to lose it all again so soon. Maybe he can't be any more dead than he already is, but the

Chevalier will make sure he'll never find peace. He'll break him so there'll be no coming back. His only memory will die with me.

I cry for each of my beautiful boys as the anguish gnaws at my heart, despair eating me alive. The corridors around me blur into one. Sometimes, we pass through stone; sometimes, we walk. I have no idea where we are or where we're going, and I don't really care. I'm already lost in the darkness of my mind.

At last, we stop. For a few moments, I listen to my staggering heart, that useless organ which'll never move on from this. At least, I won't be used by the Chevalier and able to keep everyone else safe; just not the ones that matter most to me.

"Thank you, Jean," I force myself to say, acknowledging his help, knowing how much it cost him.

"Don't thank me, Mademoiselle Dubois. Not for this." He sounds as heartbroken as I feel.

Breathing hurts. Hell, existing hurts. I vaguely hear people chattering and whispering around me—some busy intersection, I assume. I should probably go home. But where to? To that lonely apartment where no one but my hedgehogs await? Malou's good, but she can't heal this pain. No belly rub will ever let me forget I sacrificed my boys for the greater good. Suddenly, I long for my parents, to throw myself into my maman's arm and shed all the tears I've yet to cry.

With a deep breath, I look up to orient myself. It's still so dark. Of course. It must be the dead of night. How fitting. But then why are there so many people around me? Someone's pointing at me with three arms. Three arms... all sprouting from the same shoulder. No, not a shoulder. A hipbone.

My mind clears as I take in one horrifying ghost after the next. I'm not outside, I'm still in the catacombs, surrounded by countless heaps of bones and their hapless souls. Confused, I search for Jean.

He's next to me, eyes cast to the ground. "I'm sorry, Alix."

I follow his gaze and recognise the arcane runes of one of the Chevalier's ritual circles. Understanding hovers at the edge of my mind, waiting to crash over me like a wave of doom. "Why?"

Jean raises his gaze, looking terribly torn. "He's my commander."

"But he got you killed."

"That's part of being a soldier."

I shake my head. "No, no. You told me this—it's written in letters. He always sent you into the worst frays, the most daring conquests. Your soldiers died so he could sweep in and save the day. You lost so many friends. And then you were hit."

Jean smiles softly, as if he's proud I know so much about him. "And when I was and they took my leg, knowing I wasn't going to make it, he stood by me. He stayed until the end. Napoleon... He was my commander, but we were also friends. We shared a dream. You can't win big without risking it all."

"Risk?" Tears are forming in my eyes. "Is that what I am to you? Something to risk?" It's getting harder and harder to resist the crushing truth.

He cocks his head, full of affection. "You know this isn't the end for you. You'll probably die, yes, but that's just the beginning. You won't be forgotten."

"Of course I'll be forgotten! I haven't done anything of note and... and..."

The words stick in my throat as sobs ravage me. The people who'll remember me are probably already dead, with the rest at risk as soon as Napoleon leaves the catacombs. That little social media audience I built won't keep my memory alive—my ghost experience will be relatively short-lived, just like most ghosts, which is fine, I guess. I just don't want to die. Not yet. Not for this.

"Jean, please."

"It's time to get started, Jean."

I whirl around and find Napoleon and the Chevalier walking towards me. The Chevalier smiles. "I told you I'd have you one way or another."

Before I can find the words to reply, Jean grabs me by the shoulders and pushes me to the ground. I can't move. The runes in the circle bind me as effectively as if they were chains around my hands.

"Jean, don't do this!" I cry. "You're not like them. You know it's not worth it. You—" I hiccup, and after that, no more words make it past the sobs and gasps for air.

My arms and legs are stretched out as my body's placed in a specific direction. When I look up, Napoleon's above my head, looking down on me with a dispassionate expression.

"This will give me an army at last?"

"Trust me," the Chevalier says, kneeling at my side. "She's got a way with ghosts, and I have a way with blood and bones." Suddenly there's a knife in his hands. Methodically, he cuts away the clothes from my arms and legs.

"Help!" I shout. "Someone help!" There's so many ghosts around, but they're all broken. They can't even remember their own name. "Jean!" He's stepped back, watching me with a mix of shame and pity. "Alexandre!" But Alexandre has been cut to pieces. "Vi—"

"That's enough from you," the Chevalier says and sticks tape over my mouth.

Panic sweeps me away. One moment, I try to think of my ghostly friends, the next all I can think about is the blade glistening before my eyes. I jerk away, but my body won't move, lying completely still, while the Chevalier carves his symbols, first in my forehead and then my arms and legs. There's a low hum, which I belatedly recognise as a Latin chant. Something about bones, and war, and blood.

My blood.

"This could've been so much easier for you," the Chevalier says, not without regret. "But you made your choice, and I have to make mine."

When he starts singing again, a terrible tearing pain goes through my limbs. My forehead feels like it's splitting. My skin is cracking. Suddenly, there's something warm running down my arms and legs, something, warm, liquid, and sticky. A metallic smell fills my nose.

The Chevalier raises his arms and my blood follows him. "Rise!" he commands, then follows it up with more Latin.

The pain in my body becomes unbearable. It's like I'm turned inside out, as if I'm still attached to my blood while it's pulled in all directions. My vision grows hazy. I'm losing too much blood—maybe all my blood.

I don't think I'll survive this; I don't think I'm meant to.

Sébastien. Gaspar. Dix. I could've saved them for all the good leaving them there did. It was all in vain. The battle, the campaign, trying to make people understand.

Turns out I can't escape my destiny.

The last thing I see before my vision fails is an army of mismatched ghosts and bones rising around me.

# Afterword

Phew!

I hope you can forgive me for this terrible cliffhanger of an ending. Sadly, it had to come to this: Nostradamus' prophecy demanded it.

Of course, this isn't the end. There's still one last book to come, so don't count Alix out just yet. This is a series about ghosts, after all.

If this book felt a bit like a set-up, it probably is. When I first started to look at the plot, I was ready to bring back Napoleon fairly quickly—he was never meant for Alix—but then the resurrection kept moving further and further back, until he informed me that he didn't want a second lease on life, he just wanted to rule us all as a ghost. And well, who am I to say no to the emperor?

I promise, he'll have a more prominent role in book 9, and it'll all pay off eventually. *Ghosts of the Revolution* will be a rude awakening to everyone who's doubted Alix and decided not to listen to her. I mean, home girl has been begging to free the mismatched catacombs ghosts all series long.

It won't be too long until you can join the revolution and watch the battle for Paris unfold—and of course find out what'll happen to Alix, Gaspar, Sébastien, and Dix.

As usual, I want to thank everyone who's made this book possible: from Rajou, who listened to my plotting and writing woes and cheered me on every single day, to my beta readers, Jojo, Tina, Paula, Mathilde, Mariaan, Katja, and Perri, who always do such a fantastic job at finding inconsistencies and errors, as well as vibe issues in the original draft. Jackie, my proofreader, whom I'm not allowed to reveal spoilers to, even if I really, really want to talk about upcoming ideas, and my boys for their unwavering support.

Last but not least, I want to thank you for reading the story, for rooting for Alix (or Malou), and for being such great support, online and offline. I literally could not do this job without you.

Love,

Janna

**Book 9: Ghosts of the Revolution**

**Magic, Demons and High School Drama**

# A Force of Nature (Spirit Seeker 1)

A supernatural adventure through Europe

# About Janna Ruth

.

Once upon a time, Janna Ruth studied the plate boundaries of this world. Now, she's creating her own worlds. Born in Berlin, Germany, Janna lives in Wellington, New Zealand, writing both English and German books.

Janna's writing career kicked off when she won a writing competition for German publisher Ueberreuter. Her first self-published novel "Im Bann der zertanzten Schuhe" (Melody of Curse, coming in June 2022) went on to win the 2018 SERAPH for "Best Independent Title". She debuted in English with her witchy novella "Witching with Dolphins" in 2020 and has since published urban fantasy, YA sci-fi, and contemporary coming-of-age novels and series.

When Janna isn't writing, she has a plethora of hobbies, such as aerial acrobatics, cake decorating, drawing, reading, and anything crafty you can throw her way.

**Find out more about Janna and her books here:**

**Website:** www.janna-ruth.com

**BookBub:** www.bookbub.com/authors/janna-ruth

**Facebook:** www.facebook.com/authorjannaruth

**Reader Group:** www.facebook.com/groups/storyseeker

**Goodreads:**

www.goodreads.com/author/show/16513923.Janna_Ruth

**BlueSky:** https://bsky.app/profile/janna-ruth.bsky.social

**Instagram:** www.instagram.com/janna_ruth

**TikTok:** www.tiktok.com/@jannaruthwrites

**Pinterest:** www.pinterest.com/jannaruthwrites